THE GRAVES

Also by Pamela Wechsler

MISSION HILL

PAMELA WECHSLER

THE
GRAVES

MINOTAUR BOOKS

NEW YORK

THE GRAVES. Copyright © 2017 by Pamela Wechsler. All rights reserved. Printed in the United States of America. For information, address St. Martin's Press, 175 Fifth Avenue, New York, N.Y. 10010.

www.minotaurbooks.com

The Library of Congress Cataloging-in-Publication Data is available upon request.

ISBN 978-1-250-07788-2 (hardcover)
ISBN 978-1-4668-9022-0 (e-book)

Our books may be purchased in bulk for promotional, educational, or business use. Please contact your local bookseller or the Macmillan Corporate and Premium Sales Department at 1-800-221-7945, extension 5442, or by e-mail at MacmillanSpecialMarkets@macmillan.com.

First Edition: May 2017

10 9 8 7 6 5 4 3 2 1

THE GRAVES

Chapter One

Ten years in the district attorney's office has taught me to never let down my guard, even here on Beacon Hill. Walking on West Cedar Street, I detect the first signs of danger—footsteps and cigarette smoke. No one from this neighborhood smokes anymore, at least not in public. It could be a stray tourist, checking out the gas lanterns and cobblestone streets, but I reach in my tote and search for my canister of pepper spray—just in case. A gloved hand covers my mouth. I start to pivot around but someone yanks my shoulder and pulls me in.

"Give it up," he says.

I'm relieved. It's just a mugging. The man doesn't even seem to be armed. I palm the pepper spray and surrender my tote, which he passes to a second man, who rifles through it and tosses the contents. The key to my Prius lands under an iron boot scraper. A bottle of Chanel No. 5 shatters and splatters on the brick sidewalk.

The second man opens my wallet and pulls out the bills.

"Twenty-five bucks? You gotta have more than that," he says.

"Take the bag, it's Prada," I say.

"It's probably fake."

"It's real, worth over a thousand dollars. I have a Rolex, too."

The first man takes the bait. As soon as he loosens his grip on my body and twists my wrist to inspect my watch, I aim the pepper spray at his eyes and press down hard on the nozzle. Nothing happens. The can is empty, something neither of us expected.

I run into the street but only make it a few steps before my heel catches on a jagged brick. I fall forward, directly into the path of an oncoming bike messenger, and we both go down hard. The cyclist looks at me and adjusts his helmet. He hesitates, shrugs, and climbs back on his bike. I watch him speed away.

I look up, see my attacker's face for the first time, and he sees mine. I don't know who's more surprised.

I'm furious. "Freddie, what the hell are you doing?"

He's mortified. "Ms. Endicott? Oh, man, it's not what you think."

Although I haven't prosecuted Freddie Craven before, many of my colleagues have. He's a midlevel drug dealer who moonlights as an informant. He was a witness for me last year, in one of my murder cases. Freddie is not the most upstanding citizen, but prosecutors don't get to choose our witnesses. In most cases, we're lucky if we have witnesses at all.

"Freddie, we talked about this," I say.

"I didn't know it was you," he says.

"That's not the point."

He puts his arm under my elbow and helps me to my feet. There are specks of blood on the hemline of my slate-gray skirt, my stockings are shredded, and pieces of gravel are embedded in my knees.

Freddie activates the flashlight on his phone, and we search for my belongings. My prescription for Ativan blew into a planter full of purple pansies. My gold badge landed on a sewer grate.

"You have to stop mugging people," I say, "at least until our case has gone through the appeals process."

"I wasn't. I won't. I swear," he says.

The second man pipes up. "Hey, I know you. You're that lady district attorney."

"You remember my cousin Martin." Freddie introduces us as though we're colleagues at a cocktail party. "You met him that time you came by my mother's house in Dorchester."

"Martin, you're on probation," I say. "You still have two years hanging over your head."

"You gonna lock us up?" Martin says.

"She can't," Freddie says. "She's not Five-O. She's a lawyer."

"I should report you both, but I'm not going to let you screw up my murder case, or my evening."

"Sorry about all this." Freddie takes my tote from Martin and hands it back to me. "It was just like a misunderstanding. You know what I'm saying?"

"Go home," I say. "A detective will be by in an hour to check on you. Be there."

"Sure, it's all good."

Freddie and Martin shuffle toward the Park Street subway station. I brush myself off, apply a fresh coat of lipstick, and continue toward the Liberty Hotel, where my boyfriend, Ty, and a glass of Malbec await.

Chapter Two

The Liberty Hotel, née the Charles Street Jail, is a massive granite structure, built in 1851. Thousands of pretrial detainees, including Malcolm X and the Boston Strangler, have done time here. Now it's a luxury destination for tourists and business travelers, willing to pay upwards of $400 a night to sleep in refurbished jail cells. Real police mug shots of celebrities hang in the lounges: Clink, Alibi, the Yard. The place makes me feel right at home.

About a hundred well-heeled women and besuited men are lined up outside the hotel. I sneak to the front of the queue, prepared to badge my way inside, until I see Jimmy Vickers, stocky and balding, stationed at the front door. Jimmy and I met a couple of years ago when he was impaneled on one of my grand juries.

"Ms. Endicott, long time no see." He clocks my knees. "You're all cut up."

"It's nothing." I stretch the fabric of my skirt to cover the scrapes. "I'm clumsy."

"Someone came in here a while ago, asked me to keep an eye out for you. A black guy, about six foot two."

"That's my boyfriend, Ty. He's playing a gig."

"He said he'd be upstairs, in the Catwalk."

Jimmy unhitches the red velvet rope from the metal stanchion and steps aside. I go into the hotel; a steep escalator leads to an expansive atrium, underneath a ninety-foot-high rotunda, where a frenetic pickup scene is in progress. A thirtysomething, in a navy-blue blazer and gray flannel slacks, blocks my path.

"Buy you a drink?" he says. "Hey, wait, aren't you that—"

I cut him off before it becomes impossible to deny.

"No, I look like her, but I'm not."

He starts to challenge me, but gets distracted when a willowy brunette, in a slinky silver bridesmaid dress, glides by. I take the opportunity to disappear in the crowd.

Upstairs, Ty is seated at a table, drinking an Anchor Steam. He's wearing a black leather jacket and white button-down shirt. No matter the venue, Ty is always the most handsome man in the room.

He sees me walking toward him and stands.

"Babe, what happened?" he says.

"I fell," I say. "It's nothing."

I don't even try to sell the lie, and, kindly, Ty pretends to buy it. He wraps his arms around me and gives me a kiss. I relax for a moment, feel safe in his embrace.

There's a glass of red wine on the table; I take a sip, then quickly put the glass down.

"We can't afford decent wine anymore?" I say. "This tastes like something I'd pick up at the Clinique counter."

"Sorry, babe," he says. "The reds you like go for over twenty bucks a glass."

"We have twenty dollars."

"Not for a glass of wine."

Cash never used to be a problem. My family has plenty of money, too much money, and they've always been more than generous—until last year, when my life was threatened and Ty was almost killed. They issued an ultimatum: quit my job or forfeit my wealth. My parents never approved of my career choice. My mother called it *unbefitting*, and my father deemed it *unsafe*. The incident was the final straw.

It was an easy decision. I love what I do, can't imagine doing anything else, but it's been an adjustment. Living off my salary is no easy task, since I'm committed to a ridiculously expensive lifestyle. My condo fee alone eats up most of my income.

Ty moves to the ballroom to set up and do a sound check. He's a musician, a brilliant tenor sax player, and he's worked with some of the best, in clubs like the Blue Note and Ronnie Scott's. Tonight, however, it's not about art. It's about paying the bills.

As soon as the coast is clear, I flag down the waitress, order a better glass of Pinot and an expensive cheese platter. She returns a few minutes later and hands me back my Visa.

"Sorry, it was rejected," she says. "Want to try another one?"

I have other credit cards, but the result will likely be the same.

"No, thanks," I say.

My stomach grumbles and I reach for the bowl of free cashews. Before I can pop one in my mouth, my phone vibrates. I consider sending it to voice mail, until I see the call is from a blocked line. It's probably work.

"Abby Endicott, homicide," I say.

Ty's amplifier squeaks loudly, startling me.

"Is that a cat? Where are you, the Angell Memorial?"

The caller doesn't have to identify himself, and he doesn't have to ask if he's interrupting. Kevin Farnsworth knows I'm always happy to hear from him.

"You may need to bone up on your detective skills, Detective," I say. "I'm not looking to take in a stray. I'm at the Liberty."

"Busman's holiday?" Kevin says.

"Ty's playing a wedding."

"You're still with that guy? What's it been, like two years?"

"Thirteen months."

"That's twelve more than most of them last."

In the decade I've known Kevin, he's seen me bail on a lot of relationships. He knows the idea of a long-term commitment scares me more than most of my murderers. But Ty is different.

This past year, when my life was in danger, Ty stepped in front of a bullet that was intended for me. He spent hours in surgery, days in the hospital, and months in physical therapy. Whenever things between us start to feel permanent and I feel vulnerable, I go into default mode and search around for the eject button. Then I remember him, stretched out on a gurney, blood seeping from his chest.

My boss ordered me to stay away from the office for six months, to rest and recover. After I sat around my apartment for a couple of weeks, the boredom grew intolerable. I begged to return to work early, and my boss caved, but only under the condition that I avoid crime scenes and casework. I've been running the office training program for the past few months, which is a snooze, and I'm itching to get back to my murderers.

"Can you catch cases yet?" Kevin says. "Or are you still on supersecret probation?"

"What do you have?" I say.

"It's a good one. A woman, about twenty years old, strangled."

Ty's band starts to perform the couple's first song: "What a Wonderful World." I should hang up the phone, go and watch Ty play.

"Where was she found?" I say.

"In Eastie, buried under a pile of trash."

"Was she raped?"

The bride and groom, champagne glasses in hand, overhear as they pass by. The bride stops and looks at me, horrified.

"Someone was raped?" she says. "Here?"

"Don't worry, everything is fine," I say. "Enjoy your night. You look beautiful."

The bride has more questions, but the groom nudges her away.

"It's the same MO as Rose Driscoll's case," Kevin says. "The vic was stripped naked, dumped, and posed."

I put down my glass of sour wine. Last month, Rose Driscoll, a sophomore at Boston University, was found in King's Chapel Burying Ground, Boston's oldest cemetery, next to the grave of Elizabeth Pain, whom many believe to be the inspiration for Nathaniel Hawthorne's *The Scarlet Letter*. Rose was sprawled out, naked, her eyes open and her arms crossed in front of her.

I feel the surge of adrenaline that comes with a new murder.

"I'm not supposed to catch cases," I say.

"The doer is a potential serial killer." Kevin knows how to reel me in. "You'd go bananas, sitting around and twiddling your thumbs, while someone else tries to chase him down."

I consider the consequences. Ty has been protective since the shooting; he'll worry if I take the case. And if Max finds out I was at a new crime scene, at best, he'll give me a stern lecture. At worst, he'll extend my leave of absence.

"Are you in?" Kevin says.

"I'm on my way," I say.

Chapter Three

Black luxury vehicles idle in the circular driveway outside the Liberty. Jimmy signals the first in line, an Escalade, and helps a couple of honeymooners roll their luggage to the rear of the car. He ushers them into the backseat, wishes them safe travels, and pockets the tip.

"You need a ride?" he says.

"Yes, but not a limo," I say. "Can you get me a taxi?"

"There's a half-hour wait time for cabs."

"Uber?"

"Even longer."

Jimmy whistles to a nearby Navigator. When the car pulls up, he introduces me to Chuck, the driver. Chuck looks uncomfortable in his ill-fitting uniform; his pant legs pool around his ankles, and the sleeves on his suit jacket stop about four inches north of his wrists.

"Nice to know you." Chuck adjusts the faux leather visor on his hat. "Where you headed?"

"East Boston," I say.

"Sure thing. Which airline?"

"I'm not going to the airport."

"Oh, sorry, Eastie usually means Logan."

Chuck opens the door to the backseat and I climb inside.

"I need to go to Public Alley 257," I say.

"Never heard of it. Is it a new club?"

"No, it's a just public alley, near the tunnel, behind the old candy factory."

Chuck turns to Jimmy and shrugs. "Sorry, I don't do drug runs anymore."

"She's not a drug dealer, numbskull," Jimmy says, "she's an attorney."

"Prosecutor," I say.

The distinction is important, a point of pride. Lest I be confused with other members of the bar, like corporate litigators, ambulance chasers, or worse, criminal defense attorneys.

"You oughta see her in court," Jimmy says. "She cross-examined a guy into a full-blown asthma attack. Don't mess with her."

I suppress a smile. Chuck closes the door, gets behind the wheel, and catches my eye in the rearview mirror.

"I always follow the rules of the road," he says.

"Drive as fast as you like," I say. "As long as you don't kill anyone, we'll get along fine."

We pass Faneuil Hall, a centuries-old meetinghouse, crowned by a four-foot-tall gilded grasshopper. George Washington, Sam Adams, and Oliver Wendell Holmes delivered speeches here about the importance of American independence, and liberty and justice for all. Politicians still hold public events here, but mostly it's a giant gift shop, surrounded by T-shirt vendors and a food court.

Chuck slams on his brakes and swerves to avoid hitting a group of drunk twentysomethings who are crossing busy Congress Street, in spite of the flashing red Do Not Walk sign.

"If you don't mind my asking," Chuck says, "why are you going to a vacant lot?"

"It won't be vacant tonight," I say.

When we arrive on scene, a cluster of reporters and a couple of lookie-loos are gathered outside the perimeter, which is bound by yellow tape.

"Can you pull up across the street, away from the cameras?" I say.

Chuck nods and moves the car away from the action.

"You want I should wait for you?" he says.

"No, thanks. I'll get a ride home from one of the detectives."

Before I can tell him not to, Chuck gets out and opens my door, chauffeur-style. Carl Ostroff, the least obnoxious of the local crime reporters, clocks me stepping out of the limo— exactly what I hoped to avoid.

Carl charges at me, microphone in hand, a camera light flashes on. Even though the glare is blinding, I can still make out his porcelain veneers, meticulously shaped eyebrows, and $400 haircut.

"Carl Ostroff, Channel 7 News, reporting from East Boston, where details of a grisly murder are unfolding. Abigail Endicott, chief of homicide in the district attorney's office, just arrived on scene. In a limousine, I might add. Abby, I can't help but comment on your mode of transportation this evening."

I give him the stink eye. "Shut it down, Carl."

"Did the legislature pass a rider to this year's budget that includes vouchers for limo rides?"

"You have something green stuck in your teeth."

Carl signals his cameraman; the light goes dark. He pulls back the corners of his lips to expose his uppers and lowers, and uses the mirror app on his phone to check for stray pieces of lettuce.

"Made you look," I say.

"I still got the money shot," he says.

I duck under the yellow tape.

Carl calls out to me. "Hey, Abby," he says, "it's nice to see you back on the job."

The medical examiner's van pulls up to the alley. Assistants open the back doors and slide the gurney out.

"It's good to be back," I say.

Chapter Four

The investigation is in full swing. Technicians, detectives, and uniforms swarm around, marking distances with measuring wheels, dropping miniature orange cones, and circling pieces of evidence with chalk. Some talk on cell phones, others snap pictures.

A sergeant is positioned at the foot of an unpaved alley, which is framed by two abandoned factory buildings, both pocked with shattered windows and gang graffiti. He barks out orders. "Bag and tag that broken Smirnoff bottle. Fan out. Check inside the buildings." When he sees me, he points to the end of the alley. "ADA Endicott, your vic is behind the Dumpster."

The overwhelming stench of garbage and decomposing flesh makes me gag. I keep perfume in my purse for these occasions, to mask the odors, but Freddie and his cousin broke the bottle. I rummage around in my tote until I find a sampler of Obsession, double-check the label to be sure it's not pepper spray, and spritz the side of my neck.

I glove up and lean on the wall to steady myself as I slip a pair of paper booties on over my suede pumps, taking pains to avoid facing the cameras. My parents are disappointed enough with my career choice; no need to rub salt in the wound. I don't want them to flip on the local news and see pictures of me poking around in a vermin-infested alley.

Medical examiner Reggie Rene is a few feet away, sharing his wisdom with a couple of young technicians. "When you put her on the gurney, be sure not to dislodge anything that could be in her throat. Scrape the red stains from the side of the Dumpster. Bottle up a few of those live insects."

At five three, Reggie is a couple of inches shorter than I am, but he's a commanding force, a master choreographer, who runs a murder scene like it was a Hollywood film set. Definitely more De Palma than Capra.

"Do we have a cause of death?" I say.

"It's hard to tell because the rodents got to her, but I found bruising and abrasions on her throat."

"Strangulation?"

"Looks that way," he says. "I'll confirm after I get her on the slab."

"Sounds similar to Rose Driscoll, the BU student," I say.

Reggie nods. "Both bodies were moved postmortem, and posed. We could have a serial killer on our hands."

I'm both repulsed and intrigued. This is uncharted territory, a new level of threat. I've had double murderers before, even a triple once, but never an actual serial killer; the biggest difference being marked by a cooling-off period between attacks. If we are dealing with a serial killer, there could be more victims—past, present, or future.

Reggie reaches into the back of the van and opens up a first aid kit. He tosses me a bottle of iodine, a roll of surgical tape, and a piece of gauze. "You don't want that thing to get infected," he says. He shines his flashlight on my knee.

I stuff the items in my tote. "I'm fine," I say.

"Listen to the doc. Cover that wound." Detective Kevin Farnsworth is walking toward me. "This place is crawling with disease."

I haven't seen Kevin in months. His close-cropped hair has a new dusting of gray, and he looks taller than his six-foot-two-inch frame, especially standing next to Reggie. It looks like he's gained some muscle tone, which brings him up to about negative 10 percent body fat.

The last time Kevin and I were together was in the Mass General, waiting for Ty to get out of surgery. Kevin had just killed the man who put a bullet in Ty's chest. I was in shock, too numb to realize I was walking around on a broken ankle, and too stunned to appreciate that I had come close to losing my own life. After the incident, my boss was concerned about post-traumatic stress. I promised to see a shrink—and I will, at some point, maybe.

In the weeks after the shooting, Kevin and I talked on the phone a few times and made plans to get together, but something always came up. Or at least that's what we claimed. Really, we were avoiding each other. I was afraid of what might happen between us, because as the days went by, reality set in; Kevin had saved my life. We already had a playful attraction, but after the shooting, it intensified tenfold. I was vulnerable and not sure I could resist the temptation. I suspect he felt the same.

"Can we seize the Dumpster and its contents?" I say.

"It's your party," Kevin says. "You got a spare bedroom back in your fancy condo. How's about I ask crime scene services to haul it to your place?"

"It'll clash with the furniture," I say. "Have it towed to the garage in Southie."

Kevin is holding a surgical face mask, and he tries to hand it to me. I look around, note that I'm the only woman on scene and that no one else's face is protected. I wave him off.

"Suit yourself," he says, "but you don't have to prove you're Superwoman. The whole department got that memo a couple of months back."

I step around some used condoms and broken glass, and feel

a sharp pain in my right ankle. I hope I didn't reinjure it when the bike messenger crashed into me. Following Kevin, I try to keep my weight on my left foot, careful not to draw attention to myself.

"You're hobbling around." Kevin says. "Is your ankle bothering you?"

"No."

We stop a few feet from the Dumpster.

"Prepare yourself," Kevin says. "She's in pretty rough shape."

Kevin knows that, for me, this is the worst part of the job—meeting my client. The horror of this moment will only be equaled by seeing the expression on her mother's face when she listens to me deliver my carefully filtered description of what her daughter looked like when we found her.

Kevin and I have a system. Before I look at the body, he describes it. This always cushions the impact. The visual will make me nauseous. It always does. But worse, as soon as I see her, she'll become a part of me, another source of sorrow that I'll carry wherever I go.

"She's partially nude," Kevin says. "Her eyes are open, and her arms are crossed."

"What else?" I say.

"Her legs are buried under a pile of trash: a Campbell's Soup can, a deflated tire, an empty Windex bottle. Her flesh has started to turn green, like rotting meat." He pauses.

"Keep going."

"The tips of her fingers have been chewed off."

I inhale, exhale. "Animals?"

"Probably."

I peer behind the Dumpster and look at my victim, look away, then look back again. She's beautiful, even in the early stages of decomposition. What's left of her stylish dark pixie is wet with a curdled milk-like substance. A shredded, once-white now-brown sheet is wrapped loosely around her waist.

When I lean in closer, I see a smudged ink stamp on the back of her hand.

"Some kind of design, like a cat or something," Kevin says. "I can't make out the words."

"Crazy Fox," I say. "It's a bar in Cambridge. I went there a few times in college."

A cluster of maggots seems to have settled into the woman's left ear. I feel dizzy as a small pool of vomit swells in the back of my throat. Now I'm glad I didn't have enough money for dinner.

A bulletproof SUV, driven by a plainclothes detective, pulls up to the perimeter. My boss, District Attorney Max Lombardo, opens the front passenger door, but before his Florsheims hit the pavement, he's barraged with questions from the reporters. Like any elected official who wants to keep his job, he pauses to respond.

"Are there any suspects?" a reporter says.

"Not yet," Max says.

"What about the victim? Do you have a name?"

"Boston Police are in the process of making an identification. We're asking for anyone with information to contact our tips line. All calls will be anonymous."

Max starts to walk toward the alley but another reporter calls out.

"What can you tell us about her?"

"She was female, approximately twenty years old. Right now all we know is that she died at the hands of a monster. Rest assured, we're going to catch whoever is responsible."

Carl Ostroff steps up. "Is it true you're planning to run for mayor?"

"Now's not the time for politics, Carl."

Max breaks free and makes a beeline toward me. He looks good, sober; more the powerful in-command leader of years past, less the booze-addicted, aging basketball player of late. His tie is uneven, but that's par for the course.

"Abby, what the hell are you doing here?" Max says.

"It's nice to see you, too," I say.

I try to distract him by fixing the knot on his tie, but he waves me off.

"I don't want you at scenes until Thanksgiving—it's not even Halloween."

Most people go on vacation during the holidays. My family jets off to Saint Moritz, or one of the Palms—Beach or Springs—but I prefer to stay in Boston. Thanksgiving, Christmas, and New Year's are the busiest times in department stores, retail outlets, and the district attorney's office. The days grow shorter, the weather turns cold, and families spend lots of quality time together, cooped up inside, eating, drinking, watching football, and reminiscing about past slights. Tempers flare and bloodshed often results.

"I just happened to be in the neighborhood when the call came in," I say.

Max looks around, takes in a couple of raccoon-sized rats, and raises his eyebrows.

"We're a long way from the Back Bay," he says.

"Kevin's allowed back out on the street," I say.

"That's the commissioner's call, not mine."

"It's because he's a man. That's not good politics."

"Nice try," Max says, "but the gender card isn't going to work. I'll pull the case from you and assign it to Cassandra."

Surprised that he's called my bluff, I change tacks. "How about a compromise?"

Max eyes the reporters. "Fine. Keep it, but you don't need to be out in the field. Let the detectives do the shoe leather."

"Deal," I say.

The medical examiner's assistants hoist the woman onto a gurney.

"I have your word," Max says. "You're going straight home."

"Absolutely." I hold up my hand as if I'm taking the oath in court. "I solemnly swear that I'll go directly to my apartment."

I call out and move toward Kevin.

"Can I hitch a ride?" I say.

He opens the passenger door to his SUV.

"Sure. Hop in. I'll drop you off at your place."

I look around, see that Max is preoccupied with the press, well out of earshot.

"Thanks," I say, "but I'm not going home."

"But your boss—"

"I can handle him. I'll say something came up, something that couldn't wait."

"He's not going to buy that."

"He'll understand." I get in the car, buckle myself in. "Let's go. We have a murder to investigate."

Chapter Five

Dunkin' Donuts on Causeway Street is one of the few places in Boston where you can get a cup of coffee at two o'clock in the morning. Kevin double-parks out front. Racks of doughnuts are visible through the windows: frosted, glazed, powdered, drizzled. The glare of the neon-orange-and-hot-pink sign gives me a slight headache.

"The usual?" Kevin says.

"I take my lattes with soy now. I became lactose intolerant after the shooting."

"Stress will do crazy things to your body."

"And to your mind."

In my bag, I have a travel mug for coffee. I dig it out and hand it to him.

"Your purse is like a bottomless pit," he says.

He gets out of the car and uses his remote to lock me in. It's not a dangerous neighborhood, but the sports bars around the TD Garden are just finishing last call, and scores of drunk hockey fans, wearing black-and-gold Bruins sweatshirts, are wandering around, yelling, looking for a fight. *We're number one. Fuck the Canucks. What are you looking at, asshole?* A group staggers and stumbles toward the parking garage. Soon they'll get behind the wheels of their cars.

Kevin returns with the coffees and a small package, wrapped in wax paper.

"Egg white flatbread," he says. "Chock-full of protein. I figure you haven't eaten in a good twelve hours."

"I appreciate it," I say, "but I would've appreciated a chocolate cruller even more."

Kevin merges onto Storrow Drive. Winding along the Charles River, we pass a series of iconic landmarks: the Hatch Shell, where every Fourth of July, the Boston Pops perform Tchaikovsky's tempestuous *1812 Overture*, and where last March, a jogger was sexually assaulted and beaten. The domed statehouse, where two hundred years ago, Paul Revere laid his copper sheathing, and where last summer, a tour guide was stabbed five times in the gut. The sixty-two-story glass John Hancock Tower, the tallest building in Boston, where two years ago, a twenty-six-year-old father of twins was shot in the chest and died instantly.

When we're parallel to Beacon Street, Kevin catches me eyeing the back of my condo building. Ty is probably home, sprawled out on the sofa, listening to jazz or watching an old black-and-white movie on TV. I feel a tinge of guilt for sneaking out of the Liberty without telling him where I was going.

"Last chance to get out while you still can," Kevin says.

"I'm not going home," I say.

"Yeah, I figured." Unlike Ty, Kevin understands the draw of a new murder.

The brownstones and high-rises in the Back Bay and Kenmore Square are dark. Even the blinking Citgo sign has been dimmed for the night. Kevin veers onto the Anderson Bridge, takes us across the Charles River, out of our jurisdiction and into foreign territory: Middlesex County.

"Hold on to your *Miranda* card," Kevin says. "We're entering the People's Republic of Cambridge."

I look out the window and wonder about my newest victim,

who she was, where she lived, how she died. Then I think about Rose Driscoll, how gut-wrenching it was to meet her parents, first when there was still hope that she might be found alive, and again after her body was discovered. In an instant, Mrs. Driscoll's frenetic energy shifted into inconsolable despair.

"You think this case is tied to Rose Driscoll?" I say.

"I hope so," Kevin says. "Otherwise, we have two maniacs on the loose."

"Did anyone call in a missing persons?"

"Not yet."

We pass the Kennedy School. The shops and restaurants that line JFK Street are dark. Stacks of magazines are piled in front of the Out of Town News kiosk.

"When I was in college," I say, "I could fall off the radar for days."

"Didn't you have roommates?" Kevin says.

"Suite mates—that's what they're called at Harvard."

"Excuse me, Miss Ivy League," he says.

"They'd assume I was in the library, pulling an all-nighter, or with a new boyfriend."

Sometimes it was neither. I'd take the Acela to New York and visit MoMA or, when I was feeling claustrophobic and decadent, I'd fly to Paris and spend hours wandering around the Musée d'Orsay. These days, a trip outside Suffolk County is rare; the last time I left town was to speak at a homicide conference in South Carolina. The only reason Max authorized the travel request was because when I told him it was in Charleston, he thought I said Charlestown.

We wait at the red light in front of Harvard Law School's student center. Kevin and I accidentally lock eyes for a split second. He clears his throat, as though he's going to say something, but remains silent. Being this close is more awkward than I had anticipated. The sexual tension between us is palpable.

I stare out the window, where a homeless woman is sleeping

on the pavement under a limestone archway. I grab the Dunkin'
Donuts bag, jump out of the car, and leave my egg sandwich by
the edge of her wool utility blanket.

As I climb back in the car, the light turns green.

"Bet you wouldn't have been so quick to give away a chocolate cruller," Kevin says.

When Kevin smiles, the corners of his eyes have a new set of
crinkles. The shooting aged us both. Recently, my hairstylist
noticed a cluster of gray along my part line.

Kevin pulls back into traffic, past the library and the class-
room buildings, where I studied torts and contracts.

"When I was a one L, I thought practicing law would be an
intellectual exercise," I say. "I dreamt of appearing before the
Supreme Court and arguing about the unenumerated rights
found in the Fourteenth Amendment."

"I'm guessing Harvard didn't teach classes on how to bitch-
slap a mobster on the stand," Kevin says.

"No, I learned that my first year on the job, watching you in
the interview room."

There aren't a lot of pedestrians in the area. A lone student
makes his way back to his dorm, or house as it's called at
Harvard.

"I always wondered what made you want to be a prosecutor," Kevin says. "I mean, with all that family dough—you could
buy an island in the Caribbean, retire, and drink piña coladas
for the rest of your life."

"Third year of law school, I volunteered in a clinic, where
I got to represent real people with real problems. My first client was a woman who wanted a restraining order against her
boyfriend. She was nine months pregnant, with a black eye, a
chipped tooth, and a sprained wrist. I listened to her story,
sat with her while she sobbed, stood with her in front of the
judge. We were in it together. For once, I was doing something
worthwhile."

"We all remember our first victim. Did you ever find out what happened to her?"

"The next day, she came to my office and practically spat at me. She was furious. She screamed and swore, accused me of pressuring her into testifying. Then she dropped the charges and threatened to sue me."

"And, still, here you are."

"Those were the good old days," I say, "when my victims could yell at me, because my victims were all alive."

Chapter Six

We pull onto Porter Street and park in front of the Crazy Fox. The neon lights in the window are dark, and the handle on the steel-reinforced door is locked, so we walk around the corner, to the rear of the building. Kevin pounds on the emergency exit.

"The bar is closed," a staticky voice says through the intercom. "Come back tomorrow."

Kevin returns to his car, lets out a quick blast of the siren, and talks into the mouthpiece of his loudspeaker.

"Boston Police, open up." His voice echoes, bouncing off the brick buildings.

A man cracks open the door. He's about my age, dry-mouthed, skinny, sweaty, and shaky—like he's popped one too many benzos.

"Are you the manager?" Kevin says.

"That's right. Hank Palermo's my name. What can I do you for?"

Kevin flashes his badge, brushes past him, and I follow. The bar hasn't changed in fifteen years. Same sticky floor, same stale beer smell, same wobbly wooden tables.

"We fixed the ventilation system. And we got a guy coming in the morning to take a look at the drains."

"Relax. We don't care about code violations," I say.

"We're investigating a homicide," Kevin says.

"Homicide?" Hank says. "You got the wrong place. People come in here to listen to music and blow off steam. The only shots we have are tequila or peppermint schnapps."

Hank is chatty, but not in a helpful way, more in a nervous, please-don't-pat-me-down-because-I've-got-a-pocketful-of-pills kind of way. Kevin takes out his cell phone and shows him a picture of our victim, surrounded by trash.

"Do you recognize her?" Kevin says.

Hank flinches but keeps his eyes on the photo.

"Jeez," he says, "she could have been in here before, but I don't know."

"Do you remember seeing her on Thursday?" I say.

"Thursday's our busiest night. You know college kids. They start their weekends early. The place was packed. But not too packed, I mean. We keep a running head count, so we're always within the occupancy limit."

"That's not an answer," Kevin says. "Do you remember her, yes or no?"

"What was she wearing?" Hank says.

"I wish we knew," I say.

Kevin looks up at the ceiling. "How many security cameras do you have?"

"Three," Hank says. "Front door, back alley, and one next to the safe."

"Let's take a look at the footage," I say.

Hank leads us into a dank, windowless office and flips on the light switch, but nothing happens. "I've been meaning to change that bulb."

He powers on a computer, and the screen provides our only source of light. When Hank steps out into the hallway and closes the door, Kevin and I are left standing, elbow to elbow, in the dark. Not having showered in about twenty hours, I feel self-conscious.

"Cramped quarters," I say.

We plant ourselves in metal chairs and reach for the mouse at the same time. I quickly pull away, as though I'd been zapped by an electric prod. Aware of my coffee breath, I pop an Altoid. Kevin twists his wedding band around his finger. His knee bobs up and down as he moves his foot. *Tap, tap, tap.*

For the next hour, we sit, straining our eyes, looking at grainy video of couples, groups, and strays entering and exiting the bar. There are dozens of people, mostly students, wearing pretty much the same outfit: jeans, T-shirts, hip-length jackets, and an occasional baseball cap.

The room is warm, and soon my eyelids grow heavy. I see a bag of Doritos on the table, tear it open. Anything to keep my body moving; otherwise, I might nod off.

"There, that's her," Kevin says.

Kevin freezes the frame, but it's hard to get a clear picture. It looks like my victim, same body type and haircut. She's chic, draped in a knee-length sweater coat. A scarf, possibly the murder weapon, is triple wrapped around her neck.

Kevin calls out to Hank, who joins us.

"That's you, stamping ink on her hand," Kevin says.

Hank goes to lean on the doorframe, but his hand slips and he bangs his shoulder.

"I relieve the bouncer sometimes," he says, "when he needs to take a leak."

"The picture doesn't jog your memory?" Kevin says.

Hank says no, leaves the room, and returns to whatever it was that he was doing before we interrupted him—flushing his drug supply down the toilet, replenishing bottles of vodka with tap water, or skimming off the till.

"Looks like our vic came in the bar alone," I say.

"I'm betting she didn't leave alone."

Kevin is right. He flips the tape back on, and about twenty minutes later, the woman leaves the bar with a man. He has his hand on the small of her back and leads her out of view. He's about six two, twentyish, with dark hair, a blue-and-white collared shirt, and a blazer. We take the video and print out a couple of still photos of the best frames.

When we emerge, Hank is at the bar, pretending to polish the brass fixtures with a dirty dishrag.

Kevin shows him a photo. "You know this guy?"

"Sure. He's in here all the time," Hanks says.

"A regular?"

"A stuck-up prick."

"Why do you say that?"

"He comes in here every Thursday night, acts like he owns the place. Last week, he asked me to put a Reserved sign on the back table so he could have his own private seating area. We don't do that for anyone. Well, maybe if Tom Brady came in, especially if he brought his wife—yeah, definitely if he brought Gisele—but that's it."

Kevin flashes a smile. "With that kind of snotty attitude, I'm guessing he's a Harvard man."

I throw him a look, *Very funny*, then turn to Hank.

"This guy, is he usually in here with the same woman?" I say.

Hank shrugs. "Not that I've noticed."

"He got a name?" Kevin says.

"Sure. He pitches his name around like it means something, like he thinks it'll get him a medal or a key to the executive bathroom."

"Who is he?" I say.

"Tommy Greenough."

I try not to react. The Greenough name is synonymous with Boston. The family is famous for their wealth, connections, and power. I think my father knows more than a few of them. Still,

there are lots other people on this planet with the same sur-
name.

"Tommy Greenough, is he any relation to the senator?" I say,
hoping the answer is no.

"Yup," Hank says. "He's his oldest son."

Chapter Seven

M y cell phone dings once, softly, and I bolt upright. My body is always at the ready, even when my eyes are closed. Homicide prosecutors can't afford to drift past the second stage of the sleep cycle into REM, especially when there's a potential serial killer on the loose.

I check the text; it's from Max: *Meet me at Victoria's in an hour.* There's no need to RSVP; an invitation from the boss is a demand, not a request. I have no idea what he wants, but it's not going to be good. Otherwise, he'd call me directly. Whatever he has to say, however, will pale in comparison to my news: Senator Thomas Greenough's son is under suspicion for murder.

When I'm done showering, I find Ty in the kitchen, drinking coffee and stirring something on the stove. He gives me a kiss and pops in a K-Cup.

"What time did you get home?" he says.

"Late. It was after four."

"I'm making oatmeal, steel cut."

When the Keurig lets out a final groan, Ty takes the coffee, adds a splash of soy from the fridge, and hands it to me.

"Sorry, I don't have time for breakfast," I say.

"I was hoping we could go out to Walden today, walk around the pond."

I sip my coffee, delaying my confession for as long as possible.

"I caught a new case," I say.

"So that's why you snuck out of the Liberty last night, without saying good night."

"You were busy, working."

"Babe, you said you were going to slow down, ease back into work."

After the shooting, I promised Ty two things: I'd try to have more balance in my life, and I'd be more forthright with him. I managed to keep my word, until now.

"This is important," I say. "It could be my first serial killer."

"Okay," he says.

If Ty is annoyed or disappointed, he doesn't show it. Past boyfriends used to complain, call me detached and unreachable. Ty seems to take it in stride. He transfers my coffee from the cup into a stainless steel to-go tumbler, twists on the top, and hands it to me.

"We're supposed to have dinner with your family," he says.

"I'll cancel."

"We bailed on them last time. Let's get it over with."

Even though my parents and my brother both have homes on Beacon Hill, less than a mile away from my Back Bay apartment, I haven't seen them in a couple of months. My relationship with my mother has always been strained, but recently, it's been tense with the men in my family as well. Even though the main issue is my job, Ty knows my family hasn't fully embraced our relationship. His response has been more mature than mine; he doesn't want to contribute to an estrangement, so he's trying to keep the lines of communication open.

He digs into his jeans pocket and hands me my car key.

"It's parked on Berkley Street, near Marlborough. It may be low on gas."

We've had to share my car since his Corolla has been in the shop off and on, mostly on. At my urging, he bought the car at a police auction shortly after we started dating. It's got a bullet hole in the trunk, and the radio is missing, but the price was right.

Outside, it's unseasonably warm, and I enjoy the short walk across Beacon Street, around the corner to Berkley. Ty isn't the most reliable witness; predictably, my Prius isn't where he said it would be. I circle the block until I find it on Clarendon Street, with a bright orange parking ticket tucked under the windshield wiper.

Someone taps me on the shoulder. I clutch my tote, ready to inflict bodily harm. Fool me once.

"Abigail? Abigail Endicott?"

I turn to see a man who looks vaguely familiar. To be safe, I don't commit to my name.

"Can I help you?"

"It's me, Chip—Chip Aldridge."

I recognize the name—the Aldridges have deep roots in Boston. They're related by marriage to many family friends: the Roosevelts, the Coolidges, and the Grants. I've probably met him more than once.

"Sure," I try to bluff. "You grew up on the Hill, right?"

"No, but my cousins did. I grew up in Manhattan. My family used to summer near yours on the Vineyard."

He extends his hand and gives me a firm, proper handshake. I have a weakness for strong hands; it's a sign of confidence. Chip looks like someone who could have spent his youth on Martha's Vineyard: tall and lanky, with the hint of a suntan and expensive loafers.

"We belonged to the Edgartown Yacht Club," he says. "I met you at one of the dances, but you always had so many guys chasing after you, you probably don't remember me."

He's starting to look familiar.

"How have you been?" I say.

"Great," he says. "I've seen you on TV a few times over the years. You're a lawyer, right?"

"Prosecutor. How about you? What do you do?"

"I'm a surgeon." That explains the hands. "I live a couple of doors down from here, on Comm Ave." He sneaks a look at my unencumbered ring finger. "How about we get together sometime?"

I'm tempted to accept, but think about Ty, at home, cleaning up the breakfast he made for me.

"I've got a crazy schedule," I say.

"Me, too," he says, "but I'm sure we can figure something out. Come on, there's no harm in two old friends getting together for lunch."

He makes a compelling case, and not just because he reminds me of my high school crush—the tennis coach at Winsor. Besides, it won't be a date—it'll just be a lunch. I stuff Ty's parking ticket in my bag and pull out a business card.

"Give me a call," I say.

I get in the car and head up Mass Ave. to Victoria's. It's only a fifteen-minute ride, but it might as well be a million miles away. I drive past the Back Bay brownstones and gourmet grocers toward some of my other favorite haunts: Boston Medical Center's emergency room, the first stop for some of my victims. The Pine Street Inn, where many of my witnesses reside. And the morgue.

I park in front of Victoria's, an old-school diner, open 24-7, ideal for law enforcement types. There's a black-and-white checkerboard floor and barstools are lined up at the counter, where gooey blueberry pies and fluffy coconut layer cakes are displayed under glass domes.

Max is seated in a booth, pounding the bottom of a Heinz bottle, splashing gobs of ketchup onto his home fries. He glances up at me, looks down, and stabs a fork into his omelet.

"I told you to go home last night," he says.

"We had a late break in the case."

I look around for the waitress and hold up my empty coffee cup.

"You're taking on too much too soon."

"Come on, Max, you've known me for over a decade. Did you really think I was going home to sleep, in the middle of an investigation?"

The waitress comes to our table, fills my mug. Assuming Victoria's doesn't supply soy milk, I take a sip of the black coffee. She clicks her pen and takes down my order: corned beef hash and biscuits. I've lost a lot of weight since the shooting last year, and don't eat very often, so I'll take the calories when I can find them.

"I spoke with Cassandra," Max says once the waitress is gone. "She offered to help with the case."

This is an annoyance but not a surprise.

"Before or after it made the national news?" I say.

Max plays it straight, which concerns me. We're always mocking Cassandra for her love of the spotlight.

"She could second seat you, carry some of the load."

"I don't need help," I say.

"You might, after you hear the reason I called you here." Max takes his time, finishes his plate of food. Then he looks around, leans across the table. "Ray Harris is resigning."

He's got to be wrong.

"No one gives up being mayor of Boston," I say. "Once you're in, it's a job for life."

He smiles weakly. "Unless you get indicted."

"Ray is getting indicted?"

Max sticks out his hand, signaling me to lower the volume.

"The U.S. Attorney charged him with patronage violations," he says. "She's unsealing the indictments on Monday."

I put down my coffee, anxious about where this is going. Max has made no secret about his political ambitions.

"You're going to do it, run for mayor?" I say.

"I'm assembling a committee, filing my papers this week," he says.

The waitress delivers my food. It looks delicious, with just the perfect amount of grease, but I've lost my appetite.

"You love being DA. You're seriously going to resign?"

In Massachusetts, elected officials often step down before they've served out their term. They break their promise to the electorate and cash in their political capital, while it's still worth something. Sometimes there's a lofty presidential appointment, like secretary of state or ambassador to the Vatican, but mostly it's about money. Either way, the governor will appoint someone to fill the seat until there's an election. That person will have the advantage of incumbency next November, when the voters decide.

"You should go for it," Max says. "You'd be a shoo-in. You're the hometown hero, with a million-dollar smile and an Ivy League education. The party will endorse you, the police union will support you, and the victims' rights groups will rally around you."

My disapproving family members flash through my mind.

"It's not that simple."

Max signals for the check.

"It's a fucking no-brainer."

"My family has been pressuring me to get out of public service since the day I was sworn in."

"They'll get over it when they see you up on the platform, giving an acceptance speech, hobnobbing with all the muckety-mucks."

He crumples his paper napkin, puts it on the table, takes out his wallet, and starts to count bills. I have to tell him my news before he leaves.

"Every politician in the state is going to distance themselves from me," I say.

"What are you talking about?"

"Our suspect from last night's murder is Tommy Greenough."

He looks up, unsure if he's heard correctly.

"Senator Greenough's kid?" he says.

"We have a picture of him with the victim, leaving a bar a few hours before she was found. Right now, he's our best suspect."

The waitress drops off the check. Max plasters a smile on his face and waits for her to leave.

"Slow down and choose your words wisely," he says. "That doesn't make him a suspect. It doesn't even make him a person of interest. At most, he's a potential witness. That's what we're calling him. Got it?"

I lean in close, forcing him to meet my eyes. "You want me to give him special treatment?"

He doesn't blink. "That's exactly what I want you to do."

"But you always say: just worry about the cases, let me worry about the politics."

He drops three tens on the table and repeats his new catch-phrase: "Tommy Greenough is a potential witness. Period."

"You've got egg on your shirt," I say.

"Screw you."

"No, I mean literally."

I dip my napkin into my water glass and wipe the goop off the front of his oxford. He stands, slides in his chair.

"Keep me in the loop," he says.

I follow him out the door. When I reach my car, I check my phone and see that there are two missed calls from Kevin. I hit redial.

"We got an ID on our victim," Kevin says.

"Who was she?"

"Caitlyn Walker, aged twenty-one, scholarship student from Missouri. She went to Wellesley."

Four girls from my graduating class at Winsor went to Welles-ley, as did my cousin Hattie and my aunt Lukie. Flustered, I drop my car key, and as I bend to pick it up, I fumble and drop my phone.

"You okay there?" Kevin says.

"Let me know when you reach her parents and make the notification."

I start the ignition, switch the phone to hands-free.

"What's our move?" His voice fills the car.

"I'll e-mail you a target letter," I say. "Let's invite Tommy Greenough to testify before the grand jury."

"Bold move. Did you run it by Max?"

"He's got a lot on his plate. Besides, Max won't be calling the shots much longer."

"Sounds like he's not calling them now."

Chapter Eight

My parents live in Louisburg Square, on the south slope of Beacon Hill, a couple of doors from where Louisa May Alcott lived and died. It's in the heart of Boston, but feels like a small, self-contained village. The local shops sell everything from tutti-frutti tarts and organic ostrich meat to seersucker doggie outfits and gold leaf andirons. There's hardly a reason to ever venture beyond Charles Street.

Ty and I walk past the liquor store, or packie, as it's called in Boston.

"I feel weird showing up at your folks' place empty-handed," he says.

"Don't worry about it."

"I should stop in and pick up a bottle of wine."

"My parents are very particular about their alcohol. Whatever you buy will be regifted to the postman or newspaper delivery guy."

We make our ascent up Mount Vernon Street and turn left onto the Square, which hosts Boston's only remaining private park—a plot of green, surrounded by a wrought iron fence, accessible only by key. Tomorrow is my favorite holiday, Halloween, and the perimeter of the park is decorated for the occasion, outlined by dozens of candlelit jack-o'-lanterns.

A boy, about six years old, wearing a vampire cape, races by, his nanny in tow. He's shouting, jumping up and down, rehearsing his shtick.

"Trick or treat, smell my feet, give me something good to eat."

Ty notices me staring. "Do you know that kid?" he says.

"That was George's favorite mantra," I say. "No matter the season or the holiday, he would belt out the words, over and over, until our nanny caved and gave him a handful of M&M's."

As a child, my younger brother, George, had an insatiable appetite for chocolate. As an adult, it was drugs. He died of an overdose eight years ago.

Ty puts his arm around me, pulls me close. "I wish I'd met him," he says.

"George got so jazzed about Halloween. It was practically a national holiday in our house."

"Let me guess. You dressed up as Sherlock Holmes."

I shake my head. "Most years, I'd go as a skeleton, Charlie would be a sheriff, and George would be a ghost." I picture George, with a sheet draped over him. "His life still haunts me," I say.

"You mean his death?" Ty says.

"No, I mean his life."

We stop at my parents' doorstep, Ty smiles, gives me a kiss, and raps the heavy brass door knocker. I press the bell; like many of my parents' possessions, the door knocker is just for show.

Serena, my parents' live-in housekeeper, greets us in the foyer. She's been with the family since I was a child, and she's protective. When I introduce her to Ty, she gives him the once-over. Her disapproving eyes stop at his scuffed-up cowboy boots. I hook my arm into his and give her a tight-lipped smile, signaling: *Keep your comments to yourself.*

"Something smells amazing," Ty says.

"Claude is making Dover sole." Serena takes my Burberry

trench, inspects the lining, and clucks her tongue. "There's a tear in the sleeve. Leave it. I'll have it fixed."

I consider putting up a protest, but the coat could use mending.

"Is everyone upstairs?" I say.

"The men are in the library. Missy is with your mother, in her dressing room."

I lead Ty up the staircase to the second floor, where my father is mixing a batch of martinis in a monogrammed cocktail shaker. They greet me with warm hugs and Ty with welcoming handshakes.

"I see you more on TV than in person," Charlie says.

He doesn't mean it as a dig. He and I are close; he's always considered his role as oldest sibling as a serious responsibility. When we were kids, he taught me how to pop a wheelie on my Schwinn, and how to negotiate a successful Pokémon card trade. As an adult, he tries to guide my career decisions, and he views my current position as his own failure.

My father hands me a glass of Pinot and offers a martini to Ty, who accepts. I've never seen Ty drink anything other than beer and an occasional glass of wine. He's making an effort to fit in, and I love him for it. Never having visited my childhood home before, he scans the room: the hundreds of books, mostly collectibles; and the artwork, mostly early nineteenth-century oils.

He stands in front of a portrait. "Is this a Sargent?" he says. "An original?"

Normally, it'd be tacky to ask about authenticity, and by inference, value, but Ty's unapologetic enthusiasm make the inquiry charming.

Charlie seems to agree. "Good eye," he says.

Initially, Charlie was opposed to my relationship with Ty, but after the shooting, his position shifted. He finally stopped trying to fix me up with his colleagues and former classmates.

Ty admires the painting. "The subject looks a lot like Abby," he says.

"It's Abigail's great-grandmother, on her father's side," my
mother says, sweeping into the room.

Her glossy hair is in a blond bob, and she's wearing a cream-
colored silk suit.

She walks toward the bar and stumbles slightly. My sister-
in-law, Missy, is right behind her, in a smart navy A-line dress.
Missy grabs my mother's elbow to steady her, throws Charlie a
look: *Do something.*

"Have a seat, Mom, I'll get you a drink," Charlie says.

Charlie and my father don't seem concerned about my mother's
increasing alcohol consumption. My mother has always enjoyed her cocktails; as teenagers, we used to joke that her best
friends were Brandy Alexander and Dom Pérignon, but it's no
longer funny. Her drinking became worse after George's death,
and I worry that my own near-death experience is the cause of
her recent spiral.

"Abigail, you look wonderful," my mother says, "but I think
it's time to retire that blouse."

She never misses the opportunity to critique my wardrobe,
even when she's three sheets to the wind.

Missy gives me a kiss. "I think you look fabulous, as always,"
she says.

I gotta give Missy credit; six months into the marriage, and
she's already defying my mother.

My mother sinks into the sofa, and my brother hands her a
cocktail. Serena enters the room, escorting our dinner guests, a
man in his late sixties and an attractive woman in her early
forties—definitely not a first wife. My father gives him a hearty
backslap and makes the introductions.

"Larry is the managing partner at Norton and Standish. And
this is his wife, Suzanne."

"Abigail, I've heard a lot about you," Larry says. "Your father
tells me you're looking to make a career change."

I turn to my father, then to Charlie, but they're smiling,

encouraging me. When my parents cut off my trust fund disbursements, I thought they'd end their crusade to get me out of the DA's office, but apparently they're still trying.

"We're always looking for new talent," Larry says. "Give my office a call, and we'll set something up."

I smile politely. My parents are famous for their "accidentally on purpose" encounters; I should have predicted we were invited here for more than a simple dinner. They mean well; I don't plan to leave the DA's office, but if I did, I'd sooner join the French Foreign Legion than a corporate law firm.

Ty nudges me. "Babe, I think you're vibrating," he says.

My cell phone is buzzing. I pull it out of my pocket, check the caller ID.

"I've got to take it," I say.

I walk into the living room, past a shelf of family pictures: Charlie and Missy, in swimsuits, on the beach in Saint Barths. George, in a jacket and tie, at his boarding school in Switzerland. Me, dressed as Lady Macbeth for my seventh-grade class play at Winsor. *What's done cannot be undone.*

"Hi, Kevin," I say. "What's up?"

"I wanted to let you know, our vic's mother is flying to Logan in the morning. She's coming to pick up the body," Kevin says.

I accidentally bang my elbow on the piano, igniting a pitch-perfect C-sharp. "Has she been autopsied?" I say.

"Yup—I just got off the horn with the doc."

"What's the COD? Strangulation?"

"Get this: she drowned. There was water in her lungs."

I look out the window at Louisburg Square; the candles on a couple of the jack-o'-lanterns have been extinguished by the wind.

"Was it fresh or salt water?" I say.

"Fresh, probably tap. Looks like she was killed in a bathtub," he says.

"Did you serve Tommy Greenough with the subpoena?"

"I handed it to him an hour ago."

I peek into the library, survey the scene. Suzanne is sucking up to my mother, asking for help getting on the symphony's board of trustees, while my mother polishes off her martini, pretending to care. My father, my brother, and Larry are yammering on about mergers and acquisitions. Ty is thumbing through a book of Turner landscapes.

"Swing by and get me," I say. "We can prep for grand jury."

"It's Saturday night," Kevin says.

I catch Ty's eye, look toward the door: *Want to get out of here?* He raises his eyebrows and smiles. He'd love an excuse to cut out. My father will be disappointed, but he has guests to entertain. My mother won't care. I've made an appearance, and to her, that's what matters.

"I'm getting paid overtime," Kevin says. "You should enjoy whatever you're doing and jump back in on Monday."

"That's okay," I say. "I don't have anything important going on."

Chapter Nine

Suffolk County grand juries are made up of twenty-three citizens, but it only takes sixteen votes to secure an indictment. Today's panel is well into their second month of hearing cases, at a rate of about seven felonies a day. They get a steady diet of stabbings, shootings, robberies, rapes, and murders. While the witnesses testify, the jurors sit in worn leather chairs listening, reading the newspaper, snacking, and doing the sudoku.

I walk into the grand jury room and flip on the recording device.

"I'm opening a John Doe investigation into the facts and circumstances surrounding the death of Caitlyn Walker, whose body was discovered in Public Alley 257 in East Boston."

A juror seated in the back row, a graphic designer from Hyde Park, unwraps a fresh batch of coconut brownies and takes one for herself. She offers the plate to her seatmate, a retired postal worker, who takes two and passes them on.

"I read about this case in the *Herald*," the postal worker says in between bites. "This is about that girl from Wellesley College."

A few jurors start to stir and whisper to each other. I turn off the recorder.

"You're allowed to consider outside sources," I say, "but please wait to hear the evidence as it unfolds."

A very pregnant fortysomething ignores my reprimand.

"Is this case connected to that other girl who got killed, the one from BU?" she says.

Before the panel makes up their minds and issues indictments, I'd better put in some evidence. I turn the recorder back on.

"I'm going to call my first witness: Thomas Greenough Jr."

The room quiets. A man in the first row sets his knitting aside. The postal worker sits up straight in his chair and brushes crumbs off the front of his sweatshirt. A few members of the panel take out their notebooks.

Tommy Greenough enters the room, followed by his lawyer. I'm not surprised he's represented by counsel. It's someone I recognize, but wasn't expecting: Josh King, a former law school classmate. Josh and I were on law review together. We dated for a few months, but he found me *avoidant and elusive*, and I thought he was a crashing bore. Smart move by the Greenoughs, choosing someone who is equal parts competent and annoying.

I raise my right hand, signaling Tommy, who mimics the gesture.

"Do you solemnly swear the testimony you will give in this hearing will be the truth?" I say.

He sits back and says something unintelligible.

"Please keep your voice up," I say. "The microphone records, but it doesn't amplify."

Josh whispers to him. Tommy nods and then speaks loud enough for all to hear.

"I swear to tell the truth," he says.

"Do you understand you have the right to remain silent, and anything you say can and will be used against you?"

Tommy looks at Josh, who urges him on. "Yes," Tommy says, "I want to testify. I'm here to help."

After the preliminary warnings, admonitions, and introductions, I hold up a picture from the Crazy Fox security tape.

"I'm showing you what has previously been marked as grand

jury exhibit one. Do you recognize the two people depicted in the photograph?"

"Yes and no," he says.

"Please explain."

"The man, that's me."

"And the woman?"

Tommy picks up the water pitcher, fills his cup, and takes a series of small sips.

"I can't say for sure," he says.

"Can't or won't?" I say.

He pours another cup of water, downs it in one gulp.

"I'm unable to identify her," he says.

"Your hand is touching her back," I say.

"That doesn't mean I know her. Women approach me a lot."

Josh puts his hand on Tommy's arm, hoping to shut him up.

"You didn't leave the Crazy Fox with this woman?" I say.

Tommy raises his voice and rolls his eyes. "Obviously, we both left at the same time," he says.

"Where did you go after you left the bar?"

"Where did I go?"

Josh stands and says, "Even though my client would like to respond, I am advising him to assert his Fifth Amendment right and decline to testify further."

Josh would never walk his client into a murder indictment, but I had hoped to get a little more out of Tommy. Now that he's invoked, I can't ask any more questions unless I offer him immunity, and that's not going to happen.

I shuffle some papers, try to gather my thoughts.

"You are excused, Mr. Greenough," I say.

The panel seems disappointed when I tell them that's the only witness for today. Outside the grand jury room, Kevin is seated on a bench, waiting for me. We walk to the elevator in silence and get on an empty car.

"You think we jumped the gun by calling him to testify so soon?" Kevin says.

"No, I was able to lock him into a story. The minute we prove he knew Caitlyn, talked to her, bought her a drink, or anything else, he's screwed," I say.

"Why do you think he was so eager to come in and testify?"

"Usually, I'd think it was a ploy to try to get immunity, but Josh knows I'd never fall for that. There's gotta be another reason."

We get off the elevator. The lobby is buzzing with lawyers and defendants.

"We need to find where Tommy went after he left the bar," Kevin says.

"There was no one else on the tape with him," I say.

"Maybe we're going at it the wrong way. Let's see if we can figure out who went into the bar with him."

Outside the courthouse, there's a full-blown press conference going on. Tommy and Josh are surrounded by cameras and microphones.

"Who put the word out?" Kevin says.

I survey the crowd, point to a woman who is positioned behind a layer of reporters. She's petite, in the middle of the pack, but you can't miss her in her trademark peacock-blue suit.

"That woman is Sally Springer," I say. "She runs the biggest crisis communications firm in town. She was probably up all night, scripting every syllable of Tommy's testimony."

"The best defense starts with a good presser," Kevin says.

We listen to Josh play fast and loose with the truth. "My client extends his deepest sympathy to the Walker family and will do whatever he can to help bring her killer to justice. We have cooperated fully with investigators. Unfortunately we don't have much information to offer."

Josh knows I can't refute anything he's saying; prosecutors aren't allowed to talk about what went on inside the grand jury room, not even to correct a lie. That's why they came to the grand jury—so they could claim they're helping, even though they're not. Clever move.

Reporters shout out questions. "Tommy, what were you doing at that bar?" "Who were you with?"

Josh puts his hands up, gestures dramatically. "Tommy was enjoying a glass of beer. We've supplied the grand jury with all relevant information."

"Tommy, isn't there anything you want to say?" a reporter says.

Tommy crosses his arms, looks at the pavement. "Yes, of course," he says, even though his body language screams *no*. "I wish there was something I could do to help."

"What about the other girl, Rose Driscoll? Did you know her?" Carl Ostroff says.

Sally Springer steps in. "That's all. Thanks, everyone. The police have asked us to limit our access to the press, to allow them to do what they do best—solve this horrific crime. This is the only public comment we'll be making."

When the Greenough posse is done misleading the media, a couple of reporters notice me and smell blood.

"Abby, do you want to comment?" Carl Ostroff says.

I break through the mass of microphones and cameras, walk away.

Carl stays on my heels. "Off the record?"

Kevin and I ignore him, cut across the plaza, and descend the steep stairs. I check my text messages, skipping past most of them. An unfamiliar number catches my eye. *Feeling like an impromptu lunch? Meet me at the Four Seasons. Chip Aldridge.* I should say no. My life is complicated enough. Besides, things are going better than ever with Ty. There's no sane reason to mess with that. I text Chip back. *Sure. See you in fifteen minutes.*

Somehow my encounter with Chip, however brief, struck a chord. He's charming and handsome, but it's more than that.

He reminds me of the fun parts of being an Endicott. Summers on the Vineyard, sailing, bodysurfing, eating fried clams. It will be fun to reconnect, reminisce. It won't go any further than that.

I tuck my hair behind my ears, reapply a coat of lipstick, and check my teeth in the mirror. As soon as I snap my compact closed, I notice Kevin is watching me.

"Hot date?" he says.

"Just a lunch," I say. "Do you mind dropping me off at the Four Seasons?"

"Fancy schmancy. My lunch meetings usually take place at Finagle a Bagel."

"It's not what you think," I say.

"Baloney," he says.

Kevin is a human lie detector, which is probably why he has the highest solve rate in the city. And he's relentless.

"Are you stepping out on that boyfriend of yours?" he says.

"For the thousandth time, his name is Ty. And, for the record, no, I am not stepping out on him."

I check myself, knowing that my agitation is evidence of my consciousness of guilt.

Kevin looks at me and shrugs. "Fine. If that's how you want to play it, that's how we'll play it," he says.

Chapter Ten

The maître d' escorts me into the Bristol Lounge, and I fiddle with my phone as we cross the dining room, pretending to check e-mails—anything to avoid eye contact. There's a strong possibility someone will recognize me; I'd rather not have to explain my presence.

Chip Aldridge is seated at a table overlooking the Public Garden. He's casual compared to the other diners, in a cashmere sweater and corduroys; a sign of irreverence and confidence—qualities I find most attractive in a man. I should duck out before it's too late.

He stands and surprises me with a kiss on the cheek. Not a fake air kiss; his lips actually make contact with my skin, and it feels good enough to make me drop my phone. He picks it up and hands it to me.

"I was beginning to think you weren't going to show," he says.

"Sorry, I was tied up in the grand jury."

"That's the best excuse I've ever heard, and the most intriguing."

He smiles and pulls out my chair. When he touches me on the shoulder, I feel the excitement of possibility that comes with a first date. As the waiter takes our orders, I remind myself this is not a date. It's just two old friends catching up.

I take in the view across the street at the Public Garden. The bronze statues of Civil War heroes and abolitionists, perched atop granite bases. The weeping willows that surround the lagoon. The two men engaged in a drug transaction, cash in exchange for a small glassine envelope that most likely contains heroin.

"When I was ten, my grandmother used to take me here for tea," I say. "I felt grown-up, special. I'd always get the same thing: a pot of chamomile, a plate of scones, and a side of lemon curd."

"Sounds like a nice ritual."

"We'd chat for a while, then she'd disappear, for about an hour. I'd sit at the table, reading or drawing. It didn't occur to me until years later, when my grandfather filed for divorce, that she was having an affair and she was using me as her cover."

"We have a lot in common. I was my father's alibi, but he used to take me to the track. We'd come home and lie to my mother, tell her that we were at the ball game."

I try not to sink too deeply into the comfort of compatibility. We enjoy our lunches, lobster salad for me and scallops for him, and the waiter delivers dessert menus.

"The blood orange sorbet looks tempting," I say.

Chip orders a bowl and two spoons.

"Your job sounds exciting, prosecuting murderers," he says.

"Sometimes a little too exciting."

He leans in, eager to be in the know, and lowers his voice. "Are you involved in the Wellesley student's abduction that's been all over the news?"

"I am, but I can't talk about it."

"Attorney-client privilege?"

"Something like that."

The waiter delivers our sorbet, and I dig in.

"Tell me about your work," I say.

"This morning, I operated on a concert pianist who shattered his elbow in a skydiving accident. The surgery went well, but it'll be a long time before his next performance."

Talk of musicians and concerts makes me think about Ty. After he was shot, it took months for his shoulder to heal. His physical therapy ended a few weeks ago, but he's still having a hard time maneuvering the sax. A flash of guilt lands in the pit of my stomach. I put down my spoon and check my watch.

"I've got to get back to work," I say.

I take out my wallet and offer to split the bill, to make it seem less like a date, but Chip acts as though he doesn't hear me. As we walk through the dining room, he places his hand in the center of my back, igniting a spark of electricity. I tense up and look around.

"I'd like to do this again," Chip says.

I would love to do it again. By any objective standards, Chip is attractive, but I think there's more at play. Maybe I'm trying to sabotage my relationship with Ty.

"That's not a good idea," I say.

He looks at me for a minute and flashes a high-wattage smile.

"It was good to see you," he says.

We pass through the lobby in silence. As we near the door, I start to walk a little faster, and he keeps pace. The doorman flags down a taxi, and I take the short ride back to Bulfinch Place. On the way back to the office, I promise myself to tell Ty about the lunch. He'll be curious about Chip, because he's interested in my past, but I doubt he'll ask a lot of questions. My criminals have taught me the best way to avoid fallout from a bad decision is to get in front of it.

Chapter Eleven

My victims, Caitlyn Walker and Rose Driscoll, have taken over my office. Their crime scene photographs and autopsy diagrams are spread out on the desk. Their grand jury transcripts line the windowsills. Their case interview notes and police reports cover the floor. I sit and think about where to start.

Kevin taps on the door and takes a seat across from me.

"How was your date?" he says.

"It wasn't a date," I say a little too abruptly.

"Just so you know, I'm all for you playing the field."

I take a beat, try to relax, knowing he has my best interests at heart.

"Why don't you like Ty?" I say.

"Plain and simple—I think you're too good for him," he says.

"If anything, he's too good for me."

Kevin shakes his head in disbelief. "You could have anyone. Why him?"

"We've got a yin-yang thing going," I say. "Nothing seems to faze him, which makes me slightly less neurotic."

"You're dating him because it saves on Prozac?"

"Ty is smart, handsome, talented, and a great guy," I say, more to reaffirm my own feelings than to convince Kevin. "You'd like him."

I wonder if Kevin is jealous of Ty. I bristle every time Kevin mentions his wife.

He drags his chair in front of my computer screen and looks through the Crazy Fox security video, hoping to discover who Tommy came into the bar with. I use my laptop to research the Greenough clan. Thomas is the senior senator from Massachusetts, elected twenty-two years ago. His wife, Elizabeth, teaches French literature at Georgetown. They have two sons. Tommy, the oldest, runs a nonprofit for veterans—a sure sign of political ambition. Robert, the youngest, is a senior at MIT, studying urban planning.

Kevin sees something on the computer screen.

"Bingo," he says.

The video shows Tommy, holding up his ID as the bouncer inspects it. He gets his hand stamped and pays the cover charge. Behind him is a man with the same aquiline nose, broad brows, and square chin.

"That's gotta be Tommy's kid brother," Kevin says.

I compare the video with the family picture posted on Greenough's website. "It's definitely Robbie Greenough," I say. "Let's take another look and see if Robbie was around when Tommy left the bar."

Kevin finds the tape of Tommy and Caitlyn leaving the bar and hits play.

"There he is. That's Robbie, off to the side," Kevin says.

"That means all three of them were in there together," I say. "And all three of them left together."

We're distracted by chatter in the hallway. I check my watch; it's exactly five. The DA's office has a lot of clock-watchers, but a mass exodus is unusual. Cassandra Lester strides past my office.

"Where's everyone going?" I say. "Is it another bomb scare?"

Cassandra made a play for my job while I was out on leave, and she was not a member of the welcome committee when I returned. She stops, hesitates, then swivels around to face me.

She's like a flashing neon sign, demanding: *Look at me*. Her hot-pink suit, her chunky gold-plated necklace, her overprocessed blond hair. She's not half-bad in the courtroom; what she lacks in intellect and preparation, she makes up for in theatrical performance.

"Everyone is headed to the Parker House," Cassandra says. "Max is announcing his run for mayor."

I turn to go back in my office, but Kevin blocks the doorway.

"You should get over there and show your mug, let people know you're interested," he says.

"Who said I'm interested?"

"The *Herald* is naming you as Max's most likely successor," Cassandra says.

If someone from the media is tossing my name around, it's flattering and affirming, but not plausible. I'd never get the political support, especially with the Greenough investigation looming. Besides, I don't want the job.

"They're probably batting everyone's name around," I say.

I stand aside to let a group of gang prosecutors get by.

"If you don't want the appointment," Cassandra says, "let me know."

"Why?" I say.

"Because I want it."

She smiles at the thought, fastens the rhinestone buttons on her coat, and jumps on the elevator.

"You're nuts," Kevin says. "You'd be great at Max's job."

"I'm a trial attorney, not a politician."

I walk back into my office, and he follows.

"It's not brain surgery. You can learn that stuff. You ask for money and kiss some keisters," he says.

"The governor will never appoint me," I say, "not in a million years."

"You should give it a shot. Think about it: Wouldn't you rather have Cassandra work for you, than vice versa?"

I consider the idea of Cassandra as my boss, and don't like what I see. I stand, take my coat from a hanger on the back of my door, and slip it on.

"I'll be back in an hour," I say.

I walk quickly, across City Hall Plaza, onto School Street, and through the revolving doors of the Parker House. The hotel is an all-purpose venue for prosecutors. The ballroom is where we host fund-raisers. The lounge is where we celebrate guilty verdicts and commiserate over acquittals. The rooms upstairs are where we stash our witnesses.

I nudge my way into the Kennedy Room. The space is small, the air is stale, and it's jammed full of people—perfect campaign optics. I grab a *Lombardo for Mayor* button and pin it on, careful not to rip a hole in my jacket. Armani doesn't grow on trees, not anymore.

Max is at the podium, his wife, Cindy, by his side. Their son is next to her, looking wholesome and supportive. They know the drill.

"Ray Harris's resignation comes as a shock to all of us," Max says. "Corruption, a violation of the public trust in any form, is unacceptable. I've spent my entire professional career fighting crime at all levels, in the streets, in the boardroom, and in the statehouse. I take my role of chief law enforcement officer as sacred. And I'll do the same when I'm elected mayor."

Max pauses for a booming round of applause; he doesn't take questions from the press. He knows to quit while he's ahead. He and Cindy work the crowd by dividing and conquering. Cassandra elbows her way to his side, making sure to hijack as many photos ops with him as possible.

Carl Ostroff sidles up to me. "Word on the street is Cassandra has been working her contacts, lobbying for Max's job."

"Have you heard if anyone else is interested?" I keep my voice to a whisper.

"All the usuals: a community organizer, a couple of city councilors, and a nutcase."

"They're not mutually exclusive," I say. "Don't quote me on that."

"You already sound like a politician. For what it's worth, the statehouse press corps is giving you the odds," he says.

I smile, clench my jaw, and do my best ventriloquist impression, in case anyone is lip-reading.

"Do me a favor," I say. "Fan the flame."

Carl opens his notebook, flips to a blank page.

"Any movement on the coed killer invest?" he says.

"Yes."

"Can you be more specific?"

"No."

He closes the notebook. "Throw a guy a bone. Have you interviewed anyone else in the Greenough clan? How about Robbie?"

"Not yet, but he's next on my list."

Chapter Twelve

Tommy's brother, Robert Greenough, lives in the Alpha Beta Zeta house in the Fenway section of Boston. The fraternity was chartered eighty years ago and has a rich history of brotherhood, community service, and binge drinking. The neighbors call police regularly to complain about loud parties, trash, and drunk students passed out in the front yard.

We circle the block until we find an empty parking space in front of my favorite museum, the Isabella Stewart Gardner. Kevin and I walk around the corner to the Alpha house, a three-story brick building. I've been here twice. The first time was for an assault that put a sophomore engineering student in a coma for six months. He suffered permanent brain damage and had to relearn how to hold a fork and tie his shoes. The second time I was here, the victim wasn't as fortunate. A seventeen-year-old pledge was hazed, forced to drink until he passed out, and died.

Other than that, my experience with fraternities is limited. At Harvard, men don't pledge fraternities; instead, they punch final clubs. Generations of Endicott men, including my father and brother, were members of the ultraexclusive Porcellian, along with Theodore Roosevelt, Henry Cabot Lodge, and the Winkelvoss twins. I never had much interest in what went on inside the clubhouse, or Old Barn as it's called. I imagine that, like all male-only clubs, there was drinking, networking, and more drinking.

The shades at the fraternity house are drawn and the windows are closed, but we can hear Maroon 5's "Moves Like Jagger" from the sidewalk. Kevin presses on the bell, bangs on the door a couple of times, counts to ten, and turns the knob. It's unlocked.

"Hello?" Kevin says.

We step inside to find a young man in the foyer. He's holding a red plastic cup of beer.

"Can I help you?" he says.

Kevin flashes his badge. "We're looking for Robert Greenough."

The man directs us into a large, wood-paneled room, where clusters of students are talking, shooting pool, and playing a competitive round of beer pong. A banged-up metal keg is on the floor, in front of a fireplace. Robbie Greenough is in the center of the room, chalking a pool cue, boasting about his game. He's disheveled, in a privileged kind of way: tousled hair, torn khakis, and a T-shirt that says *ACK*, which is the abbreviation for the Nantucket airport.

"Robbie, the cops are here to talk to you," the man says.

Robbie hesitates, puts down the stick, and moves toward us.

"My lawyer says if you're here to search the place, you need a warrant."

He's been well prepped.

"We're not here to execute a warrant," I say.

Kevin eyes a purple bong on the floor. "At least not tonight."

Kevin staked his claim on bad cop, which means I play good cop.

"Is there somewhere we can talk privately?" I lower my voice. "You don't want everyone to know your business."

Robbie nods to a woman with shiny black hair and Clark Kent glasses.

"Emma is going to come with us," he says. "Nothing personal, but my lawyer said I should have a witness."

He walks us into what must have been the smoking room, back when people smoked. The walls are mahogany, the chairs are leather, and the bookshelves are dusty.

"Were you in the Crazy Fox last Thursday, with your brother?" I say.

I look at him hard, try to gauge his reaction, see if he'll admit to what we already know.

"I go there sometimes," he says.

"It's a yes-or-no question," Kevin says.

"Yes."

Emma elbows him. "You told me you were studying," she says.

"What time did you leave the bar?" I say.

"Why did you lie to me?" Emma says.

Emma has gone rogue, and Robbie's not sure how to handle it. He looks at her, then at me, as though he's trying to assess who poses the greatest threat. He chooses Emma.

"I didn't lie," he says. "I went to the library earlier. Then I went to the bar." Robbie turns to me. "I stayed there until around closing."

Kevin shows him a photo of Caitlyn Walker. "Do you remember seeing this woman?"

Robbie glances at the picture, then at the floor. Emma can't take her eyes off the photo.

"That's the woman from Wellesley, who was killed." She grabs Robbie's arm. "Did you see her? Tell me. Did you know her?"

Robbie shakes her off, throws her a look. *Shut up.*

"I know you think she was with me and my brother, at the bar," he says.

"Was she?" I say.

"No."

"Where did you go after you left the bar?" Kevin says.

"I came back here. Emma can confirm that."

"I was asleep in Robbie's room," Emma says. "When I woke up at around three to go to the bathroom, he was passed out next to me."

Emma isn't as willing an alibi witness as Robbie had hoped.

"Where did Tommy go after he left the bar?" Kevin says.

Robbie shrugs. "You'll have to ask him."

"We're asking you."

"Look, I didn't kill that woman. And neither did Tommy." Robbie stands and takes his phone out of his pocket. "I'm not answering any more questions, until I've called my lawyer."

"Why?" Emma follows him into the hallway. "If you don't answer them, they're going to think you're hiding something."

Robbie stops at the front door, opens it, expecting us to leave. Kevin and I continue to the party room. Robbie, unsure of what to do, follows. The room has been tidied; the bottles, keg, and bong have been removed.

"Can I see some ID?" Kevin says to the group.

"This is a private club," Robbie says.

A young woman looks like she's about to burst into tears. "I'm nineteen. If you arrest me, my parents will kill me."

"My lawyer wants to talk to you." Robbie hands me his phone.

"You're harassing my client," Josh King says. "He had nothing to do with that girl's murder."

"So he said." I take the phone with me as I wander into the kitchen, where there are dozens of empty beer bottles and a scattering of cereal boxes. "The fraternity is chock-full of underage kids, and they're all drinking," I say.

"News flash, Abby: college kids drink. You may have been a law-abiding, perfect-GPA-holding student, but most kids aren't."

I fight the urge to remind Josh that *I* was the one who broke up with *him*.

"Being a minor in possession of alcohol is a crime," I say.

"You're going to give a bunch of Rhodes scholars criminal records?"

"Have you met these clowns? They're hardly MIT's best and brightest."

I imagine Max's disapproval of what I'm about to do. *You arrested a group of teenagers because you couldn't get what you wanted out of Greenough. You can't abuse your authority to satisfy your own ego.*

I hang up and turn to Kevin. "We need leverage. Let's arrest them."

"They're not exactly public enemy number one." Kevin inspects the liquor supply, an assortment of bottles containing high-octane grain alcohol. "Plus, arresting a senator's kid is not going to help your chances of becoming DA."

"I don't care. Besides, I've already pissed Greenough off. He'd never support me, and neither would his cronies."

"No one will ever accuse you of being one of the good old boys."

We look around the room. The walls are lined with framed yearbook-type photographs; each one shows the fraternity members for a particular year. Pictures of the leaders are on the top row, with their name and position: president, treasurer, social chairman, pledge captain.

Kevin lifts one of the pictures off the wall.

"They look like the board of trustees at a bank," he says.

I inspect the photo. It gives me an idea.

"If these guys want to act like a corporation, then let's treat them like one. We don't have to charge the teenagers for drinking. Let's charge the fraternity as a corporate entity."

"No offense, but you're starting to sound like a fed," Kevin says.

"Exactly," I say. "It's like when they charged Enron, or the international soccer executives at FIFA."

"Okay, I'm liking it, but if we charge a corporation, then who wears the cuffs?"

"The chapter president, who just so happens to be Robbie Greenough."

Kevin and I walk into the party room. He unlatches the handcuffs from his belt.

"You have the right to remain silent," Kevin says.

Robbie starts to breathe audibly, eyes the door like he's about to bolt, and takes a step forward.

"Don't even think about it," Kevin says.

Chapter Thirteen

I made my bones in the Roxbury District Court about twelve years ago, and I have a lot of fond memories here. It's where I argued my first motion to suppress, arraigned my first serial rapist, and offered a plea on my first mayhem case. The courthouse has undergone extensive renovations, security has been improved, and people no longer urinate in the stairwells, but its bread and butter remain the same: drugs, guns, and more drugs.

The sidewalk outside the building is packed; courthouse personnel, lawyers, defendants, victims, and witnesses all try to navigate around the crush of reporters. Extra deputies guard the front door. The line to get inside is at a standstill.

Carl Ostroff elbows his way through the scrum.

"Abby, you seriously arrested Senator Greenough's kid for drinking a Heineken?" he says.

"Check your facts. It's not about drinking a beer. The charge is serving alcohol to minors." I keep moving, my eyes fixed on the front door.

Carl follows me. "Homicide prosecutors don't arraign alcohol violations. My hunch is that you're thinking he might be the serial killer."

"See you inside."

"You're pretty touchy this morning," he says. "Is it nerves, or do you have a case of buyer's remorse?"

I force a smile, ignoring the rest of the pack, who are waving and shouting questions at me. *Do you plan to ask for jail time? Shouldn't you be chasing real criminals? What's next, you're going to arrest Malia Obama for jaywalking?*

A court officer comes to my rescue, escorts me inside, and waves me around the line. I skirt the metal detector, pass through the lobby, and take the stairs up to the third floor. As soon as I open the door, I see Max, arms crossed, foot tapping.

He directs me into a side office, and on the way, we pass Cassandra. She's standing in front of a window, doing her best imitation of a concerned public servant; furrowed brow, pursed lips, and index finger pressed against her chin. She's posing, with the hopes that she'll make it onto the B roll of this evening's newscast.

As soon as I step in the conference room, Max slams the door. His face is red, his forehead sweaty. I don't wait for his reprimand.

"I know I should have called before we made the arrest, but there was a crime being committed right under my nose." I hope if I keep talking, it'll give him a chance to calm down. "I couldn't just walk away, and neither could Kevin. We have legal, ethical, professional responsibilities."

"Fuck that. Your responsibility is to me." His finger has a slight tremor as he wags it in my face.

"Come on, Max. If the guy's name was Robbie Green, instead of Robbie Greenough, we wouldn't be having this conversation."

"I'm still the goddamned DA. I call the shots." A spray of spit comes out of his mouth.

"I didn't mean any disrespect. I made a judgment call."

"You've lost your marbles. I knew you came back to work too soon."

This conversation is veering in the wrong direction; I have to stop it before it's too late.

"You don't want to end up like Ray Harris," I say.

Max grips the back of a chair, and looks like he's going to pick it up and hurl it at me.

"What the fuck is that supposed to mean?" he says.

I should change course and retreat, but I can't help myself.

"Playing footsie with the rich and powerful, that's what got Ray indicted."

Max takes a breath. I take a seat, hoping he'll follow. He doesn't.

"You're making me look like a goddamned Keystone Cop," he says.

"If you're worried about saving face, blame it on me."

"You got that right. As soon as you leave this room, you're going to file a nolle pros and withdraw the charges. Then Cassandra is taking over."

"You mean the drinking case, not the murder investigations."

"I mean the whole enchilada. I'm pulling you from the game."

I assumed that Max would be angry, but I didn't expect him to yank me off the case entirely. Maybe I've overestimated both his allegiance and my value.

There's a light knock on the door, Kevin is looking in the window at us. Turning my back to Max, I mouth: *Please, come in, interrupt us.* He opens the door and eases into the room.

Max doesn't let up. "This was the final straw. You're out."

"Whoa, hold off," Kevin says. "This is my fault. Abby warned me that you'd blow a gasket, but I wouldn't listen."

"Bullshit. This has Abby's prints all over it. She ignored my directive, went ahead and did exactly what she wanted to do. Do you see all the press out there? They don't care about your damn judgment calls. This is going to land on me."

"Max, I hear you," I say. "I promise I won't do it again—"

"You're fired."

He's not bluffing. I don't know how to respond. Fortunately, Kevin does.

"Max, hear me out. There isn't going to be any stink on the DA's office."

"Kevin, you're a stand-up guy, but this has spiraled beyond your control," Max says.

Kevin holds up his cell phone. "No, it hasn't. Check your newsfeed."

Max scrolls through his phone and reads out loud: "The *Globe* is reporting that: *unnamed sources claim this was a police tactic, a clever move, designed to further the investigation by squeezing information out of the Greenoughs.*"

"See there, they don't even mention you," Kevin says.

Max continues reading. "They're calling it: *bold and decisive. It shows strong leadership, in the face of powerful interests.*" His face drops. "Son of a bitch. The commissioner is getting all the credit."

Max's rage has shifted away from me, toward the police department. Seeing an opening, I take a comb from my tote and hand it to him.

"There are cameras all over the place," I say.

He runs the comb through his hair, then calls his press secretary to try to get some airtime. When he's done, he turns to me.

"You're lucky this didn't go south," he says.

"I've got to do the arraignment," I say.

He blocks my exit. "If you go against me again, that's it, you're done."

On my way out the door, I squeeze Kevin's elbow. He got me out a jam—again. And I'm grateful.

Downstairs, the arraignment session is bursting with reporters, lawyers, police officers, and defendants, all here to see the show. Even my favorite court watcher, Harold, has taken the Orange Line from downtown to catch the live performance. A news camera, which might as well be an Uzi, points in my direction, following my every move. As soon as I take my seat at the prosecutor's table, Josh King walks in. He looks like a half a million bucks, which is probably what he's getting paid.

"Where's your client?" I say.

"All rise," the court officer says. "This honorable court is now in session, Judge Patrick Lafferty presiding."

Judge Patrick "Lightweight" Lafferty bounds in, chest first, feigning confidence. He's a former defense attorney, a worka-day ham-and-egger, recently appointed to the bench because he used to coach the governor's kid in peewee hockey. His greatest fear in life is being called upon to issue a well-reasoned decision. He's been safe up to now, since district court judges are more akin to school yard referees than Nobel laureates.

"Be seated." Judge Lafferty smiles at Josh. "Nice to see you, Mr. King. It's been a while."

In most instances, prosecutors have the home field advantage and command of the courtroom. A $750-an-hour attorney from a white-shoe firm is like a unicorn in state district court. When one deigns to make an appearance on a misdemeanor, almost everyone, prosecutors included, suck up to him as though he might leave a trail of hundred-dollar bills in his wake.

"It's a pleasure to be in your courtroom, Your Honor," Josh says.

I catch myself rolling my eyes and try to break up the love-fest.

"This is the matter of Commonwealth *v.* Alpha Beta Zeta fraternity, alleging providing alcohol to a minor," I say.

"Where is your client, Mr. King?" Judge Lafferty says. "Call him in here so we can proceed."

"The so-called defendant is not in the building and, consequently, unable to partake in this hearing."

A few members of the audience chuckle. Judge Lafferty isn't sure which of us Josh is mocking, him or me. It's definitely me. Screw him.

"Robert Greenough is president of the corporation. It appears that he has voluntarily absented himself from the proceedings," I say. "I'd request that a default warrant be issued."

Lafferty looks down, shuffles some papers. Uh-oh, he may have to make a decision.

"Was Mr. Greenough given proper notice?" he says.

I don't wait for Josh's answer. "Detective Farnsworth served him personally, in my presence. The Commonwealth submits that Mr. Greenough is in default, and requests that an arrest warrant be issued."

Judge Lafferty looks around, fidgets with his pen. His biggest nightmare has come to fruition; a simple bail argument has evolved into a legal dispute, requiring resolution. He tosses the hot potato to Josh.

"What do you say, Mr. King? Why shouldn't I issue a warrant?"

Josh grins. "Your Honor, the fraternity disbanded this morning. Therefore, there is no corporation and, consequently, no corporate president. And no one or nothing to charge."

Judge Lafferty spins his chair around and pulls a law book from a shelf behind him. He thumbs through it, turning the pages slowly, pretending to read. He probably wishes it were entitled *Corporate Dissolution for Dummies*, but it's not. The book is a collection of statutes that have nothing to do with either corporations or criminal law; he's perusing a collection of regulations from the 1800s that pertain to child labor regulations. He slams the book closed, takes off his reading glasses, and looks up as though he found precisely what he was looking for.

"Would you like to be heard, Ms. Endicott?"

"Mr. Greenough is president of the corporate entity. He can't evade responsibility for its actions."

"*Was* president," Josh says, "but the entity doesn't exist anymore."

Josh takes out a file, hands me a copy of the Articles of Dissolution. Nice move. I didn't think he'd be able dissolve the fraternity this quickly.

I try to recover. "The defendant can't escape responsibility by waving a magic wand and making it disappear."

"Apparently, he has done just that. The matter is dismissed." Judge Lafferty stands, eager to make a swift exit.

Josh rises. "Your Honor, Ms. Endicott is relentlessly harassing my clients, using them to gain attention as part of her efforts to become district attorney. I'd ask that she be admonished for her outrageous behavior."

"Ms. Endicott, reacquaint yourself with the rules of conduct, or I'll refer you to the Board of Bar Overseers." Judge Lafferty decided the best way to get out of the spotlight is to hurl it at me.

Josh pushes on. "Since this was an unlawful arrest, the fruits of the poisonous tree—namely, Mr. Greenough's fingerprints and DNA—must be suppressed."

"It was a lawful arrest. There is nothing unethical—"

"That's it. I won't allow any grandstanding in my courtroom. The defendant's motion is allowed. I'm ordering you to destroy Mr. Greenough's fingerprints and DNA. They are not to be used in furtherance of any investigation."

A photographer memorializes the disaster. *Click, click, click.*

"We are adjourned," the judge says.

Judge Lafferty practically sprints off the bench. A serial murder case is going down the tubes because I drew the laziest judge in the Commonwealth.

Josh packs his briefcase. "Offer him immunity or leave him alone," he says.

"Robbie Greenough is backing himself into an accessory to murder charge," I say.

"Keep it up and I'll file a civil restraining order against you."

Josh turns and walks through the swinging doors. The courtroom empties. I sit, shuffle my papers, anything to avoid going outside. The door clacks open; I can hear snippets of courthouse chatter coming from the hallway.

A defendant talking to his lawyer: *The cops got it wrong. I didn't hit her. She hit me.*

Josh King giving an interview: *The prosecution is acting out of desperation. My client is an innocent man.*

A court officer directing traffic: *Sir, put on your shoes. You can't clip your toenails in the corridor.*

I turn and see Kevin, walking toward me. Feeling the shame of defeat, I can't bring myself to meet his eyes.

"Lafferty tossed our evidence," I say.

"This isn't a game for wusses," he says.

"I got my head handed to me on a silver platter."

He picks up my case folder. "There's no time to lick your wounds. Our vic's mother is waiting downstairs."

Chapter Fourteen

While I was being humiliated in arraignment court, Kevin drove out to Logan to pick up Caitlyn's mother, Karen Walker, and bring her to the courthouse. On the ride over, they passed the alley where Caitlyn's body was found buried under trash. Now they're seated in a sterile conference room, in the Roxbury District Court. Welcome to Boston.

Kevin and I stand in the hallway, looking through the glass opening in the door. Karen has her back to us, head in hands.

"How is she holding up?" I say.

"She's numb," Kevin says.

"Does she know what happened at the arraignment?"

"She was scanning the news in the car, on the way over here."

I hoped to talk to Karen, explain what went on in court, before she heard about it through the media.

"It already hit the airwaves?" I say.

"NECN ran a live feed from the courtroom," Kevin says.

When we walk into the conference room and take seats, Karen barely looks up. Kevin introduces me, and I sit next to her and try to bring her up to speed on the investigation. It's difficult to tell whether or not she's absorbing my words.

"Do you have questions?" I say.

She looks up and speaks quickly. "Some reporters called and

asked me if I thought Caitlyn and that girl from BU are connected to each other. Are they? Or is this random? Is he a serial
killer?"

I try to comfort her with competence, which is a challenge
given the state of the evidence. "We don't have any indication
that Caitlyn and Rose knew each other, but the circumstances of
their abductions do have similarities. We're not sure who killed
your daughter, not yet, but he isn't going to get away with it."

Karen is about sixty, my mother's age, but the deep crevices
around her forehead, eyes, and mouth make her appear decades
older. She hasn't had the benefit of regular visits to the spa for
facials, dermabrasion, and age-defying injections. Her roots are
gray, her hands are chapped, and her eyes are swollen from crying. It's obvious she hasn't had it easy up to now, but at least
she had her daughter.

I put my hand on her arm. "Caitlyn sounded lovely."

"She was my only child. Her father passed when she was a
baby."

"Do you have pictures?"

I know what Caitlyn looked like, but I always make a point
of asking survivors to share a happy memory. It diminishes their
pain, however slightly, and it sharpens my resolve.

Karen scrolls through the photos on her phone, a series of
candids. Caitlyn, at the state fair, holding a half-eaten corn dog.
Caitlyn, wearing a wrist corsage and lavender bandage dress, sitting next to an awkward teenage boy. Caitlyn, grinning, cradling
a small turtle in the palm of her hand. Karen continues to scroll,
stopping at a picture of herself with Caitlyn, who is wearing a
cap and gown. Karen is almost unrecognizable; she's happy, her
arm proudly wrapped around her teenage daughter's shoulder.

"She was the first in our family to go to a four-year college."

I look at the picture and think about my own high school
graduation. Winsor girls didn't wear cap and gown; we wore
simple white dresses of our own choosing and a garland of

flowers in our hair. My grandmother and nanny stood in for my parents, who couldn't make it because they had more pressing matters: tickets to the U.S. Open.

"It must have been difficult, having her so far away," I say.

She coughs back the pain in her throat. I find a bottle of water in my tote, untwist the top, and hand it to her. She takes a couple of sips.

"Do you feel up to answering a few questions?" Kevin says.

"If it will help."

"Do you know if Caitlyn was dating anyone?" Kevin says.

Karen shakes her head. "She wasn't. She would have told me."

"Did she ever mention anyone she was afraid of?"

"No."

"Do you know if she had any new friends?"

Karen looks at Kevin, as though she's worried that she's failing a test.

"I don't think so," she says.

While they continue to talk, I get a text from the medical examiner. *Caitlyn Walker autopsy completed. Body ready for identification and retrieval.* I put the phone away and deliver the news, one more bit of sadness.

"We need you to identify Caitlyn's body, for the official records," I say. "Then they can release her for burial."

Kevin drives us to the medical examiner's office, and we spent most of the ten-minute ride in silence. I fight the urge to make small talk, allowing Karen some time to prepare herself for what she's about to experience. When we arrive at the morgue, the receptionist buzzes us into the visitors' room, where an assistant medical examiner is waiting. We take seats around a table, and the assistant displays an edited photograph of Caitlyn that was taken after she was placed on the gurney. The picture is cropped so only Caitlyn's face is visible; her eyes are closed, and her skin discolored.

Karen examines the picture and lets out a hiccup.

"That's my baby," she says.

The assistant flips the photo over, shielding it from further view, and asks her to sign some documents.

"I'm going to bury her next to her father," Karen says.

My throat swells. "We have you scheduled to fly out in the morning."

"We're not flying," Karen says. "My sister is on her way from Pittsburgh to pick us up and drive us back to Missouri."

"It's a long trip. If you're concerned about the fare, the office will cover it."

"I appreciate the offer, but I'm not putting Caitlyn in the cold belly of an airplane, like a piece of luggage."

Our next stop is Leary's Funeral Home in Mission Hill, where Caitlyn's body has been embalmed. We pull into the parking lot, Karen steps out of the car, and Kevin and I linger a minute.

He reaches over and squeezes my shoulder. "You okay?"

It feels like a million years ago that Tim Mooney was waked here, but it has actually only been about six months. I tell my victims' families that time makes things easier. Turns out, I've been lying all these years. Time doesn't heal all wounds; sometimes it barely makes a dent.

"I know you miss him," Kevin says.

Karen is standing in the parking lot, staring at the funeral home.

"I'm fine," I lie.

I get out of the car, put my hand on Karen's back, and lead her inside, where we find the funeral director. We sit in a family room, while Karen fills out forms and talks about arrangements. About a half an hour later, her sister, Arleen, arrives.

"The car's out back," Arleen says.

"You need a permit to transport the body to Missouri," the funeral director says.

Kevin passes him some paperwork. "I stopped by the Hall yesterday. We have authorization to do a private transport."

While Karen is not unusual in her devastation and grief, she is unusual in her devotion. Few if any families would want to drive their child's dead body halfway across the country in the back of a van. I know my parents wouldn't.

When we're finished filling out forms, Arleen pulls her minivan up to the back of the funeral home. All but the two front seats have been removed. She opens the rear door, and there are a few scattered clues about her family: a crumpled-up bag of Goldfish crackers; a few stray LEGO pieces; a small orange life jacket.

Three men slide Caitlyn's casket onto the floor of the van. Arleen grabs a fleece blanket from the front and hands it to Karen, who wraps herself up in it. Karen climbs into the back and lies down, next to the casket.

"You're going to stay back there?" I say.

"She's my child," Karen says.

Karen crumples up a sweatshirt that will serve as her pillow. She stretches out next to the wooden box, where she will remain until her family reaches Missouri. Arleen climbs into the front seat, starts the engine, and looks over her shoulder to check for oncoming cars. When all is clear, she pulls out of the parking lot and eases into the flow of traffic.

Chapter Fifteen

Caitlyn's lung tissue contained water and traces of soap, leading the ME to opine that she was likely killed in a bathtub. Water served dual purposes: it killed her, and it washed away evidence of her killer's identity. We can't tie the murderer's DNA to Caitlyn, but if we can locate the bathtub, maybe we can tie Caitlyn's DNA to her killer.

We need to find out if Tommy or Robbie Greenough have bathtubs and, if so, snake the drains for evidence. The only way to get a forensic team inside Tommy Greenough's apartment, or the Alpha Beta house, short of committing a felony, is by obtaining a search warrant.

Kevin and I go back to my office. He writes up an affidavit, and I research relevant case law, with the hopes that clever legal maneuvers will compensate for lack of evidence. By the time our application is ready for judicial review, the courts have closed for the night.

"Who's the on-call?" I say.

"Rebecca Hynes," he says. "Do you know her?"

"She's a former constitutional law professor, apolitical, and brilliant."

"Just our luck. We pull Oliver Wendell Holmes when we need Bozo the Clown."

I call Judge Hynes to let her know we're coming, and we set out to Brookline. As we pass Taberna de Haro, one of my favorite tapas bars, my stomach gurgles. Kevin reaches into his glove box and hands me an unsweetened granola bar. I appreciate both the gesture and the nourishment, but I would have preferred a Snickers.

Judge Hynes lives on prime real estate in Brookline, between John F. Kennedy's birthplace and the Country Club, the nation's oldest and snobbiest. Word is that Tom Brady was denied membership here. It's dated, elitist, and expensive. My great-great-grandparents were among the founding members.

Judge Hynes's gingerbread-style Victorian looks grand, with wraparound porches, two chimneys, and a turret. We ring the bell and are greeted by two barking Dobermans; they jump up on their hind legs, their front paws scraping against the door. We wait on the porch as Judge Hynes yells at the dogs and corrals them into a side room.

I've never seen her without her black robe. When she opens the door, she looks more absentminded professor than superior court judge. She has unapologetically gray hair and a tattered brown sweater dotted with dozens of pulls and pills. She reminds me of my uncle Minty, who lives in a $10 million estate in Dover but refuses to set his thermostat above fifty-five.

I introduce her to Kevin, and she leads us down a dimly lit hallway, littered with yellowing newspapers and half-full trash bags. Kevin and I take seats around the kitchen table. I put my hands in my lap, careful not to touch the grimy Formica tabletop. She fumbles around, searching under books and papers, looking for something.

"Do you need a pen?" I say.

Maybe she's going to be more of a pushover than I thought.

"I can't find my peepers," she says.

I subtly tap my forehead to clue her in on the whereabouts of her glasses. She takes them off the top of her head, puts them on, and flips through Tommy Greenough's search warrant affidavit. When she's done, she folds the warrant in thirds and hands it back to me, as though she just discovered it has cooties.

"You're lacking probable cause," she says. "It's not even a close call."

I helped her find her glasses; maybe I can help her find probable cause.

"Tommy Greenough was one of the last people to have seen the victim alive," I say.

She's not buying it. "There's no evidence the victim was ever inside his apartment," she says.

"I'll concede that point, but nonetheless, the apartment could contain valuable evidence."

"Be more specific."

I direct her to various sections in the affidavit, speaking quickly and jumping around from paragraph to paragraph.

"His computer could have e-mails or Google searches. His phone could have voice mails or texts."

"It's entirely speculative."

Not ready to concede, I keep pressing. "The bathtub could contain the victim's hair or DNA."

She pushes her glasses back on top of her head. "There's no evidence that the apartment even has a bathtub."

I knew the warrant for Tommy's apartment was a long shot, but I had to give it a try. Some judges might have signed off on it, especially at this time of night, shortly before bedtime but after cocktail hour. Not dissuaded, I put the papers in a folder and pull out the application to search the Alpha Beta house.

"Would you consider authorizing a warrant to search the fraternity?"

"Not based on the same set of facts."

"There are differences. The fraternity has shuttered its doors. No one lives there anymore. The expectation of privacy and level of intrusion have been significantly diminished."

"Are you familiar with Sisyphus?" she says.

"We'll see ourselves out," I say.

Heading to the car, I imagine Karen Walker, still lying in the back of her sister's van, stretched out next to Caitlyn. They're probably somewhere in Connecticut by now.

"We have to get inside the fraternity," I say.

"Can we treat it as abandoned property?" Kevin says.

"Nice try, but that rule is for trash, like chewed gum or used tissues. It doesn't apply to real estate."

"How about a consent search?"

"How are we going to find the building's owner at this hour?"

Kevin smiles. "I know a guy."

We head over to Boston City Hall, a shining example of brutalism. The cement bunker is dark, closed for the night, but Kevin's uncle's wife's brother-in-law works there as a security guard.

Kevin's guy looks like he's old enough to have been with the City since the Curley administration. He lets us inside, leads us up to the eighth-floor assessing department, and logs us on to a computer terminal. It only takes Kevin a few minutes to search the database and find the property owner, Otis Thurman.

"Is he in Boston?" I say.

"Better. He lives in the land of the liberals: Cambridge." He smiles. "I'm guessing he's not a fan of our conservative senior senator."

"I'll give him a call," I say.

"I'll assemble a search team."

As anticipated, Mr. Thurman is happy to assist in our efforts to solve the murder and, as he said, *to stand up to the D.C. power structure.* It's a sure sign we're up against a formidable opponent when the police and prosecutor are considered the underdog.

We arrive at the Alpha Beta house to find it stripped bare and wiped down. The students got rid of everything that might contain DNA: clothing, dishes, books, furniture. The search team goes room to room, confirming what we already know: there's nothing to collect. Even the lightbulbs have been removed from the ceiling fixtures. Last week, the place reeked of booze; now it smells of bleach.

Jack Rater, a civilian who oversees the crime lab, approaches. "There's no bathtubs, just showers. I don't see anything to sample."

"Take some pictures of the empty space," I say. "I can try to spin it as consciousness of guilt."

I climb the back staircase, up to the fourth floor. The steps are narrow and steep. Between the third-and fourth-floor landings, my ankle buckles, and I fall backward, grabbing hold of the railing just before I hit the ground. A sharp pain runs from my foot to my knee, reigniting the injury I got the night that Ty was shot. Serves me right; the doctor warned me about removing the cast too early.

At the top of the stairs, there's a shadowy hallway that leads to three rooms. The ceiling is low and slanted. I open the doors, one by one. The first room is an empty storage closet, with warped shelves and a built-in set of drawers. The second room could have been a bedroom, large enough to fit a single mattress. The door to the third room won't budge. I jiggle the handle, try to force it open. Behind me, the floor creaks; footsteps startle me. I'm not alone.

I whip my head around and see Kevin.

"You scared me," I say.

"What are you doing, besides contaminating the scene?" he says.

"There's nothing to contaminate."

"What's behind door number three?"

"I don't know. It's jammed."

Kevin twists the knob.

"It's not stuck, it's locked," he says. "Interesting. It's the only room in the house with a lock on it."

Kevin leans his shoulder into the door and pushes, but it won't open. He takes a couple of steps back and kicks it in.

"Oops," he says.

He walks inside the room, looks around, then signals me to follow. It's a bathroom, with a hot tub. Kevin calls Jack Rater, who comes upstairs, removes the trap, inserts a drain auger, and twists it around.

"I don't feel anything," he says.

"Please, dig deeper," I say.

He grips the snake with both hands and pushes down on it, to lower the cable. He twists the snake around clockwise, until it stops. "Got it." He draws back the snake until we see a clump of brown hair, hooked onto the end.

"Let's get it tested," I say.

Chapter Sixteen

When I arrive home, Manny, the night doorman, is in the lobby of my condo building, at the reception counter. I wave to him from outside and he opens the sliding glass doors. He was on duty when I left for work, about fifteen hours ago.

"It's barely past midnight," he says. "You're slacking."

I check my mail, which consists of a bunch of catalogs and a handful of bills. My Visa is past due. Comcast is threatening to shut off the cable. Neiman Marcus is giving me thirty days to settle my account. Stuffing the envelopes in my tote, I hop on the elevator. When I get upstairs, I pour a glass of Malbec, plant myself on the couch, and open my laptop. There are a dozen messages.

From Chip Aldridge: *I hope you'll reconsider, I'd really like to take you to dinner.* Delete.

From Max: *I want an update on the search warrants. ASAP.* Delete.

From the governor's legal counsel, return receipt requested: *Please contact us at your earliest convenience. We'd like to arrange a meeting to discuss your candidacy for district attorney.* I read the message two more times, then print it out.

I kick off my shoes, lie back, and imagine myself standing at a podium, giving a campaign speech to a large audience. My colleagues are pretending to be excited, but each one secretly wishes it had been him or her on the stage. Charlie and Missy are enthusiastic and supportive, but privately wondering how I ended up in such an unsavory line of work. Ty is front and center, smiling proudly and cheering me on. My parents are noticeably absent.

A few hours later, I'm awakened by the clicking of the dead bolt on my front door. Disoriented, I open my eyes and see Ty walk into the living room, carrying his saxophone case, singing to himself. *I can't give you anything but love, baby. That's the only thing I've plenty of, baby.*

He takes off his coat, notices me. "What are you doing up?"

"I fell asleep on the couch. How was Wally's?"

"Full house, great crowd."

I sit up, rub my eyes, and try to focus. "What time is it?"

"Almost five. I stayed way later than I should've." He gives me a kiss, then another. "How's it going? Any progress on your case?"

"Some, a little, not really."

My cell phone vibrates; the display shows my father's name. He's an early bird, probably about to jump on a conference call with someone in Asia. I let it go to voice mail. A few seconds later, Ty's cell phone rings.

"What's everyone doing up at five in the morning?" I say.

Ty checks the caller ID. It's my brother. He takes the call, has a brief conversation.

"You should talk to him," Ty says. "Your mother had an accident."

Shaking the sleep from my head, I take the phone.

"Charlie, what's wrong? Is everyone okay?"

"Mom fell down the stairs last night. She broke her arm. They think she could have a concussion."

"Was she drunk?"

He lets out a sigh. "Very."

"This is getting out of hand. We need to get her into treatment."

"Good luck with that," Charlie says. "Can you stop by the house and get some things for her?"

I shower and dress quickly. Ty and I drive over to my parents' house, he pulls up to a hydrant, and I jump out of the car. Before I reach for the buzzer, Serena opens the door.

"I've been so worried." Her eyes are heavy, and her voice is shaky.

I put my hand on her arm. "She'll be fine."

"I was in my room, asleep. I heard screaming and found her at the bottom of the stairs." Serena notices Ty out in the car, he waves at her, and she looks away. "Your mother doesn't approve of your boyfriend. She thinks he's after your money."

I look at Ty and smile. "Trust me, Ty is not after money."

She glances at him again and reconsiders. "He is handsome."

My mother's Celine weekender is on the table in the foyer, packed and ready to go. Serena hands it to me. I unzip the bag to be sure she has all the necessities for a short stay in the hospital. A tub of La Mer moisturizer, a silk La Perla robe, handcrafted Bottega Veneta slippers. Looks about right.

The sun is rising when we pull up in front of the Mass General, and a shift change is in progress. The security guard recognizes me from when Ty was shot and we were both patients here. He allows us to park the car in the ambulance bay.

The hospital holds about 950 beds, but there's no need to stop by the information desk and ask for the location of my mother's room. My family always stays in the Phillips House, the section of the hospital that offers deluxe private rooms, with flat-screen TVs, daily newspaper delivery, and mini-fridges, which my mother usually has stocked with wine and cheese.

When we get to the room, we find my father and Charlie seated on a sofa. They look exhausted. My father gives me a hug and shakes Ty's hand.

"She's downstairs in recovery. They had to set her arm," my father says.

"She should go directly from here to McLean, for inpatient treatment. I can make some calls," I say. "I've worked with the head of their addiction program."

"That's something your mother has to decide on her own." My father turns his back to the room and looks out the window. "This is a helluva view," he says. "You can see all the way to Harvard."

I redirect my appeal to Charlie. "She could have killed herself."

He's not jumping on my bandwagon. "Don't be so dramatic."

"This is not going to end well," I say.

"Have some compassion." My father is still gazing out the window. "She's not one of your defendants."

Ty comes to my aid. "I think Abby's trying to help—"

"This is a family matter, Tyson."

I take Ty's hand, letting him know I'm grateful for his support. As he starts to speak again, I squeeze so hard I almost crush his fingers, signaling him to stop. Charlie calls Missy to give her an update, and my father calls his assistant to let her know his whereabouts. I unpack my mother's bag, hang her robe in the closet, and arrange her toiletries in the bathroom.

"We've got to go," I say.

"We're around if you need anything." Ty is unperturbed by my father's rudeness.

I take his arm, and we enter the hallway, where I'm surprised to see Chip Aldridge walking past the nurses' station, heading toward us.

"I heard your mother was brought into the OR last night," he says. "I was about to stop by and check on her."

My body stiffens with both attraction and guilt. "I . . . I . . . appreciate that, Dr. Aldridge."

Chip gives Ty the once-over and extends his hand, which Ty accepts.

"Chip Aldridge. Nice to meet you."

"You look familiar," Ty says.

"Chip is a surgeon here," I say, much too quickly.

"No, that's not it. I've seen you someplace, but it wasn't here."

"Maybe we've crossed paths in the Back Bay," Chip says.

If Ty is taken aback by Chip's disclosure that he knows where we live, he hides it well.

"Dr. Aldridge and I had a case together," I say. "He testified for me as an expert witness."

I'm surprised by my spontaneous lie, and how easily it came out. I look down. Chip, who is unfazed, rolls with it.

"I've been trying to get in touch with you," he says. "I heard that the case is up on appeal. If you have any openings next week, maybe we could schedule some time to discuss it."

Chip flashes a conspiratorial smile, and I almost smile back, but then I see Ty has moved to talk to a nurse, probably checking on my mother's condition. There's a chance he may have stepped away in anger; Ty is pretty astute—maybe he senses something is up. Or, just as likely, he's preoccupied with my family situation, and he's genuinely concerned about my mother. Feeling like a traitor, I move away from Chip, stand with Ty, and listen to the nurse describe the extent of my mother's injuries.

Chapter Seventeen

The mayor traded in his city hall office for a jail cell, and Max is the odds-on favorite to replace him, with a well-oiled machine of volunteers and a dozen campaign offices spread out across the city. Today's mandatory volunteer meeting is in Max's home turf, West Roxbury, a neighborhood with reliable voters and desirable jurors.

Since Ty and I are in the midst of our own campaign, designed to avert bankruptcy, he gives me a ride to the meeting, saving a thirty-two-dollar cab fare. He's so excited about what he has deemed my newfound *mindful spending* that I can't cop to the fact that, yesterday, I plunked down thirty-eight dollars for a tube of lipstick.

He pulls the Prius up to the curb, and I clock a few small groups of familiar faces. A couple of detectives carry stacks of Dunkin' Donuts boxes inside the headquarters. A cluster of probation officers distributes Max's campaign propaganda. Two investigators and a defense attorney hold up LOMBARDO FOR MAYOR signs. The lawyer is doing double duty; he dips into his jacket pocket, pulls out one of his business cards, and slips it to a pedestrian. I've seen the cards: *Reasonable Doubt at a Reasonable Price.*

Ty and I idle in the car as people start to gather inside.

"If Max wins, they'll have to appoint someone to fill his job," I say.

"So you'd have a new boss."

"The governor's counsel is considering naming me for the job."

"That'd be awesome, babe." Ty leans in and surprises me with a passionate kiss.

He's never been shy about public displays of affection, but this feels urgent and insecure, as though he's staking a claim. A burst of sadness explodes in my chest, and I wonder if he picked up on the vibe between me and Chip at the hospital.

One of the new gang unit paralegals parks in front of us and struggles to retrieve lawn signs from the trunk of her Kia. Ty gets out of the car and helps her move an armful of the splintery wooden posts.

"Thanks, I owe you." Her smile is a little too eager. "Maybe we should sign up to do a lit drop together this weekend. We could have a beer afterward, my treat."

Determined to break up their tête-à-tête, I join them.

"Thanks for the offer, but Ty is going to San Francisco for work this weekend. Another time."

I slip my arm into Ty's. She turns red and moves away. A passing motorist blasts his horn and yells at the sign holders across the street: *You all belong in jail. Politicians are a bunch of crooks.* I give Ty a kiss, wish him safe travels, and join the group inside.

This space used to be occupied by a RE/MAX franchise. Everything looks temporary: metal folding chairs, collapsible tables, exposed phone sockets, burned-out lightbulbs. Boxes of coffee and doughnuts are strategically placed near the dozens of to-do lists, one for each volunteer. I resist the crullers, grab a Styrofoam cup, and fill it with coffee. There's a volunteer packet with my name on it, containing voter lists and campaign brochures for my neighborhood, Ward 5, Precincts 6 and 7. I tuck it under my arm, keeping my hands free so I can write my name on the sign-in sheet. There's no point showing up if you don't get credit.

There are about ten rows of chairs, occupied by government employees, students, local businessmen, and private defense attorneys. Everyone has one thing in common—they're all here out of self-interest, to curry favor. Before the last vote is even counted, they'll try to cash in by hitting Max up for something. The law students will ask for a job. The prosecutors will seek a promotion. And the defense attorneys will expect a good deal on a case.

I move toward the back of the room and plant myself in an aisle seat, next to a uniformed court officer. His legs are stretched out in front of him, and head is tilted back, like he's about to doze off. Cassandra is behind me. I can't see her, but I can smell her gardenia perfume.

She leans forward and talks to the back of my head. "Did the governor's office call you?"

I breathe through my mouth. "Yes, they did."

"Me, too."

I twist around to face her. She's smiling, but she's not kidding.

"They did?" I try to sound casual.

"I decided to throw my hat in the ring," she says. "I figured why not."

"Sure, why not."

Cassandra told me she'd only be interested in applying for the job if I didn't want it, and, stupidly, I took her at her word. My knee is moving up and down nervously, so much that the manila envelope slips off my lap and onto the floor. I use my foot to slide it closer to me.

"I made a couple of calls, and next thing I knew, they invited me in for an interview," she says.

I lean over and pick up the envelope. A minute ago, I was ambivalent about seeking political office; now I am 100 percent sure that I want to be DA. And I'll fight for it to the death.

I plaster on a fake smile. "You'll make a great candidate."

She fake smiles back. "That's exactly what the governor's scheduler told me."

Max's campaign manager blows a whistle and steps up to the front of the room. He thanks everyone for coming and delivers a canned pep talk. *This election will be a close one. Every vote is going to count.* No need to waste enthusiasm on this group of hacks.

As the speaker drones on, a text comes up on my phone. It's from the crime lab: *Hair from the Alpha Beta house was analyzed. Preliminary results are a match to victim Caitlyn Walker.* This is the break we've been hoping for.

My seatmate snorts; his head bobs up and down. I elbow him to let him know the candidate has arrived. Max steps into the room, bringing a gust of energy with him. Everyone sits a little taller, hoping to be noticed. The lucky ones get a smile and a nod of recognition.

Max's campaign manager amps up the enthusiasm. "We're leading in the polls. Councilor O'Neill is our closest competitor. We've got six points on her, but we can't take anything for granted."

Max takes his place, front and center. "I don't want to see any of you out campaigning during business hours."

Max wants to make the record clear. There's always at least one mole in the audience, surreptitiously recording everything, eager to tweet out any missteps or blunders. When the meeting winds down, I sign up for two phone banks and one knock-and-drop, careful not to overpromise. I refill my coffee cup and head out the door, looking for a ride back to the office.

Max follows me to the sidewalk and pulls me aside. "What's the latest with the Greenoughs?"

"The hair from the fraternity hot tub is a match to our victim. I've gotta get back to the office."

"What's your move?"

"Both Greenoughs are lawyered up, and Josh King won't let me near them. He's made it personal."

"Cases like these, with so much at stake, are always personal," Max says. "Whether or not the prosecutor and defense attorney have rolled around in the sheets."

I'm not surprised he knows about Josh. Boston is an intellectual hub, attracting a variety of professionals from around the globe, but it has a small, incestuous legal community. There are no secrets. I often think about relocating to a less parochial area, like Mayberry or Smallville.

An unmarked police SUV pulls up. Max holds up a finger and mouths: *Give me a minute.*

"Josh is blocking access," I say. "I can't get to his client."

"Josh King isn't the one pulling the strings. Refocus your lens."

"You're talking about the senator?"

"Give him a ring. Tell him you'll call your media contacts and leak his lack of cooperation."

Max's shift in attitude from last week's lapdog to today's pit bull can only be attributed to one thing: his pollsters must have done a survey. He starts to move toward his car when I notice Cassandra is nearby, eavesdropping, looking for an opening. Determined not to let her beat me to the punch, I turn my back to her and follow Max to his car.

"Have you thought about who you're going to endorse as your replacement?" I say.

He lets out a sigh and looks at the sky as though he's never considered the issue.

"It's premature," he says. "My seat isn't vacant yet."

"Everyone knows you're going to win. Your support will be important."

His shoulders tense. He doesn't want to commit, but I'm not going to let him off the hook this easily.

"You've got a huge base, and your popularity rating is through the roof," I say.

He tosses his half-filled coffee cup up in the air; it arcs and lands in the trash can, which is at least fifteen feet away. "Three points," he says. This is his go-to move, when he wants to remind everyone, including himself, that he was a college hoops star and he's still got it. I'm not impressed by his aim or his attitude.

"Max, we've known each other for eleven years."

"You've gotta understand, I've known Cassandra a long time, too."

My stomach drops. "You're the one who told me to get in the race."

"And you should." He steps away and gets in the car.

There's mud on the shoulder of his jacket, but I don't point it out. This time he's on his own. As his driver takes off, I look around for a ride back to the office. Seeing no one, I go inside, where Cassandra is perusing the volunteer sign-in sheets.

"I saw your boyfriend earlier, He's cute." She pauses, but I know she's not done talking. "Didn't Middlesex County prosecute him a while ago for drugs?"

She's trying to get in my head, and it's working. I reach for the last cruller in the box, even though I'm not hungry, and take a bite.

"Ty's arrest was over fifteen years ago, and it was for pot," I say.

"Did the governor's office ask about it yet?"

My throat is dry. I down a gulp of coffee too fast, and it goes down the wrong pipe. I cough, try to clear my throat.

Cassandra takes out her car key.

"Do you need a ride back to the office?" she says.

"No, thanks," I say. "I'm all set."

Chapter Eighteen

I Uber back to the office. As we pass Brigham and Women's Hospital, I think about the last time I was here, when a crazed patient stabbed a brilliant neurosurgeon. The patient is in a secure psychiatric hospital, awaiting trial. The doctor is in Mount Auburn Cemetery.

We stop at a traffic light next to the Fenway, where a group of women my age are pushing baby strollers, smiling and laughing. I wonder what it would be like to have a carefree afternoon with friends, or a carefree minute by myself.

I use the downtime to call Senator Greenough's office in Washington. I'm not surprised when his assistant tells me he's not available. Five minutes later, Josh King calls.

"I represent the senator. All contact should go through me," he says.

"Can we set up a meeting?" I say.

"That depends. Will it be a meeting or a fishing expedition?"

"Your quote in the *Herald* says the Greenoughs are cooperating with investigators. It was so convincing that I almost believed you."

Josh knows I won't leak information about the grand jury, but I'm not above putting out the word that he refused a sit-down. He agrees to meet, but the logistics and location are the subject of strenuous debate. We spar back and forth, exhibiting all the maturity and finesse of a couple of first-year law students, engaged in a moot court competition.

Josh strikes first. "Let's have it in my office. We have in-house stenographers. That'll save the government a lot of money."

"I can use the audio recorder on my iPhone," I say.

"My office is bigger and can accommodate more people."

"There's only going to be four of us. Our conference room is more than adequate."

"My assistant can order in from Abe & Louie's. The firm will pick up the tab."

This line of argument gives me pause. I love Abe & Louie's signature salad, with apples and pistachio nuts. I weigh my options as an ambulance speeds past, siren blaring.

"I can't accept lunch," I say. "It'd be considered an unlawful gratuity."

"I've paid for your meals before. You didn't protest when I took you to L'Espalier."

His tone is playful, bordering on flirtatious, but I have no interest in revisiting the past. Any kind of relationship with opposing counsel, even a platonic one, is asking for trouble. Besides, I've already got my hands full of non-romantic flirtations.

"That was fifteen years ago, before I took an oath of office."

He's not ready to concede. "We have free parking."

Time to shut this down. I fire my best and final shot.

"We can't validate parking, but we can issue indictments," I say.

"See you later," he says.

Josh is stubborn, but not at his client's expense. I'd rather have won last week's bail argument than today's venue debate, but I'll take my victories when I find them. I call Kevin and let him know the plan.

"What's the catch?" he says.

"There isn't one."

"Everybody's working an angle."

"It fits their narrative. His press aide can send out a release, saying that the whole family is continuing to cooperate with the investigation."

"You bring the coffee," Kevin says. "I'll bring the handcuffs."

I can barely hear him. There's loud clanging and groaning in the background, like someone is being tortured.

"I don't even want to know where you are," I say.

"It's called a gym. People come here to stay healthy and blow off steam. Google it."

"For your information, I went to SoulCycle last week."

This is technically true; I did go there. What I don't reveal is it was to meet Ty after his spin class, before we ate plates of pasta at Toscano. Kevin knows he doesn't have the full story.

"If you say so, but you're going to have get into fighting shape. Campaigns take a lot out of you."

He's right; campaigns are strenuous both physically and psychologically. As we talk, I log on to Yoga Plus and sign up for a beginner's class. Then I check out Lululemon's website. I'll need to be properly outfitted; I order $98 yoga pants, a $108 hoodie, and a $78 mat. After we hang up, I rethink the yoga commitment, cancel the class and the mat, but keep the clothes.

A couple of hours later, Kevin comes by.

"There's a slew of cameras out front of the office," he says.

"Josh must have tipped them off so they could document his arrival."

When Josh arrives, I'm not surprised to see he brought his own stenographer to transcribe the meeting. It's a small power play, a signal he doesn't trust us and that his clients have deep pockets. He shouldn't have bothered; I'm well aware of his mistrust; the feeling is mutual, and his Brioni suit is evidence enough of his exorbitant billables.

Senator Thomas Greenough strides in after Josh. He's about six two, with a shock of gray hair and a killer handshake.

"Abigail Endicott, it's nice to finally meet you," he says.

He takes a seat at the head of the table and settles in, as though he's about to carve the Thanksgiving turkey. I have to assert control or he'll commandeer the meeting.

"As you know, I've been conducting an investigation involving your sons," I say.

He acts as though he didn't hear me. "You know, your father was a couple of years ahead of me at Exeter. He was a helluva football player."

Even though my father never mentioned anything about knowing Greenough, it's likely they travel in the same circles.

"We've been by your son's fraternity house," I say.

I want to unsettle him, put him on the defensive, but he keeps talking. "I don't know if your old man told you, but I dated your aunt Percy, took her to her junior prom at Emma Willard. I was the one who introduced her to your uncle."

"Which uncle?" I say. "She's been married six times."

Josh nods to the stenographer, signaling it's time to start typing.

"How can we help you today?" Josh says.

I turn to the senator. "In the spirit of cooperation, we'd like your consent to access computer drives and financial records."

"That's what subpoenas and search warrants are for. Should I assume that a judge already turned you down?" Josh says.

I try to bluff. "We thought you could expedite the process."

Josh grins. "Anything else we can do for you, counsel?"

I didn't really expect him to agree to the request, but we've both accomplished our goals. The lines are drawn; I let them know that I'm not backing down, and Josh let me know that he's going to say one thing and do the opposite. I stand; Kevin and Josh follow. The senator remains seated, shakes his head at the stenographer, who puts away her machine.

"How's your mother?" he says.

My heart pounds. "Fine, thank you."

"Alcoholism is a terrible addiction."

The senator's strategy has emerged. He's going to make this personal by threatening to expose and embarrass my family. I have to beat him to the punch. Game on.

Chapter Nineteen

After Rose Driscoll went missing, her parents, Ed and Delia, traveled from Indianapolis to Boston, spending most of the fifteen-hour drive on the phone with me, asking the same heartbreaking question again and again. *Could she still be alive?* I told them about the search, the police officers and scores of volunteers, and I tried to prepare them for the worst. Still, we all held out hope until the bitter end.

There was reason for optimism. Rose, a junior at BU, was by all accounts both book-smart and street-smart, not one to wander off into dangerous neighborhoods alone. She was last seen leaving the Mugar library; security cameras captured images of her walking out of the building, onto Commonwealth Ave. Other cameras picked her up, entering Pavement and emerging a few minutes later, coffee cup in hand. She was last seen walking in the direction of Kenmore Square. Then she vanished.

There was no evidence of an abduction or robbery. Two days later, her body was discovered, a few miles away, in King's Chapel Burying Ground. To her parents, Rose is a memory, but I'm just getting to know her.

Ed and Delia returned home, to Indiana, and buried their daughter. That was before Caitlyn went missing, before we thought it might be part of something bigger. Now the Driscolls are back in Boston to collect her belongings. Kevin gives me a ride to Bay State Road, a quiet tree-lined street tucked between chaotic Kenmore Square and the Charles River. I ask him to drop me a few blocks away from Rose's dorm; the short walk allows me time to shift gears, from aggressive prosecutor to compassionate advocate.

When I arrive at the dorm room, the Driscolls greet me with familiar zombie-like hugs, the same lifeless hugs I get from most of my victims' families. They're surrounded by boxes, evidence of Rose's unfinished life. I take a seat on the single bed, and we talk while they continue their packing; both seem set on autopilot. Delia folds T-shirt after T-shirt, no matter that they're tattered and stained. Ed removes framed photographs from the wall.

I tread lightly. "How's your family holding up?"

Delia seals a box of T-shirts and moves her attention to a pile of sweaters.

"Our youngest keeps asking when she can visit Rose. She doesn't understand what's happened. I'm not sure I do either."

"Did you speak with the grief counselor?"

She shakes her head. I know enough not to push; everyone has their own timetable. They continue to work quietly for a few minutes until Delia stops and looks over at me, as though she'd forgotten that I was there.

"Do you think it was one of those Greenough boys?" she says.

Ed pries a nail from the wall with his bare fingers.

"That's what they're reporting on the news," he says.

Even if I could tie the Greenoughs to the murders, I wouldn't be able to reveal it to anyone outside law enforcement. I'm not here to provide details of the investigation. I'm here to give reassurance that I'm invested, and to show I care.

Ed untacks a snapshot from a bulletin board above the desk:

Rose, eating a drippy blue Popsicle, dressed in an armadillo costume.

I look around for something to do, some way to help, and begin to sort through a mound of sweatshirts. I smooth, fold, and stack them, handling each one with more care than I give to my most elegant silk blouses. Near the bottom of the pile is a gray hoodie with a bulge in the front pouch. I turn my back to the Driscolls and pull out an uncapped aspirin bottle. Inside, there are about fifty round white pills; one side is branded: *OC*, the other side is marked: *80*. I'll send the pills to the crime lab for an official chemical analysis, but I don't need a scientist to tell me what they are: 80 mg OxyContins.

"Did your daughter have any old injuries?" I stuff the pills in my pocket and turn around. "Was she ever treated for pain?"

"Freshman year, she was biking to class, fell, and hurt her shoulder," Ed says.

Often that's how a habit starts—treatment for an injury turns into an addiction. I open a drawer, pull out a stack of blue jeans, and feel inside the pockets. Finding nothing, I pile them into a cardboard box. Maybe Rose's murder was a drug deal gone bad. At this point, every motive is still on the table.

Sounds from other dorm rooms fill the silence. Music, laughter, chatter. *Can I borrow your poli sci notes? Are you going to the Delta Tau party? I was like sooo wasted last night.*

"What is the other girl's name?" Ed says. "The one from Wellesley?"

"Caitlyn Walker," I say.

"Did she and Rosie know each other?" Delia says.

"We haven't found a connection."

Delia takes a threadbare sweatshirt, hugs it close to her chest, and inhales, filling her lungs with what remains of her daughter's scent. I wonder if Caitlyn used drugs, too. I'll have to look into it.

Ed removes textbooks from a shelf, one by one, and examines

the spines: *Freeing the Natural Voice, Fundamentals of Abnormal Psychology, Introduction to Logic.* Delia pulls a strip of duct tape from the roll, rips it off with her teeth, and seals the last of the boxes. A few minutes pass until the silence is interrupted by a knock. Some of Rose's hall mates offer to help carry things out to the car.

"We've got to get on the road, hon." Ed rubs Delia's back in small circles.

As the students load the last group of boxes onto dollies, Delia surveys the room one final time, her eyes stopping at the *Keep Calm and Call Your Mom* poster on top of one of the piles.

I take a Starbucks bag out of my tote and clear the rasp of sadness from my throat. "You have a long drive ahead of you."

I hand her the bag, my standard care package, filled with biscotti, fruit, and bottles of water. She thanks me and smiles, using only her mouth; her eyes remain expressionless. I promise to keep them apprised of any developments in the investigation and wave good-bye.

Outside, it's turned dark and raw, and it's starting to drizzle. I jaywalk across Commonwealth Ave., passing a lone student; her eyes are glued to her phone, earbuds in. Someone could snatch her off the street before she knew what hit her.

I stand in front of her, blocking her path. She looks at me, more annoyed than startled, and removes one of the buds.

"Be careful," I say. "You should be aware of your surroundings."

She rolls her eyes, puts the bud back in her ear, and continues on her way. I'm not surprised. Most college students think they have absolute immunity to danger, whether it's alcohol poisoning, date rape, or murder.

Thunder rumbles in the distance, and the sky explodes, spewing pellets of icy rain. I fish around the bottom of my tote for the compact umbrella that I keep with me at all times. One thing in Boston that's less predictable than the murder rate is the weather.

A car hits a pothole and splashes a puddle of dirty water all over me. A gust of wind overtakes my umbrella, flipping it inside out. I try to push it back into place, but the metal stretchers are too mangled. An empty taxi drives toward me, slows, and flashes its lights, but I wave it off and walk the rest of the way home.

Chapter Twenty

The next day, Kevin and I drive to Wellesley College to interview Caitlyn Walker's roommate, Nadine Franklin. Detectives have taken Nadine's statement, but we want to meet her, see where Caitlyn lived, and get a sense of what her life was like. Wellesley is about a half-hour drive from BU and couldn't be more different. BU is urban and coed; Wellesley, suburban and women-only. BU has more than 18,000 undergrads; Wellesley has fewer than 2,500. But the schools share something in common: the shock and grief over the loss of two promising students.

Nadine lived with Caitlyn in a three-story apartment building on the outskirts of campus. We ring the bell and hear a lot of yipping and scratching coming from inside. Nadine opens the door and greets us; behind her are an unidentifiable number of shaggy dogs that are sniffing and snorting and scrambling to get out.

"Stop it, you guys. Chill." She extends her leg to block their escape.

Once they appear to have calmed down, we slowly step inside. An enormous, furry, something-doodle jumps up excitedly, licks my hand, and shreds my hose.

I let out three sonic sneezes. "I've got really bad allergies."

"They're rescues," she says as though her benevolence will bolster my immune system.

The apartment is tiny, and the floor is cluttered with slimy tennis balls, metal water bowls, and dogs, lots of dogs. Milk crates serve as bookshelves, a cable spool substitutes as a coffee table, and low-back beach chairs provide enough seating for three.

Nadine gestures to one of the chairs. "Have a seat."

Easier said than done, especially in heels and a pencil skirt. I bend backward, grab hold of the rickety aluminum arms, and drop into the webbed seat; it's so low that my butt touches the floor. Kevin, clearly the brains of the operation, remains standing. I'm tempted to grab his leg and hoist myself back up.

"The dogs and I have been staying with my father in Pittsfield. After Caitlyn was killed, I took the rest of the semester off." Her hand trembles, and she tears up. "I just came to pick up some of my things."

"Do you feel like you might be in danger?"

She hesitates, chooses her words. "I don't know, maybe. I didn't want to come back here at all, but I needed my stuff."

I wonder what she's holding back.

"I understand. You must be pretty shaken up. We were hoping you could give us a sense of what Caitlyn was like as a roommate, as a person."

"We were really close sophomore and junior years, but this semester we each kind of did our own things."

"Did you have a falling-out?"

As we talk, I alternate between coughing and sneezing. I have to blow my nose, but my packet of tissues is in my tote, which a German shepherd has dragged to the other side of the room. Kevin reaches in his pocket and hands me a white handkerchief. He's the only man I know, besides my father and brother, who still carries a cloth handkerchief.

"Caitlyn and I got along fine, but we hardly ever saw each other," Nadine says.

"Why is that?" Kevin says.

"I work part-time in an animal shelter, so I'm up and out early. Caitlyn didn't get home until late, and she was usually still asleep when I left in the morning."

"Do you know where she went at night?" I say.

"All I know is that she wasn't dressed for the library."

"You mean like she was going out on the town?" Kevin says. I throw him a look. *Out on the town?*

"More like she was going to a party or something, always in a short skirt, a crop top, that kind of thing." She pauses, then adds, "She was really pretty."

A bulldog, gnawing on a red stiletto, rubs up against me. Nadine wrestles the shoe from the dog.

"This was Caitlyn's shoe." Her voice cracks. "The dogs miss her, too."

My eyes itch; my throat constricts. I need to take a break. I clumsily lean forward onto my hands and knees, and Kevin helps me stand. The conversation continues as I head into the bathroom.

I hear Kevin say, "Did Caitlyn have a boyfriend?"

"She didn't really talk about guys."

My suite mates at Harvard would have said the same about me. Not because my dating life was a state secret, but because most of my boyfriends in college and law school weren't worth mentioning; they were overconfident, overcapitalized, and underwhelming, like Josh King.

"Did men ever stop by the apartment?" Kevin says.

Nadine doesn't respond. He continues to probe.

"Did you ever hear her talk to anyone on the phone?"

"No, not really."

In the bathroom, I splash cold water on my eyes, then snoop around in the medicine cabinet and open the drawers. Hidden beneath a couple of washcloths is a soap dish with a dozen loose pills. Some are marked *GG 258*—which is another name for Xanax—and the rest are Oxy. I take the pills and rejoin Kevin and Nadine; this time, I have the good sense to remain vertical.

"Was Caitlyn into drugs?" I say.

"No way."

I show her the soap dish. She's not impressed.

"Everyone takes something—Adderall, Ativan, Vyvanse—but I'd know if she was an addict."

I doubt that. Most users, at least most educated, high-functioning users, can keep their addictions under wraps for years. My brother George being exhibit A.

We thank Nadine and make our way across the five-hundred-plus acre campus, around the golf course, back to the car.

"I'd like to send my daughter to a place like this," Kevin says.

"It's a good school."

"Yeah, and it's all women. If I'm going to fork over seventy grand or whatever it costs in five years to send my kid to college, I want her attention on the books, not the boys."

I look around, take in the conifers and the calm waters of Lake Waban. All this serenity makes me nervous.

"How about we head to the morgue?" I say.

"Let's stop for lunch on the way," Kevin says. "I'm starving."

I direct him to Blue Ginger, an upscale Asian-fusion restaurant in Wellesley. Kevin has the salmon, and I get the sablefish. If I were with Ty, I'd skip the entrée and go right to the bittersweet chocolate cake, but I don't want to be judged by Kevin, who seems to have appointed himself chief of the nutrition police.

Kevin takes a few bites of his fish, then puts down his fork.

"You gotta admit it seems funny that both our victims had all those loose Oxy pills."

"Drugs could be one more thing that ties these cases together," I say.

"I hope we don't have another rape murder on our hands soon," he says.

A couple of professorial-looking men, with facial hair and oxford shirts, stop eating and look over at us.

I shush Kevin. "Indoor voice. Restaurant behavior."

I look around the restaurant, at the other diners, who are enjoying their meals. The most pressing issue on their minds is probably whether they'll get tenure or how they did on their orals. Kevin looks at my plate; I haven't touched my fish. He slides sweet potato fries in front of me, and I grab a few. Then a few more.

"They've got to have suppliers," I say.

"I can call the drug unit and see if they can line us up with a snitch."

I think about my favorite informant / drug dealer: Freddie Craven. "I know someone who's been pinched a bunch of times for selling to college kids, and he knows most of the local slangers," I say.

"Do you think he'll talk?"

The last time I saw Freddie, he had his left hand wrapped around my throat and his right hand on my Rolex. I never turned him in to the police, and now that seems like a wise decision.

"Freddie Craven will talk," I say. "I'm positive."

Chapter Twenty-One

I don't tell Kevin about my encounter with Freddie Craven. There's no need to get him all riled up. I'm over it; my knee has healed, and it was a good reminder that I need a new can of pepper spray. I am, however, still mourning the loss of my last bottle of Chanel No. 5, which is too expensive to replace right now.

We drive to the Dorchester health center where Freddie's mother works as a receptionist. At a traffic light near Emerson College, two twentysomethings link arms. They step into the crosswalk, captivated by each other, oblivious to the Mercedes zooming toward them, almost plowing them down. The squeal of the brakes and the blast of the horn bring them out of their amorous trance. I'm envious. I've only felt that kind of unambivalent attraction once, with Tim, and I'm doubtful that I'll find it again. I love Ty, but I don't know if I'll ever stop doubting our relationship. I hope Caitlyn and Rose got to experience a moment of carefree abandon.

When we arrive at the clinic, the waiting area is packed with people suffering from a variety of ailments. I imagine the possible diagnoses: influenza, conjunctivitis, lice. My stomach turns, my eyes water, and my head itches.

Kevin knows that, for me, a room full of germs is like a torture chamber.

"This must be hell for you," he says, "all these sick people, spreading their diseases. You're taking one for the team."

I shiver, then worry that I've got a fever. "I think I'm catching a cold."

"This is a step up from our last case, with the roach-infested apartment and sewer rats."

Kevin is always the optimist. I see a box of tissues, take one, and hold it over my mouth, in an attempt to filter the germ-infested air. A woman sees me walking in her direction and catches my eye. She leans back, crosses her arms, and sneers. "Shouldn't you be downtown, putting away innocent people?"

I don't recognize the face, but I'll never forget the voice. She was a hostile witness in one of my first felony trials. I cross-examined the stuffing out of her. The defendant, her boyfriend, is now serving a seven-to-ten for pistol-whipping and robbing a grocery clerk.

Kevin puts his hand on my back and guides me toward the reception area.

"I can't take you anywhere," he says.

Freddie's mother is at the desk, on the phone. I met her last year, when I was prepping him for trial. There's no need to re-introduce myself.

She covers the mouthpiece of the phone and rolls her eyes. "What's he done now?"

Apparently, I'm not a fan favorite at the clinic.

"We need to talk to him," I say.

"Me, too. I haven't heard from him in over a week."

"Any idea where he might be?"

"Nope."

"We'd appreciate it if you could let him know we're looking for him."

"Same here."

We turn to leave, but she calls out. "Wait a minute." She scribbles something on an appointment card and hands it to me. "If you see him, tell him he's got a dentist appointment on Tuesday."

We make our exit, just in time to avoid getting coughed on by a toddler with a runny nose and chicken-poxed face. As soon as we're outside, I remove a bottle of Purell from my tote and slather it on my hands, all the way up to my elbows. If it wasn't toxic, I'd pour the rest of the bottle down my throat.

Kevin and I drive around the city, checking out places where Freddie has been arrested or seen recently: South Station, Mission Hill, the Boston Common. Then we visit areas where we know students go when they want to score drugs: the Theater District, the Fenway. We come up with nothing, or bubkes, as Kevin calls it.

On my third lap around the Victory Gardens, my feet start to ache; I regret my choice in footwear. Today was supposed to be an office day, with a quick stop at Wellesley College. If I'd have known what we'd be doing, I'd have worn something more appropriate, like combat boots.

"Should we call it a day?" Kevin says.

"Let's try one last place, Beacon Hill."

"What makes you think Freddie is hanging out there with the highfalutin folks?"

"Just a hunch."

We circle the Hill, traveling down Charles Street, up Mount Vernon, past my parents' house on Louisburg Square. I feel a tinge of guilt that I haven't been by to check on my mother.

We're about to give up when I spot Freddie on Joy Street, sneaking out of a driveway. I hope he was just peeing in the alley, but it's just as likely that he was doing a home invasion.

"There he is," I say.

Kevin pulls onto the sidewalk, bolts out of the car, and chases after him. Freddie is no match for Kevin. Freddie is young and slippery, but Kevin has spent the last twenty years at the gym, doing sprints and squats for just this purpose. When Kevin catches up with him, he grabs Freddie by the shoulders and yanks him in, just as Freddie did to me a few weeks ago. I hope he experiences the same fear. Kevin pats him down and pulls a wrench from Freddie's back pocket. I roll down the window.

"Possession of burglarious tools is a crime," I say.

Freddie notices me for the first time. His face falls. If he was scared a minute ago, he's petrified now.

He clears his throat. "I wasn't doing anything, I swear."

Kevin opens the back door and gestures him into the car.

"Tell it to the judge, Mr. Goodwrench."

Freddie climbs in the car, and Kevin takes off.

"Where are we going?" Freddie says.

We don't respond, choosing to let him sweat it out. Kevin cuts across Cambridge Street, onto Storrow Drive, and comes to a stop in front of the Nashua Street Jail. The location isn't lost on Freddie. I turn to face him.

"Maybe we can help each other out," I say.

He fidgets, takes out a pack of Newports, slaps it against the palm of his hand, and removes a cigarette from the box. He fingers it, rolls it in his palm, then puts it in his mouth.

"That's not a cigarette, Freddie. You have a joint in your mouth," I say.

"Oh, shit."

Kevin puts out his hand, and Freddie surrenders the marijuana.

"We want to ask you about the college girls who were murdered," I say.

"That wasn't me, I swear."

Kevin turns off the engine.

"Any idea where they were getting their Oxy?" I say.

He shakes his head. "I'd tell you if I knew."

I show him a picture of Tommy Greenough.

"Have you seen this guy before?"

He looks at Tommy's photo, his eyes widen slightly, revealing a hint of recognition.

"You know him."

"Sure. He's been all over the news."

A couple of uniformed corrections officers pass the car and walk up the steps to the jail. Kevin is losing his patience.

"Get out of the car and put your hands behind your back."

"Enjoy your stay at Nashua Street. I hope you get a cell with a water view," I say.

Freddie stays in the car, fidgets with his Timex, which is probably stolen.

"Okay, fine. I've seen that guy around LaVerne Street," he says.

"Have you sold to him?" Kevin says.

"Maybe."

Kevin takes out his handcuffs and flips them open. Freddie sits on his hands. "Okay, yeah. I sold to him. Who hasn't? That guy is always out there. He buys from lots of people."

"We're going to need a formal statement. And you're going to have to testify in the grand jury," I say.

"Whatever you want. Can I go?"

"Go ahead. Screw," Kevin says.

Freddie looks at him, unsure.

"Get out of here," Kevin says.

Freddie, a felon who doesn't have to be told thrice, gets out of the car, starts to take off toward the Science Park T stop.

I shout after him. "One more thing!"

He freezes and comes back to the car window. "What?"

"Your mother wants you to know you have a dentist appointment on Tuesday."

I hand him the appointment card through the window, and he watches us drive away.

Chapter Twenty-Two

Later, on my way home from work, I stop by my parents' house to see how my mother is doing and to talk to my father. Odds are fifty-fifty that I'll find them at home—a broken arm isn't likely to slow my mother. The last time she stayed home and missed an event due to *illness* was after her brow lift. She's a pro at concocting self-serving excuses to explain stitches and bruises. She'll probably go with: *I was dashing off to organize a charity event at the Vincent Club and I tripped on a squash racquet.*

Serena, the sanest member of the household, lets me in. She gives me a hug and takes my coat.

"How is she?" I say.

She wraps her hand around an imaginary glass, brings it to her lips, and tilts her head back. *Drunk.*

"They're having dinner," she says.

My parents are in the dining room. They never eat in the kitchen, even when it's just the two of them. Growing up, my brothers and I were banned from that section of the house. My mother told us it was a place for *staff*, not family. I'd never cooked a meal or loaded a dishwasher until I was in law school, living in my first apartment.

"Abigail, what a lovely surprise." My mother's words are welcoming, but her speech is slurred, and her tone is forbidding.

My father musters up a smile. "Muffin, come join us."

I give my mother an air kiss and my father a real kiss, and then take a seat at the table. It looks like a normal night at home, except for the sling on Mother's arm and the bags under my father's eyes. Serena sets me a place and passes me a platter of roast lamb, rosemary potatoes, and green beans. I help myself to a large portion of everything.

"How are you feeling?" I say.

"Busy, busy, busy," my mother says. "Our calendar is filled to the gills."

I take a bite of the lamb; the meat is rich and tender. My mother, more interested in the wine than the food, uses her fork to pick up a potato, inspects it, then puts it down.

"Your friend popped in earlier," she says.

I'm not sure who she's talking about.

"Ty was here?"

"No, your doctor friend. He stopped by my room. Right before I checked out."

"Before you were discharged, dear," my father says in between bites. "It's a hospital, not a hotel."

"His name was Aldridge."

I take a sip of wine. "Chip Aldridge?"

"Yes, exactly."

I downplay the connection to avoid further discussion. "He's not really a friend. He's more of an acquaintance."

She doesn't let it drop. "He seems like a fine young man, and quite eligible."

My father backs her up. "His father was at Exeter a few years before me."

"We know his aunt and uncle, Nick and Nicki Lowell," my mother says.

My parents would love to have someone like Chip as a member of the family. He and Charlie could play tennis at Longwood. Our mothers could drink martinis while our fathers traded tips on insider trading and corporate greed.

"He seems to fancy you." My mother taps the rim of her wineglass, signaling my father that she wants a refill.

I occupy myself by finishing my plate of food, hoping she'll change the subject. She usually has conversational ADD, flitting from topic to topic, but tonight she's glommed onto the subject of Chip Aldridge and won't let go.

"Maybe we should invite him for Thanksgiving," my mother says.

"We'll be in Positano," my father says.

After dinner, I help Serena take my mother up three flights of stairs and change her into her nightgown. When she's safely in bed, thumbing through the latest issue of *Town & Country*, I pour myself another glass of wine and join my father in his study. He's seated behind his enormous mahogany desk, reading *The Wall Street Journal*.

I slip into one of the leather club chairs.

"Did you know Max is running for mayor?" I say.

He looks up from the *Journal* and peers over his reading glasses.

"I already cut him a check," he says.

I'm surprised Max went directly to my father.

"He should have told me before he hit you up for cash."

"I thought you'd be pleased."

"Max hasn't exactly been supportive of my efforts."

"What efforts?" my father says.

I finish my wine and consider having another, but set the glass aside.

"I'd like to be named as Max's replacement," I say.

My father removes his reading glasses and takes his time folding the newspaper.

"You want to be the district attorney?" he says.

I rub my sweaty palms together. I can stare down the most vicious of criminals, but tonight I feel like a nervous schoolgirl.

"I don't expect you to support it, but I'm hoping you don't work against me."

He sits back and smiles. "I've always said you're a born leader."

"Really? I thought you wanted me to leave the DA's office."

"I do, but if you insist on staying there, you might as well be the boss. You won't have to be out at those miserable crime scenes, at all hours, chasing down felons. How do we secure that appointment?"

"It's up to the governor."

I know my father plays squash with him at the Harvard Club every Thursday, but I can't bring myself to make the ask.

He nods, a smile spreading across his face. "I'll give him a call."

When I came in the room, I was hoping my father wouldn't sabotage my chances. I didn't imagine that he'd tap his direct line to the governor. This is exactly what I need to push my candidacy past Cassandra's and over the edge.

"Don't forget," he says, "your great-uncle was in Reagan's cabinet, and your grandfather worked for Bush."

"You know I'm a Democrat, right?"

"Public service is an honorable profession, even for Democrats."

"Mom may not be as enthusiastic."

"Your mother isn't your biggest obstacle. Tyson's the one you should be worried about."

I take a breath, unsure of how to respond. I'd always wondered if my father hired a private investigator to look into Ty's background, as he did when Missy and Charlie got engaged. I think I have my answer.

"He's grown on me," my father says, "but it's hard to present yourself as the chief law enforcement officer for the county with an ex-con boyfriend."

I cringe at the description. "He can't change the past."

"No, but you can plan your future. There are other men out there, men who are just as attractive and won't put limits on your potential. Think about it."

When I get up to leave, my father offers to call his car service to take me home, but I prefer to walk. I tell him I want to get some air. I walk around the Public Garden, and when I reach Arlington Street, I take a small detour that lands me in front of Chip's building on Commonwealth Ave. The lights on the third floor are on, the curtains drawn. I pause for a moment and think about how much less complicated life could be if I was with a guy like Chip Aldridge.

Chapter Twenty-Three

My alarm sounds at five, but I've been awake for hours, thinking about Caitlyn and Rose, imagining how they felt during the final moments of their lives. I consider the options: panic, pain, resignation, peace. And I worry about who could be next.

After my shower, I make coffee, turn on the TV, and flip through the local news stations. Channel 4 is running a story about campus safety, offering stale advice: *Carry a whistle. Be aware of your surroundings. Walk in pairs.* Channel 5 is featuring a creepy-looking martial arts expert who is demonstrating self-defense techniques. I think I prosecuted that guy for child abuse a couple of years ago. On Channel 7, Carl Ostroff is positioned in front of city hall, reporting on the election. I up the volume.

"District Attorney Max Lombardo is ahead in the polls, but his opponent, City Council President Brenda O'Neill, is chipping away at his lead. If Lombardo wins, his highly coveted seat will be up for grabs. Two women are emerging as the front-runners to replace him: Cassandra Lester, who specializes in white-collar crimes, and Abigail Endicott, the battle-scarred homicide prosecutor who, last year, was a victim herself. Currently, Endicott is assigned to the high-profile coed-killer investigation, involving the Greenough family. The outcome of the case could make or break her efforts."

My phone sounds. I grab it.

"Carl Ostroff is a dimwit. Don't listen to him." I can hear the disgust in Kevin's voice.

"Who's Carl Ostroff?" I say.

"Exactly."

We agree to meet at Bulfinch. I hang up, turn off the TV, and start to dress. When I bunch up my pantyhose and slide in my right foot, the fabric catches on a broken fingernail and snags. So much for saving money on manicures. A dab of clear nail polish stops the run from advancing, but when I step into the other leg, I discover a longer run. I toss the hose in the trash. This is the fifth pair in as many weeks; it's another luxury I can't afford, but I'm not ready to sacrifice the delicate shimmer of Donna Karan for the cheaper, more durable brands. I take off my skirt and put on a pantsuit.

Kevin and I arrive at my office at the same time; each of us stopped to pick up coffee for the other. I went a few blocks out of my way for Kevin's favorite: coffee, regular, from Dunkin' Donuts. He went to Starbucks to pick up mine: grande soy latte.

He hands me the green-and-white cup, plus a paper bag.

"I'll see your coffee and raise you a chocolate croissant," he says.

I take a bite. "You win. I fold."

Case folders are stacked on my desk: forensic reports, autopsy results, the FBI profiler's analysis. I grab a couple of files.

"Let's put the papers aside," Kevin says, "and go out in the field."

"I've got my walking shoes on."

We decide that the former Alpha Beta members are a good starting point. Since the fraternity has been vacated, we drive to the former vice president's new residence, a dilapidated apartment in East Cambridge. His girlfriend tells us he's not here, he's gone home to Michigan for the rest of the semester. When I call his house in Grosse Pointe, his mother answers and says he's going to take the Fifth. Kevin locates the fraternity ex-treasurer's new apartment in Brighton. He answers the door and tells us he's lawyered up.

"I'm detecting a pattern," Kevin says once we're back in the car.

"I can call his attorney and try to negotiate," I say.

"No offense, but you're thinking too much like a lawyer. We're going at it all wrong. The frat boys may look like a bunch of preppies, but they're really just an organized group of scum-bags covering up a crime. We need to ask ourselves, if they were drug dealers or gun runners, what would we do?"

Kevin is onto something. But for the khakis and the boat shoes, the Alpha Beta guys are no different from any other gang we deal with. They don't merit special treatment.

"Let's start at the bottom rung and work our way up," I say.

Back in the office, I pull the file with the names of the newest members of the fraternity. Ned Halstead is the youngest pledge, and he has the highest GPA. Hopefully he'll cave quickly.

MIT police help us track him down on campus, in the Hayden Library. He's seated at a desk overlooking the river, cramming for an astrophysics exam. When we approach, he sees the gold badge clipped to Kevin's belt, jumps out of his chair, and raises his hands over his head in surrender, as though it were a stickup. It looks like he's mocking us, and I'm about to scold him for being disrespectful when I realize he's about to hyperventilate. He's completely serious.

"We're not going to shoot," Kevin says. "You can put your hands down."

"Please, I'll do whatever you want. Don't arrest me."

A couple of students are watching; one takes out his phone and videos us. The MIT police officer asks them to find another place to study, and they pick up their books and move away.

Kevin hands Ned a subpoena. "This is for the grand jury."

Ned studies the paper; his hand trembles. "I have class in the morning, and my experimental study group meets in the afternoon."

"We'll talk to your professors," I say.

He wipes sweat from his forehead. "Can I have the questions ahead of time?"

Kevin doesn't want to waste any more time bargaining with a nerdy nineteen-year-old. "This isn't a take-home exam," he says.

In most cases, we sit down with our witnesses and review their testimony. Right now, Ned seems like he'll go with the program, but by tomorrow, he could turn out to be a hostile witness. We want to catch him off guard, before he has time to map out his answers.

"Can't I just give you a statement?" he says.

"If you don't show up, I'll be back to arrest you," Kevin says.

Ned slumps down into his chair, head in his hands. Another satisfied customer.

Chapter Twenty-Four

The next day, Ned Halstead arrives at the courthouse wearing his best suit, looking like he's here for a job interview. I'm not surprised he brought a lawyer, most likely retained and financed by the fraternity. The lawyer asks to speak with me alone. We leave Ned in the waiting room, sandwiched between a jittery junkie and a gangster who has bulging biceps and a teardrop tattoo under his eye.

Ned shuffles a few inches closer to the junkie, who nudges him.

"Hey, man. You know where I can score some crystal?"

Ned crosses his arms and stares straight ahead.

When Ned's lawyer gets me alone, he does what he's paid to do; he tries to dissuade me from calling his client as a witness. I smile and think for a few seconds, pretending to mull over his argument.

"Sorry, Ned is a necessary witness," I say.

In the grand jury room, I let the panel know we're about to get started. They had a bake-off earlier, and they're passing around the last plate of treats, my favorite: old-fashioned Toll House cookies. I can't resist taking one. I gobble it down, make sure I don't have chocolate on my teeth, and call Ned to the stand.

When I raise my right hand to swear him in, he ignores me. There's something he has to get off his chest.

"I told them it wasn't right. I told them to stop." His voice cracks. "I did, I swear."

I look at the lawyer, who whispers. *You have to wait for her to ask a question.* Ned looks at me, and I guide him through the preliminaries: his education, his fraternity affiliation, how he knows the Greenoughs.

"Did you see Caitlyn Walker on the Thursday night before her body was discovered?" I say.

He leans in to the microphone, eager to get the ordeal over with. "Yes, she was at the fraternity."

"Was there a party?"

"It wasn't really a party. We were drinking, playing pool. Tommy told us to come upstairs. There were five of us. I didn't even know Tommy that well. I know his brother, Robbie." He's trying to tell the story in one breath.

I toss him a softball, try to slow him down. "Did you go upstairs?"

"We all did."

"What did you see?"

"The dead girl. She was there."

I'm not going to let him off the hook by depersonalizing my victim. She had a name. "Caitlyn Walker?"

He nods. "Robbie was with her."

"On the third floor?"

"Yes."

"What were Robbie and Tommy Greenough doing?" I say.

"They were drinking, straight out of the bottle. I think it was rum. They were both pretty wasted."

"What about Caitlyn Walker? Was she drinking?"

"She wasn't drinking, but she seemed like she was on something." He takes a breath. "They were, you know, doing sex acts." Ned starts to mumble, looks down at the floor. "At first it was just Robbie and Tommy, but then a couple of the others joined in."

"Did Caitlyn say anything?"

"She . . . Caitlyn . . . told them to stop."

A couple of the jurors flinch; one looks down and shakes his head.

"Did they rape her?" I say.

"Rape her? No, it wasn't like that. She told them to stop because she wanted more money from Tommy."

"Money?" says the postal worker in the back of the room. "You mean the girl, the one who went to Wellesley, was a hooker?"

There's not a lot that surprises me anymore, but this catches me off guard. I wonder if Rose was also getting paid for sex. I push forward as though I've been expecting his disclosure.

"Do you know the nature of the financial arrangement that Caitlyn had with Tommy Greenough?"

"He said he had already paid her for two guys. She wanted extra because there were a few more. Tommy agreed. That was it."

I resist the urge to run out into the hall and grab Kevin, let him know that we have a huge break in the case. Sometimes having everything recorded is inhibiting, but today I welcome the device. I want to capture every word.

"Did you see Caitlyn leave the fraternity?"

"Yes, I saw her. She walked out the door."

So much for our theory that she was killed in the hot tub. The killer, whoever he is, forced her underwater someplace else and washed away the evidence.

"Did anyone leave with her?"

"She left alone."

Even though we don't have a smoking gun, Ned's testimony has been more fruitful than I could have imagined.

I start to wrap up. "Is there anything else that you can tell this grand jury, to assist in their efforts?"

Ned thinks, then looks at his lawyer, who nods him on. "You saw the video, right?"

The postal worker and I speak at the same time: "Video?"

Ned looks down, ashamed. I want to shake him and ask why he pledged that fraternity. Was it simply peer pressure, the desire to belong? Worse, what caused him to go upstairs to witness such despicable activity? Whatever the reason, I'm glad he did.

He takes out his phone and holds it up. "Do you want to see it?"

I grab an evidence bag and tell Ned to drop the phone inside. Then I take a yellow evidence sticker, affix it to the bag, and seal it.

"This shall be marked as grand jury exhibit number one," I say.

Chapter Twenty-Five

Kevin and I go to police headquarters, where we sit in his cramped cubicle and watch Ned's cell phone video. The images on the screen make my skin crawl. The quality of the video is poor, the faces are blurry, and the background has streaks of glare, but it's clear enough for us to see exactly what's transpiring: one lewd act followed by a lewder act. I squirm in my chair.

Caitlyn is naked; Robbie is clothed. She doesn't speak, but there are four distinct male voices on the recording, including Tommy's and Robbie's. They cheer each other on. *Go. Go. Go. Go. Robbie. Robbie. Robbie. Robbie.* The instant Robbie unzips his pants, I look away, wishing I could get up and leave. I've listened to my victims recount the horrific details of sexual assaults, and witnessed their injuries, but I've never seen actual video of an attack. Even though the encounter is technically consensual, it's violent and demoralizing.

The scene quickly devolves into chaos. Naked men, each taking their turn with Caitlyn. At one point she stops to argue about money.

"This wasn't our deal." Her speech is slow, and her words are slurred.

"Don't worry, I'll make up for it," Tommy says.

She looks around the room. *"It's $200 for each guy."*

Tommy agrees to the new terms, and the activity resumes. Kevin and I sit elbow to elbow, frozen in place, until the last frame. After the video is over, Kevin busies himself with his computer. I take some water out of my tote and drink a series of small sips, capping and uncapping the bottle each time.

"It's depraved, but consensual," I say.

"There's got to be something we can lock them up for," Kevin says.

"Like what?"

"How about drunk and disorderly?"

"They're inside their own home."

"They videotaped her without authorization. That could be a violation of the wiretap laws."

"Without Caitlyn's testimony, we can't prove lack of consent."

He turns off the computer.

"The Greenoughs had something to do with her murder."

"You're singing to the chorus," I say.

We go downstairs to the computer forensics lab, where we find Sasha Phelan, the department's cyber sleuth. Sasha spends her days trolling through other people's computers, reading their e-mail, examining their Google searches and website clicks. She is seated at a table behind three computer screens. The room is musty and windowless, reminding me of a solitary confinement cell. There are at least two hundred plastic spuds scattered around her desk, windowsill, and bookcases; each figurine is outfitted with its own accessories. Mustaches, glasses, top hats, baseball mitts, holsters. It's hard to take her seriously until she speaks.

"Rose Driscoll and Caitlyn Walker were definitely paid escorts."

"Can you link them to any men in particular?" I say.

She nods. "They had ads all over the Internet. Backpage, Craigslist, Seeking Arrangement. They were sugar babies, targeting old guys who would help pay their tuition and give them spending money."

Sasha clicks a website and brings up Rose's profile. We scroll through the photos, which are rated PG, compared to the video that we just watched. Caitlyn has her own website, where she offers herself up for dates and parties.

My stomach turns at the thought of telling the Driscolls and Karen Walker what their daughters were doing to earn money. I'll have to make the call soon, before the tabloid reporters do it for me.

"Did you find a connect with Tommy Greenough?" Kevin says.

Sandra nods. "He was in contact with both of the women."

"When did he meet Caitlyn?" I say.

"Their first communication was on the night she died."

Sasha shows us a screen. Tommy: *Meet me at Crazy Fox in Cambridge.* Caitlyn: *Cash up front.* Tommy: *If chemistry is good, we'll have a party.* I keep scrolling.

"That's it? That's the only communication between them?" I say.

"So far," Sasha says.

"What about Rose?"

"Rose was more of a regular. She met Tommy through one of her personal ads. He e-mailed her, and they met at the same bar to discuss the arrangement. Then he brought her to sex parties."

"Where did the parties go down?" Kevin says.

"Mostly private clubs, fraternities, and people's homes."

"Who'd they invite?" I say.

"CEOs, athletes, Secret Service agents, a couple of congressmen, and a governor."

Tommy Greenough was a pimp with an exclusive client list. A large percentage of the names will probably be familiar. I may even know some of them personally. I hope none are relatives.

Sasha shows us a spreadsheet. "He arranged for parties, brought in the girls, but instead of charging per encounter, he charged the huge fees. There was a membership fee and an entry fee to the parties."

"Sounds like the Harvard Club, minus the hookers," I say.

Tommy doesn't strike me as a deep thinker, but he's not as dumb as he looks. Clearly, he's savvy enough to have consulted with someone who advised him how to skirt the solicitation laws. He made his business appear legal, as though he were hosting parties. Once inside, consenting adults can do what they want.

"It makes sense," Kevin says. "Greenough was one of their own. That's who you trust when you're doing something illegal? Someone who has as much to lose as you do."

"How many women were involved?" I say.

Sasha pulls open a file. "I don't have a final tally yet, but there were a lot, dozens. And he split the profits fifty-fifty."

"He had a partner?" My heart pounds. "Please don't tell me Josh King is involved."

"I didn't see that name."

"What about Tommy's brother, Robbie?" Kevin says.

Sasha shakes her head.

"It's got to be someone with knowledge of the law," I say. "And someone who has a way to launder the money."

"Like a small business," Kevin says.

"Or a political campaign," I say.

I ask Sasha to search through the records, using the senator's name. Kevin leans over his shoulder, eyes the screen.

"Our senior senator has his paws all over this," Kevin says.

"Why would he take a risk like that?" Sasha says.

"For a guy like Greenough," I say, "it's about three things: money, power, and secrets. He's got dirt on a lot of rich and powerful guys. He could bring them down with a phone call. Which means he owns them."

Chapter Twenty-Six

Ty takes the red-eye back from California. He's been away for a few days, and we haven't spoken since he left, and I've barely had time to send a couple of texts. I'm half asleep when I hear the lock on the door click open. I roll over and sit up in bed.

"Hey, babe," he says.

"Join me," I say. "I missed you."

He gives me a kiss, and I allow myself to get lost in the warmth of his embrace and the softness of his skin. I feel a rekindling of the desire that I experienced when we first met, before my fear of connection and rejection set in.

After showering, I find him in the kitchen, making breakfast: organic coffee, cage-free eggs, artisanal sausage, and gluten-free toast, most of which he picked up at the Ferry Building in San Francisco. So much for his lectures on economizing. Ty's financial weakness is food; mine is everything else.

"Today is my meeting with the governor's office," I say. "Do you think this shirt looks okay?"

"You look great," he says.

"You don't think it's too much?"

"Too much what?"

"Too flashy, too expensive looking."

"Babe, it's a white shirt."

"Actually, it's cream, and it's silk. Maybe I should wear cotton."

I pull a dozen outfits from my closet, finding fault in each. The dress is too dressy. The suit is too suity. The skirt is too sexy. I decide to stick with the cream blouse and black skirt suit. It's hard to go wrong with Armani.

It's impossible to find parking near the statehouse. Even the illegal spots are occupied. It's about a mile and a half from my apartment, so I decide to walk. On the way, I get a call from Kevin.

"Do you have time to take a trip to the ME's office?" he says.

"I have something personal to do this morning, then I'm all yours."

I don't reveal where I'm going. Telling Kevin about my interview ahead of time will just add to the pressure.

"Relax," he says. "You'll do great."

"How do you know where I'm going?"

"I don't sell shoes for a living."

I decide to stop at the Starbucks on the corner of Beacon and Charles Streets for one more jolt of coffee. At the counter, I place my order and, as I'm putting my wallet back in my tote, hear the sound of Chip Aldridge's deep, confident voice. I shouldn't be surprised to run into him here; it's the midway point between his apartment and the hospital.

He's behind me, in line. "A double espresso, please."

My heart beats a little faster, and it's not from caffeine. I turn to say hello.

He does a double take. "Hey, I've been thinking about you."

He pays for his order, accepts change from the cashier, and drops two dollars in the tip jar. When he smiles, a surge of warmth rushes though my body. It's undeniable; there's a crackle of chemistry between us.

"I have a meeting up the street at the statehouse," I say as though I have to explain my presence.

We move to the pickup counter.

"How's the murder business?" he says.

"Booming," I say, "unfortunately."

There's a loose eyelash on his upper cheek; without thinking, I press my index finger to his face and hold it out for him to see.

"Make a wish."

He exhales a stream of air on my finger, catching the lash and sweeping it away. I find myself making a wish, too. *One kiss. Just one—to see how it feels, to get it out of my system.*

A voice calls out. "Abby? Is there an Abby here? Grande soy latte for Abby?"

Chip touches my arm. I look down at his hand, and he points at the barista. "They're calling your name."

I take the coffee, say good-bye, and flee so quickly that I forget to snag a couple of sugar packets. This is bad. I cheated on Ty once, and when I confessed, he broke up with me. It was painful, and it's taken a while to repair the damage. Yet here I am, flirting with the idea of doing it again.

When I arrive at the governor's office, the legal counsel's receptionist tells me they're running behind schedule. I take a seat in the reception area, out of sight from the doorway. I'd rather not be noticed by the reporters and gossipy statehouse hacks as they pass by.

After about twenty minutes, the door to the conference room swings opens, and I'm surprised by who pops out: Cassandra. She smiles as though expecting to see me, and I try to do the same.

"They're so nice," she says. "You'll love them."

"Them? I thought it was just a meeting with one person."

"There's three. Oh, I have to tell you—it was so funny, turns out the chair of the search committee is best friends with my aunt. It's such a small world."

I know I shouldn't be nervous; both my connections and my capabilities trump Cassandra's.

She points to my mouth and makes a circle. "Your lipstick is smudged."

I look around for a ladies' room so I can do a quick makeup check, but the receptionist calls my name.

"They're ready for you."

I rub my index finger across my teeth, try not to smile, and hope that there's not a streak of lip gloss covering my front teeth. Cassandra was probably just messing with my head.

In the conference room, there are six, not three, people. I'm introduced to them quickly, and I try to commit their names to memory by focusing on something about them that will stick in my mind. I shake hands, wondering if they're looking at my enchanting smile or my smeared lipstick, and take a seat at the head of the shiny mahogany table.

Lennie Potter, a man with a polka-dot pocket square, speaks first. "Your qualifications as a litigator and a manager are impressive."

Potter: polka dots. "Thank you, Mr. Potter," I say.

Jenna Overmeyer, a woman with an underbite, speaks next. "We're concerned about your electability. We want to appoint someone who can win the election next November."

Overmeyer: underbite. I try to stay on message. "I understand your concerns, but I have significant fund-raising commitments and I've worked on numerous campaigns, including both Max's and his predecessor's."

"The Back Bay and Beacon Hill don't carry enough votes to get you elected county-wide," says a man whose name I've already forgotten. "Our concern is Roxbury, West Roxbury and Hyde Park."

I hold my ground. "I've been working in the neighborhoods for a decade. I've been a fixture in the district courts, neighborhood-watch meetings, and churches. I have a strong base of support."

That seems to placate the group, albeit slightly. They pepper me with a series of policy questions about mandatory minimum sentencing, three strikes, and the death penalty. I'm against all of them, but the committee doesn't really seem to care. They're itching to get to the next subject.

Polka Dot takes the lead. "We understand you have a case involving Senator Greenough's son."

I don't tell him that the case now involves the senator himself. "I'm sure you appreciate that I can't comment on an ongoing investigation."

Underbite pipes in. "I'm sure you appreciate that he's a very powerful and influential player."

I lean forward for emphasis. "I didn't choose this case. I'm just following the evidence. I have to go where it takes me."

Forgot-her-name smiles. "If you throw a punch at Senator Greenough, it'd better be a knockout."

An assistant taps on the door and sticks in her head; she reports that the meeting has run over and it's time to move on to the next candidate. I stand, shake hands, and thank everyone for considering me.

Polka Dot walks me to the door. "We've also learned that your fiancé has a criminal record. This could have significant impact on your candidacy."

Fiancé? Cassandra must have told them that Ty and I are engaged in order to heighten their concerns and rattle me.

"Tyson, my boyfriend, is a good man who made a mistake. He's accepted responsibility and moved on with his life. Isn't that what a DA asks others to do? Rehabilitation is a cornerstone of the criminal justice system."

"That's true, at least in theory." He stands in the entryway, nods, and smiles at a passerby. "The governor is looking to appoint someone who will win come election time. He's not looking to ally himself with a loser."

"I don't plan to lose," I say.

He starts to speak, hesitates. "Look," he says, "if you really want to be the district attorney for Suffolk County, then you should rid yourself of any encumbrances."

Chapter Twenty-Seven

My next meeting is at the medical examiner's office, but I have time to kill. I could walk back to Bulfinch, but I'd rather not. Cassandra is probably roaming the hallways, bragging about her interview with the governor's counsel, telling everyone that she saw me in the waiting room. I don't want to subject myself to an interrogation. The past few weeks have been stressful, both inside and outside the office—the investigation, the victims' families, my family, the election. I need to decompress.

Saks Fifth Avenue is my Prozac. Some people visit therapists or go to the gym; I head to Saks. It's a family tradition, and it starts early. When I was in seventh grade, nervous about a Latin test or the school play, my mother knew exactly what to do. She'd phone my father's driver, tell him to let me off in front of the Prudential Center, and I'd go to the Endicott version of the Happiest Place on Earth: Saks.

The store was mesmerizing back when I was thirteen, and it holds the same appeal today. The piercing glare of the artificial lights, the impenetrable clouds of perfume spritzes, the cacophony of sales associates.

I Uber over, promising myself I'll just look around, visit with my old friends Stella McCartney and Carolina Herrera. I don't need anything, which is fortunate because I can't afford any-thing.

Before I'm halfway up the staircase to the second floor, a couple of sales associates see me and light up. The two women practically trip over each other.

I try to lower expectations. "I'm just looking."

They back off a little, but they've both waited on me dozens of times, and they're not dissuaded.

"Abigail, it's been a while! Is everything okay?"

"We just got in a new shipment of suits."

People in here know me by sight, name, and vice. Favorite designer: Prada. Most flattering makeup foundation: Laura Mercier. Shoe size: seven and a half. Dress size: six, except when I'm on trial, when it drops to four.

"There's an aubergine Loro Piana cashmere sweater. It'll look fabulous on you," one of the women says.

"It sounds divine." And expensive. "But I'm really just brows-ing."

Her face drops in disappointment. "Let me know if I can help."

In the shoe department, I'm practically assaulted by a salesman, touting a spectacular pair of Pierre Hardy boots. My willpower is waning. I think about the pile of unpaid bills and final no-tices in my apartment. I have to get out of here.

I take the escalator down, and on my way to the exit, I pass the men's department. Ty turned thirty-six a couple of weeks ago. We celebrated with dinner at the Beehive, a neighborhood restaurant in the South End that offers his favorites: oysters, Red Betty IPA, and live jazz. We had a fun night, but he deserves more.

I scan the display cases, filled with sunglasses and wallets, and peruse the shelves, stacked with blue jeans and messenger bags. I sort through racks of coats until a Rick Owens leather jacket sings his name. It's perfect: soft, rugged, and beautifully constructed, just like Ty. Before I can get it off the hanger, a salesclerk sprints to my side.

"Gift wrapping?" she says.

I have no business buying this.

"Please," I say.

While she puts the coat in a glossy red box, I notice a rip in the side of my Prada tote, probably from Freddie's assault. I move to a case of women's bags. A laser-cut Givenchy satchel catches my eye. The salesclerk sees me ogling the bag.

"We just got it in."

"How much?" I say.

"It's $2,895."

The bag plus Ty's jacket will cost the same as two months' condo fees. I'm not sure how late I am on my most recent bill, but I decide to take a gamble.

"Put it on my house account."

I hold my breath while she punches some keys and looks at the screen. She frowns, tries again.

"The computer is saying that there's a stop-hold on your account."

Maybe I can get out of here before she calls security. I look at the door and consider making a run for it.

"Never mind," I say. "I'll come back later."

She's determined to get the commission on the sale, and she's not giving up.

"It must be a glitch. I'll put in an override," she says.

As she rings up the coat and the satchel, a call from Kevin comes in.

"Ready to see some maggots?" he says.

She ties a white ribbon around Ty's gift box.

"Maggots?" I say.

She looks up, then back down, pretending not to eavesdrop, and slides the box into a shopping bag.

"Where are you?" Kevin says.

"I'm in the middle of Saks." The line goes quiet for a minute. "Are you still there?"

"Sorry to interrupt. Call me when you're done." He sounds tense, abrupt.

Kevin has never been judgmental about any of my shortcomings, including my spending habits. This seems like an odd time to start taking my inventory.

"Why are you being weird?" I say.

"How do you want me to act? You just told me you're in the middle of sex."

I laugh so hard that I startle a makeup artist, who smudges eyeliner on the lid of her client.

"I'm in the middle of a store—*Saks*, not *sex*."

"Even worse. Do yourself a favor: put down the merchandise, turn around slowly, and come out with your hands up."

"I'll surrender, but I'm taking the contraband with me."

Kevin picks me up outside the front door; I toss Ty's box into the trunk of his car and keep the new satchel up front with me. I use the ride time to transfer my most essential belongings from my old tote to my new one. A packet of tissues, a bottle of hand sanitizer, two bottles of water, a scarf that needs to go to the dry cleaner, a pair of gloves, my badge, my wallet.

"That sack is like a clown car," Kevin says.

When we arrive at the ME's office, Reggie introduces us to the forensic entomologist, Floyd Carver, a twentysomething with sweaty palms and a limp handshake. Every time we meet Floyd, it's like *Groundhog Day*; he never seems to remember either one of us, even though we've had at least a half-dozen consults with him.

Floyd's lab is one of my least favorite places on the planet. There are dead bugs everywhere: centipedes, cockroaches, caterpillars. Everything in here makes me gag. There are even a few live worms, squiggling around in glass cases.

"That Dumpster was a gold mine," Reggie says.

Floyd pries open a petri dish, uses tweezers to remove a dried-up maggot, and puts it under the microscope. I don't need to get up close and personal with the legless larva; I'll put that off for as long as I can, until closer to trial prep. For now, I want the bottom line.

"Were you able to make an assessment about Caitlyn's time of death?" I say.

Floyd looks through the scope, turns the focus knobs, and waves me over. Not wanting to appear uninterested, I lean over the instrument and think about Caitlyn. Kevin knows that insects and corpses are not my favorite part of the job.

"Let me take a look." He squints into the scope, looks back at me, and shrugs. "Yup, looks like a dead maggot."

"Can you summarize your findings?" I say.

"Suffice it to say, you've been operating under a false assumption." Floyd is enjoying his rare moment in the spotlight and wants to drag this out.

Reggie cuts to the chase. "Caitlyn Walker might have gone missing on Thursday night, but she was murdered on Friday, within a couple of hours of when her body was discovered."

"How does that jibe with the autopsy results?" I say.

"Decomp and rigor put her time of death between Thursday and Friday. These insects narrow the time frame to Friday evening," Reggie says.

I sit on one of the stools at the counter. I accidentally bump my elbow against a glass case filled with fruit flies, causing them to buzz around, trying to escape.

My phone vibrates; so does Kevin's. We check the screens, then look at each other.

"We've got to go," I say.

"What's up?" Reggie says.

I show him the text. *Missing Person: Valerie Jackson, Tufts freshman. Last seen yesterday at 9 p.m. Possible victim #3.*

Chapter Twenty-Eight

Kevin and I drive to the Tufts campus in Medford, about twenty minutes outside of Boston. Tufts is tough to categorize. Size-wise, it's somewhere between BU and Wellesley, not quite big and not quite small, with five thousand students. The vibe isn't quite bustling urban or bucolic suburban. It's not as internationally known as its neighbors in nearby Cambridge, Harvard, and MIT, but it's a good school, with a competitive admissions process.

Rush-hour traffic heading north is at a standstill. When we reach the Zakim Bridge, Kevin flips on the lights and siren, and zigzags from lane to lane. I feel carsick, so I turn off the heat and crack my window. As we veer right, onto the exit ramp, I call the police chief to let her know we're a couple of minutes away.

I hang up and tell Kevin what I learned. "Valerie Jackson, eighteen years old. Video surveillance shows her going into the Tisch Library a little after seven and leaving a little after nine. That's the last time there's a record of her alive."

"Where do her folks live?" Kevin says.

"Her mother passed. Her father lives in Somerville."

"A townie."

"She's getting financial aid, like Rose and Caitlyn."

Kevin swerves around a pickup truck, and my nausea intensifies. I keep my eyes trained straight ahead, on a street sign, a trick my doctor gave me when I had positional vertigo last summer.

"Who phoned it in?" he says.

"The roommate. She noticed Valerie didn't make it home last night. She tried calling and texting her, but when she didn't get a response, she walked over to campus police and filed a missing persons."

"At least the kids are paying attention to the warnings."

We arrive at the campus police station, where Tufts police chief Stephanie Menton is waiting. She's a beefy woman who looks like she could go a few rounds against Mayweather. Her handshake makes me want to get on my knees and say *uncle*.

It's a short walk to Hodgdon Hall, where Valerie lives. Or lived. A couple of uniforms are keeping watch outside, checking IDs. For the time being, access is limited to residents only.

Valerie's room on the third floor is sealed off by yellow tape. Kevin and I go inside and look around. It's standard fare, about fourteen by fourteen, with two twin beds, two desks, two dressers, and two closets. Valerie's closet is jammed with a hodgepodge of clothes, shoes, and bags. Some things are old, some new; some designer, some discount.

Kevin pulls out an unused Proenza Schouler bag from the closet, unzips it, and pulls out the price tag.

He reveals a rare expression of surprise. "Guess how much this thing cost?"

If he had posed the question a year ago, I'd have had no idea. I never knew the price of anything. I didn't have to. Not so anymore. I inspect the bag; I've always been able to tell the difference between a real from a fake. The elaborate stitching and crisp magenta leather tell me that this one is the real deal, not a knockoff.

"Twelve hundred," I say.

"Close," he says. "Eleven fifty."

"That doesn't include the sales tax."

"You know your pocketbooks."

Kevin inspects a few more handbags until he finds something inside the flap of a counterfeit Kate Spade: nineteen white pills, wrapped in tissue. He holds them under the light and examines them closely.

"Oxy," he says.

A clear pattern is emerging. Rose, Caitlyn, and now Valerie are all young, attractive college students. They all receive some kind of financial aid. And they all have a penchant for Oxy. This doesn't bode well for Valerie's chances of survival.

When Sasha Phelan arrives, minus her Mr. Potato Heads, I barely recognize her. She sits at Valerie's desk and flips on her laptop. Kevin and I go downstairs to the first-floor student lounge, where the chief introduces us to Valerie's roommate, Lexie.

She's wearing sweats, clutching a nylon gym bag.

"Did you find her? Do you know where she is?" she says.

"Not yet," I say. "We'd like to ask you some questions."

The chief leads us to the resident advisor's apartment and leaves us alone. We take seats around a coffee table. The place smells of Lemon Pledge and looks like the floors have just been mopped. There's not a speck of dust; my kind of apartment.

"There are some expensive things in Valerie's closet. Do you know how she paid for them?" Kevin says.

"Sorry, I'm not really into clothes." Lexie looks down at her sneakers. "Unless I can wear them on the soccer field."

"Is there anyone new in Valerie's life?" I say.

"I don't mean to sound disrespectful, but we're in our first semester, freshman year—everyone is new."

"What about outside interests?"

"She wasn't into sports, so we didn't have a lot in common."

I remember how self-involved I was during college. I changed my major three times, from classics to French literature to history.

When I wasn't in class or studying, I was working for the school newspaper, the *Crimson*. And I dated more than a few guys. I was rarely in my room, and when I was, I wasn't paying attention to my suite mates' comings and goings.

"We're pretty different. I'm an athlete, she's more of a partier," Lexie says.

"What about drugs?" I say.

"I'm not a narc or anything, but I've seen pills."

"Boyfriends?" I say.

"She goes out like all the time. And her phone is always ringing."

"Any idea where she was planning to go last night?" Kevin says.

"I never asked." She tears up. "I'm a lousy roommate. I'm so into my own stuff, I haven't really taken the time to get to know her."

I put my hand on her arm. "This isn't your fault."

"Do you know if she ever went to frat parties?" Kevin says.

"I don't," Lexie says.

When we're done, we go back up to Valerie's dorm room to see if Sasha had any luck.

"Tommy Greenough sent her messages at all hours," Sasha says, "hooked her up with men, sent her the names of hotels and a couple of private parties."

"Anything in there about last night?" Kevin says.

"Not that I can tell. I'll dig deeper back at my office."

As Sasha packs up the computer, I think about Valerie's father, somewhere in Somerville. His life is about to change forever.

Chapter Twenty-Nine

Max has left me several voice mails, each one increasingly hostile. When I get to Bulfinch, I e-mail him an update, hoping that will be enough to keep him off my back for a while. I was wrong. Three minutes later, he makes a rare appearance in my office.

He stands in the doorway, out of breath. "Arrest the bastard."

Max's opinion poll results have made him trigger-happy, but I'm sticking to the plan. He's not the one who has to stand up in court and defend the arrest. I've had my head handed to me by a couple of judges already, and I don't want to risk it again. I don't care about getting yelled at; in fact, sometimes that's half the fun. I worry that a premature arrest, followed by a quick dismissal, will do damage to both my credibility and my case.

"Hold on. Let's pump the brakes," I say.

"We got Tommy Greenough dead to rights on deriving support and obstruction," Max says.

There's a knock on my door. Before I have time to respond, Cassandra opens it and walks in.

"Hope I'm not interrupting," she says, "but there's a pack of reporters outside the building. I told them we couldn't comment."

I wait for Max to ream her out for overstepping. She doesn't have authority to talk about the case to the media, not even to say, "No comment." Surprisingly, Max seems to be on board with her insubordination.

"Thanks for protecting me, Cassie." He turns to me. "I don't want to be quoted until we have some positive developments. So get me some fucking positive developments."

All three of our phones sound. It's a text from dispatch. *Another body, partially buried, in Christopher Columbus Park.*

"That's got to be the girl from Tufts," Cassandra says.

Cassandra shouldn't be on the distribution list of this case. I make a mental note to have her name removed.

She keeps talking, as though this is her business. "At least they found her. That should give the family some closure."

I don't say what I'm thinking, which is, *Spoken like a white-collar crime prosecutor.* There's no such thing as closure when it comes to murder. The case ends and life goes on, but the wound never heals and the sadness never disappears.

"Cassie, go to the scene with Abby," Max says. "Work the press. Stay in front of the cameras. Abby, you work behind the scenes."

Even though I'm angry Max allowed Cassandra to muscle her way into my investigation, it could play to my advantage. I'd rather not be quoted in the media until I have something significant to say. She can play Mickey the Dunce.

Kevin picks us up out front, and we head over to Christopher Columbus Park, which is on the outskirts of the North End. When we arrive, there are a group of reporters assembled around the perimeter. Inside the yellow tape, the usual controlled chaos of a murder scene is under way. Uniforms, detectives, technicians, and medical personnel carry out their respective assignments. A couple of men in white hazmat suits use shovels to collect soil from around the area where the body was found.

I notice a new guy in the mix, someone I don't recognize. He's taking notes, wearing a suit and a badge.

I nudge Kevin. "Who's the new detective?"

"He's a head-shrinker."

"The FBI sent a profiler?"

The man sees us looking at him and comes over to introduce himself.

"I'm Stan Alvarez, FBI."

"I didn't know we called for a profiler," I say.

"Three bodies in a span of more than a month—the bureau is considering it a serial killing," he says. "I talked to your co-counsel, she said she'd have the files sent to my office today."

I've got two turf battles on my hands. First Cassandra, now the shrink with a badge. Everyone wants a piece of my case. I'll play along for now. Otherwise, this guy will do an end run around me, to Cassandra, which will empower her even more.

"You ready to meet the vic?" Kevin says.

I follow him over to the tented area, but stop short before I can see the body. "Tell me," I say.

Kevin speaks slowly, allowing me to absorb every detail before moving on to the next one.

"It looks like her neck was broken," he says. "There's reddish, purplish bruising and ligature marks around her throat."

"Are her eyes open or closed?" I say.

"Open," he says.

I reach into my tote and take a sip of water while he continues.

"She was a fighter. There are defensive marks on her hands and pretty deep cuts on her knees."

I wish I could leave; instead I glove up. When Kevin is done describing the victim, I squint my eyes, then open them, slowly. She starts out as a blur, then slowly comes into focus. There she is, my new victim. She was once someone's loved one; now she's their memory.

"Has there been a positive ID?" I say.

"Not yet," Kevin says.

I hold my breath and take a closer look, then pull out the police report and read it.

"Something's not right," I say.

"Amen to that," Kevin says.

I hand him the report. "The description doesn't match."

He consults the report, compares it to our victim. "Five ten, one hundred and thirty pounds," he says.

"Valerie's eye color is listed as blue. This woman's eyes are brown."

"Could be a mistake."

I search my file for Valerie Jackson's college ID photo. The differences extend beyond eye color. The woman in the picture is shorter and thinner than this victim.

"This is not Valerie Jackson," I say. "We got ourselves a fourth victim."

Chapter Thirty

The feds have named a so-called task force: me, Kevin, Stan the profiler, and a press aid. The saving grace is Cassandra didn't make the list, at least not officially. The FBI issued a statement, touting their interest in lending resources, providing technical assistance, and bringing the killer to justice. It sounds good, but it's really a way to position themselves—to take credit if the case is solved or distance themselves if it's not. Stan requested a sit-down. I'd rather spend my time doing real investigative work, but Max feels otherwise.

"Go to the meeting," he says.

"Profiles never pan out," I say.

"This is the era of cooperation and coordination. At least that's what we're going to say in the press release."

"We both know profiling isn't a crime-solving strategy. It's a PR campaign." Max is as frustrated as I am, but he's all about image these days.

"If you don't want to go, I'm sure Cassandra won't mind," he says.

"What time is the meeting?" I say.

He checks his watch. "Now."

I call Kevin to see if he wants to join me, even though I think that I can pretty much predict his response. *I'm not wasting my time with a hocus-pocus mind reader. I'd rather go to that lady who sits on a bench in the Boston Common, holding a crystal ball.*

"I'll meet you there," he says.

"That wasn't what I expected to hear. Is the commissioner making you go?"

"Yup. Can't argue with chain of command."

I walk across the street, keeping my head down so I don't have to stop and talk to anyone. The murder investigation and the political speculation make this part of town ground zero for gossip.

When I arrive at Center Plaza, Kevin is in the waiting room. The receptionist gives us visitor's passes and escorts us to Stan's office. His work space is decorated with a framed diploma from Georgetown Law School, certificates from training programs, and his Ph.D. in forensic psychology. He wheels his chair from behind his desk to face me and Kevin without obstruction. The setup looks like we're about to start a couple's therapy session, which would probably be more fruitful, and would definitely be more fun.

"I've reviewed the local police accounts and spoken with the ME and the computer analyst," Stan says. "This guy is kind of a cross between the Boston Strangler and Ted Bundy."

"As you shrinks say, how does that make you feel?" Kevin says.

I stifle a laugh. Stan blows it off, which probably adds fuel to Kevin's annoyance. One of us has to play along, and it's not going to be Kevin.

"Where do you suggest we start?" I say.

"Establishing the commonality among the victims is important," Stan says.

"One thing they have in common is they're all dead," Kevin says.

"Agreed," Stan says.

Stan is taking Kevin's snarkiness in stride, which makes him start to grow on me. He's not a bad guy, probably used to being the butt of law enforcement jokes, and he seems to be a good enough sport. Still, I proceed with caution, skating the line between helping Stan and not pissing off Kevin.

"All the victims are women, in their late teens to early twenties," I say.

"What else?" Stan says.

"Attractive, college students, need money, engaged in prostitution."

"Drugs?"

"Yes."

Kevin lets out an exaggerated yawn and stretches his arms. Stan isn't discouraged.

"Is there an element of nonreactive premeditation?"

"Yes. It's not a crime of opportunity. Someone has been introducing him to his victims," I say.

"Do you know who?" he says.

"No."

I'm not ready to reveal what we learned about Tommy Greenough in the grand jury. Stan shrugs. *I can tell you're holding back, but suit yourself.*

"Regardless, there seems to be an obvious cooling-off period between attacks." He sits back, his fingers steepled, "He fits within the parameters of a serial killer. I'd categorize him as hedonistic, motivated by either thrill or lust."

Kevin takes a long look at his watch. "Can you tell us something we don't know?"

"We're looking for someone who is intelligent and probably comes from a high-achieving family, with at least one overbearing parent."

"You just described Abby." Kevin smiles for the first time since he's been here.

"If the Greenoughs are on your radar, you're on the right track," Stan says.

We start to say our good-byes, but are interrupted by a barrage of texts. My phone beeps, Kevin's vibrates, Stan's dings. We all get the same message: our third victim has been identified. *Positive ID of victim FKA Jane Doe. Britney Marshall, 20 yo, student at Northeastern.*

"This sicko is working his way through all the colleges on the East Coast," Kevin says.

"He's held true to his pattern," Stan says.

"Why would someone target students?" I say.

"That's a complicated issue. It's possible that the killer never completed his education. But it's important to note that all the victims are away from home, needed money, and turned to prostitution, which means he could have some kind of inexplicable obsession from which he derives sexual gratification."

"Or it could be simpler; these just happen to be the women who answered his ads," Kevin says.

"Regardless, he's still active," I say. "And he's getting bolder, taunting us. He dumped Britney less than a mile from the courthouse. It's like he wants to prove he's smarter than the rest of us."

"Right now it looks like he *is* smarter than the rest of us," Kevin says.

Chapter Thirty-One

After the meeting, Kevin and I go to the morgue, and on our way back, we get stuck in a massive traffic jam on Mass Ave. Kevin uses the downtime to call his wife and make a movie date. I eavesdrop on their conversation. She wants to eat at the Centre Street Cafe and see a rom com; he'd rather dine at Doyle's and take in an action flick. They settle on pizza and a game of darts at J. J. Foley's.

Sirens blare. Two lanes of cars pull to either side of the street, making enough room in the middle for emergency vehicles. Two ambulances, a fire truck, and three marked police cruisers zoom by.

"It's either a bad crash or a jumper on the bridge," Kevin says.

He turns on the scanner. I check my e-mails.

"A seven-year-old boy, riding his bike, was hit," I say.

"Dead?"

"He's at the Mass General, on life support."

Even though we're knee deep in the serial killer investigation, I can't resist a child fatality. Kevin indulges me in a way that feels intimate and oddly romantic—in a gesture of unspoken understanding, he flips on the blue flashers.

He races us to the Mass General emergency room and parks in the ambulance bay. When I'm halfway through the revolving door, I'm surprised to see my sister-in-law in the lobby of the hospital. She's upset, pacing, blowing her nose, and talking on her cell phone.

"I'll meet you in the emergency room," I say to Kevin.

As soon as I join Missy, before I can ask what's wrong, she says, "She's okay."

I'm confused. "Who?"

"It's my fault. I should never have let her drive, but you know how she can be when she sets her mind on something."

There's only one person she could be referring to. "My mother?"

"She's banged up, but she'll be fine." Missy stops, looks at me. "There was a little boy."

I take this in and start to tremble with rage. "My mother, she's the one who hit the kid on the bike?"

Missy looks out the window. "There's Charlie."

I turn to see my brother, handing cash to a taxi driver. He rushes in, and we all walk toward the emergency room. A receptionist gives us visitor stickers, and we slap them on. Missy and Charlie go to my mother's room, but I move toward Kevin.

"Aren't you coming to see Mom?" Charlie says.

I shake my head. Nothing good will come from spending time with my family right now. I'll be angry and accusatory; they'll be defensive and dismissive. When it comes to my mother, my family members are like big tobacco executives.

I join Kevin, who is on the phone, outside an exam room.

"How is the boy?" I say.

"He's having a CT scan." He points to a woman, about my age, seated in the waiting area. "That's his mother."

"Does anyone know who the driver is?" I say.

"Her name is Hollingsworth."

I look at Kevin carefully. "My mother's maiden name is Hollingsworth."

I don't have to spell it out for him. He nods. Missy probably came up with the idea for my mother to use her maiden name, but she won't be able to fly under the radar for long. As soon as she's arrested and interviewed by probation, her true identity will be revealed.

I look over at the boy's mother; she's crying, wiping her nose with the back of her hand. I grab a cup of water and a box of Kleenex. Kevin takes them from my grasp.

"You stay here."

He walks to the woman and hands her a tissue. A uniform sees me and approaches.

"I heard they caught the driver," he says.

"Did they do field sobrieties?" I say.

I picture my mother, on the side of the road, trying to walk an imaginary straight line, touch her nose, and recite the alphabet backward.

"No, the lady was banged up, so they put her in the ambulance," the officer says.

"What about the Breathalyzer?"

"She blew a .21."

That's more than twice the legal limit, which means she'll be charged with operating under the influence. I watch the doctors talk to Kevin and the child's mother, who is listening intently. She puts her hand to her chest and exhales. I can't tell if it's good news or bad news.

Kevin comes back to me. "The boy is going to be okay."

I tear up, relieved and frustrated. "Let's get out of here," I say.

"I'll pull the car around to Blossom Street," Kevin says. "Just in case there's press."

He leaves to get the car, and I walk through the lobby, toward the back door. As I pass the coffee stand, I hear a familiar voice.

"Abby?"

I look up. "Cassandra? What are you doing here?"

"Max wants me to cover the motor vehicle case that just came in."

Cassandra is assigned to the white-collar crimes division. On rare occasions, a homicide is thrown her way, but this is going to turn out to be a reckless driving case. It should be handled by a less experienced district court ADA. Max must already know my mother was the driver. If his goal is to bury the case, he picked the wrong prosecutor. Cassandra will never keep this under wraps.

She takes a sip from her coffee cup, leaving a thick pink lipstick impression on the white plastic cover.

"I understand you know the perp," she says.

I look around. "Does the media know?" I say.

"Not yet," she says.

Chapter Thirty-Two

It's after nine when I get home. Manny is behind the reception desk, watching the news stream on his tablet. He lowers the volume when he sees me.

"Did you hear about the little kid who got hit by the car over in the South End?"

I nod and move to check my mailbox, which is empty. Ty must be home.

Unaware I'm giving him the brush-off, he persists. "Is that your case?"

I shake my head. "When did Ty get back?"

"A few hours ago. He was carrying a bag from Whole Foods, so I think you're in for a home-cooked meal."

When Ty officially moved in a few months ago, Manny kept his own counsel, but I knew he didn't approve—no one did. Not Kevin, not my family, not my neighbors. They said I was selling myself short, that Ty has an inferior education and an unambitious career path. They couldn't be more wrong. Ty studied at the Berklee College of Music and is accomplished and well respected in his field. There's nothing I can do to change their minds. Fortunately, I don't have to. Ty has been winning them over with his quiet charm and easygoing nature.

When I get upstairs, he's in the kitchen, drinking a Sam

Adams, cooking dinner. He doesn't hear me when I come in; he's in his own world, listening to a Mozart piano concerto, humming softly to himself. I hang up my coat and toss my bag on the table in the foyer.

"Hey, babe." He wipes his hands on a dish towel and gives me a kiss. "You're just in time for a quick dinner, before I head to work."

"What are you making?"

"Scallops with quinoa and kale."

I pour myself a glass of red wine. A dinner of leafy greens and healthy grains is the last thing I'm in the mood for. I'll eat something decadent after he's gone. There's a pint of Ben and Jerry's in the fridge.

"It smells great, but I didn't know you'd be here," I say. "I grabbed something on my way home."

He opens the freezer, takes out a pint of Chunky Monkey, and scoops some into a bowl. I take the ice cream and wine, he plates his food, and we relocate to the dining table.

"My mother hit a kid with her car today," I say.

"Seriously? That kid on the news?"

"Yes and yes." I take a few sips of wine.

"They're saying he's going to be okay."

"He'll live," I say, "but I don't know if he'll be okay. Experiencing something that violent, at such a young age, is going to screw him up. It'll change who he is."

Ty takes a few bites of his nutrient-rich food. I alternate between sips of wine and spoonfuls of ice cream.

"It was an accident," he says.

"She was drunk."

I want him to share my outrage, my lack of compassion, my coldheartedness. For better or worse, Ty isn't the unforgiving sort.

"Face it, we've all got behind the wheel after we've had one too many," he says.

"Not me."

"Well, the rest of us make an occasional mistake." He gets up and clears the plates.

"Since when are you the champion of my mother?" I follow him into the kitchen.

"She's in trouble. You can't just show up for the good stuff," he says.

"What good stuff?"

He looks around the apartment to prove his point. "I love you, babe, but you can't abandon people because they disappoint you."

I'm pretty sure we're talking about more than my mother.

He goes in the bathroom and turns on the shower. Cassandra has probably already leaked the story to her friend at the *Herald*. I think about calling Carl to launch an offensive strike. There's time to get in front of this, but I'm not sure what the message should be. *My mother has a problem. She's going to get help.* Or: *She's like many other people, struggling with addiction.* Or: *It was an accident. Let's withhold judgment until there's been a full investigation.* Or: *Of course my sympathies are with the child and his family.*

Carl picks up on the first ring. "Sorry about your mother," he says.

"It's already out there?"

"I got a tip."

"Was her name Cassandra?"

"For what it's worth, no, it wasn't anyone from your office."

It's plausible Cassandra didn't leak the information. It could have been the court clerk whose brother I charged with armed robbery a few years ago. Or the desk sergeant whom I prosecuted for domestic violence. But my money is on Cassandra.

"Credible sources tell me she failed the Breathalyzer," Carl says.

"Do me a solid, don't humiliate her because of me," I say. "If I wasn't her daughter, this wouldn't get any attention."

"Senator Greenough could argue the same thing."

"That's on you and your colleagues—I'm not the one plaster-ing their mugs on the news every day. Besides, there's no com-parison." I hang up.

As soon as I hang up, Ty comes out of the bedroom, freshly showered, holding the box from Saks and the card with his name on it.

"What's this?" he says.

I forgot about his birthday gift. This is not how I wanted to give it to him, but nothing is going as planned this week.

"Open it," I say. "It's for you. Happy belated birthday."

He sits down, unties the ribbon, and opens the box. When he sees the Saks logo adhered to the tissue paper, he says, "It's way too expensive."

"You don't even know what it is."

"I know where it's from."

He unfolds the tissue paper, taking care not to tear it, and re-moves the coat. Suddenly, the protests stop.

"Try it on," I say.

He slips the jacket on over his T-shirt, stretches out his arms, and admires the material. He looks hot, so hot that I've already forgiven him.

"I love it, and I love you." He gives me a kiss, takes off the jacket, and puts it back in the box. "We can't afford it."

"It wasn't expensive. I got it on sale for a couple of hundred bucks."

Ty doesn't know a lot about fashion—he's happy wearing jeans and cowboy boots—but he loves a good leather jacket, and he knows that this one cost a lot more than $200, even on sale.

He puts the top back on the box and gives me another kiss. "You've got to get a grip on your finances."

"I will."

"When? Your credit cards are maxed out. The bills are piling up. As much as I'd like to, I can't afford to pay for all this."

"I didn't ask you to."

He looks me in the eye. "Babe, who do you think has been paying the bills? I'm up to my eyeballs in debt."

I stand and look out the window. "I'll pay you back."

He crosses the room, faces me, and put his hands on my shoulders. "You're the smartest woman I know. You can prosecute complicated financial fraud cases and unravel Ponzi schemes better than a CPA. But when it comes to your own money, you can't do simple math. I know it's not about intelligence, that it has to do with emotion, but you've got to figure it out."

"You're going to be late for work," I say.

He gives me a kiss and grabs his sax. After he leaves, I sit down and do some rough calculations. After taxes and deductions, I net about $50,000 a year. I don't have a mortgage, but expenses for my apartment—condo fees, taxes, insurance, utilities, TV and wireless, and maintenance—come to about $90,000. Then there's food, clothing, and other essentials. There's no room for Givenchy bags and Rick Owens leather jackets in the budget.

I'm already in the hole, and it's getting worse every day. I can't drag Ty down with me. I have to come up with a plan. Otherwise, I'm going to have to file for bankruptcy, which isn't the best route for anyone, especially someone who wants to be the next district attorney.

Chapter Thirty-Three

I go to bed early but am awake most of the night, worrying about a host of things. At the top of the list is Valerie, followed by Caitlyn's and Rose's families, then my mother, the boy she hit, my finances, and, finally, my political career. Ty gets home at around three. He climbs into his side of the bed, keeping his back to me, and we don't speak. He doesn't stir when I slip out of bed in the morning.

In the living room, I settle in behind my computer and troll the Internet, searching both legit news sources as well as gossip sites. There is a string of reports about the accident, all focused on the boy, whose condition has improved. There is no mention of the driver. I suspect this is the handiwork of a skilled publicist: highlight the good, and people will forget about the bad. It will be harder to keep the arrest under wraps, however, once she's been arraigned.

I decide to drop by and see the arraignment; otherwise, it will look like I'm hiding. When I arrive at the Edward Brooke Courthouse, just after nine, I'm surprised there are no press vans parked on the street, no reporters milling around on the front steps. It looks like a typical day in municipal court—a rogues' gallery of low-level drug dealers, pickpockets, trespassers, and prostitutes.

Inside the arraignment session, I scan the room, looking for my father, but he's not here. My brother isn't here either. Court officers nod and smile at me, giving no indication that they're aware of the reason for my visit.

Court has convened, and Judge Margo Meagher is on the bench, advising a flasher of his right to an attorney and telling him she's going to release him on his own recognizance.

She issues a stern warning. "Keep it in your pants until the next court date."

He promises to behave, but he's not very convincing; when he walks out of the dock, his fly is unzipped. I set my coat on a bench, next to a law student, and ask her to keep an eye on it. I approach the prosecutor's table, grab the call sheet, and flip through the pages, searching for my mother's name.

"Ms. Endicott," Judge Meagher says, "to what do we owe the pleasure?"

She doesn't care why I'm here; she knows about my mother, and she's trying to embarrass me. A few years ago, I appealed her ruling on a gun case.

"Do we have a murder on the docket?" she says.

"No, I'm just visiting."

Maybe she's not taunting me. My father could have pulled strings, arranged to have my mother's case called right before the lunch break, when the courtroom is the least populated. I return to the bench, search around for my coat, but it's gone.

"What are you looking for?" a court officer says.

"I can't find my coat. Did you see where that law student went?"

"Law student?"

"She had brown hair and glasses. She was watching my coat."

"That lady was no law student. She was in here for grand larceny, third offense."

I'm really off my game. That was a rookie mistake. Regardless, it's not worth making a fuss. I have to get out of here without being noticed. I sneak into the hallway to find Carl, cameraman in tow.

"Did I miss the arraignment?" he says.

"She's not on the list," I say.

"Why not?"

I shrug. "Maybe she's still in the hospital."

"She was released last night."

"Then you know more than I do."

He follows me outside, puts his nose up in the air, and sniffs. "I smell a bag job," he says.

I walk up New Chardon Street, coatless. It's cold, and a brisk gust of wind makes me shiver. This fiasco is getting worse by the minute. As I round the corner onto Cambridge Street, I call Kevin.

"Do you know why my mother isn't in court?" I say.

"Her lawyer challenged the Breathalyzer."

Faulty breath tests have been an ongoing problem, causing hundreds of cases to be dismissed. This could be one of those cases, or it could have been made to look like it was one of those cases.

"The machine was broke," Kevin says. "It's her lucky day."

"She's not being charged at all?" I say.

"She's going to pay civil penalties for negligent operation, but I don't think she'll wind up with criminal charges."

I'm not sure which looks worse. If my mother is charged, she'll be held accountable for what she did, but it will further damage my candidacy for DA. If she escapes charges, it will look like the fix was in.

I cross the street, move away from the office, and cut across the back of the hill, stopping at my parents' front door. Serena lets me in. She's in a freshly ironed uniform, but she looks tired, like she's been up all night. My mother has impacted Serena as much as the rest of us.

"Where's your coat?" she says.

"In the car."

She shakes her head, opens the closet, and grabs one of my mother's coats. I accept the garment; it's hard to resist cashmere.

"Is my mother upstairs?"

"She went to Martha's Vineyard a couple of hours ago."

"She should have gone to treatment."

Serena isn't going to fight me, but she's also not going to voice her agreement. My mother isn't afraid to fire a disloyal employee, even after decades of service.

"You're too thin. Claude can make you breakfast," Serena says.

"I don't have time."

She grabs a freshly baked corn muffin, wraps it in a napkin, and puts it in my tote. I head to the office, and on the way, my cell phone vibrates. The caller ID shows it's Chip Aldridge. Maybe he heard my mother was back in the hospital. He may have even operated on the boy she hit. Or it could be some other excuse, designed to keep the connection going. I let the call go to voice mail. His persistence is strong, and my resistance is weak. I'm about one phone call and a couple of glasses of Burgundy away from doing something I'll regret.

I stop by Starbucks for my third coffee of the day. Waiting in line, I check my e-mails. There's no message from the governor's office. I wonder if they know about my mother. If they don't, they will soon, and it will likely be the final straw. My candidacy is already hanging by a thread. I haven't heard from them in over a week, which is a bad sign. In politics, the only thing worse than being under the microscope is being ignored.

Chapter Thirty-Four

Fortunately, Valerie's disappearance has garnered more publicity than my mother's car accident. There have been stories in the papers, online, and on TV. Twitter has a couple of hashtags devoted to Valerie: #findvaleriejackson, #whereisvalerie, and #haveyouseenher. Facebook pages and websites have been established to announce local search efforts. Dozens of people have reported sightings; most turned out to be doppelgängers. The rest of the leads are hardly worth pursuing.

I'm in my office, prepping for my meeting with Valerie's father, when a knock on the door both startles and annoys me. I remain silent, hoping the intruder will assume I'm on the phone, or in a meeting, and retreat. No such luck; the banging becomes louder and more insistent.

"Go away."

"I know you're in there." Max opens the door and takes a seat. He sits back and plunks his feet on my desk, exposing a hole in the sole of his shoe. "What's the progress report?"

I'm tempted to tell him to get out of my office, that I'll fill him in when I'm ready. He's been a lousy friend lately. He shouldn't have assigned Cassandra to my mother's case, and he should have supported my candidacy to replace him. Still, he's the boss, and has a certain amount of control over my fate.

"We've looked into the victims' computers and texts. All four of them have been working as call girls," I say.

"Can forensics connect them to each other?"

"The texts are all to different numbers, all to disposable phones. The e-mails are from untraceable accounts."

He gets up to leave. "You want to sit in the corner office, solve the case."

I can't help asking, "Have you heard anything about the appointment? Do I still have a shot?"

"You've got a lot of supporters in the statehouse. The ultimate decision is up to the governor."

Max's assistant comes to the door to tell him he's late for a meeting. When he's gone, I change into sensible shoes and get in the car to drive out to Franklin Park, the location of today's search for Valerie. Volunteers have been out all week with stacks of *Have You Seen This Woman?* flyers, passing them out in shopping malls, sliding them under windshield wipers, and stapling them to trees. Yesterday, a dive team used side-scan sonar to search Jamaica Pond.

When I arrive at the search site, a couple of dozen volunteers are standing in an open field, side by side, a few feet apart from each other. They move in unison, keeping their eyes on the ground, scouring every inch of grass. In the more wooded sections, law enforcement personnel work in pairs; Boston police officers, state troopers, and FBI agents, all distinguishable by the logos on the back of their windbreakers. A K-9 officer follows his rottweiler, who is sniffing and snorting his way into the brush.

Walter Jackson is easily distinguishable. He's unshaven, wearing work boots and gardening gloves, using a metal poker to move around leaves and branches. He looks exhausted but determined. I step through brush and introduce myself. He kicks at a bump in the earth, sighs when he sees it's a rock. He looks up at me, takes off a glove, and shakes my hand. There's dirt and sweat on his forehead. I give him a bottle of water.

"You should take a break," I say.

On my way over, I picked up a Bistro Box at Starbucks. I figured feeding himself is the furthest thing from his mind. When I offer it to him, he shakes his head. He's not interested in eating or small talk.

"Did you check her bank accounts?" he says.

"There hasn't been any activity."

He hesitates and looks down, afraid to ask the next question. "They say the other girls were prostitutes, and Valerie was, too."

I soften my voice and speak slowly. "We have evidence that Valerie was involved in similar activity, but that doesn't change anything as far as we're concerned."

"She was a good girl, never gave me any trouble." He mops his forehead with a dirty napkin and takes a few gulps of water.

"Valerie sounds like she's a lovely young woman. And you have every reason to be proud of her."

A Tufts van, emblazoned with an elephant, the school mascot, pulls up. A half-dozen college students get out and look around. They walk over to the volunteer check-in: a folding table, with sign-in sheets, area maps, and whistles. The search coordinator directs them to an area of brush, and they get to work.

"Do you think we'll find her?" Walter says.

"I do, but it may take time."

"I read that sometimes college kids get stressed out and run away, then they show up a few weeks later," he says.

"That's true."

"And I heard about a kid who got kidnapped, and six years later, she escaped."

"It happens."

He looks at the ground and moves some debris around with his foot.

"Tell me, do you think she's alive?"

A search dog barks. A couple of uniforms talk on their

two-way radios. A local church group holds hands and prays. A pile of leaves scatters in the breeze.

I look Walter Jackson in the eye and tell him a lie. "Yes, I think Valerie could still be alive."

Chapter Thirty-Five

When I get home from work, exhausted and hungry, Ty is in the kitchen, cooking. We haven't fully recovered from our argument about finances and my mother. We exchange polite hellos and halfhearted kisses, and I retreat into the living room to watch the news. Media interest in Valerie's disappearance is already waning. Yesterday, someone leaked word that the women were working as prostitutes, and reporters are losing interest. It's football season, and stories about the abduction and murder of four young women have been bumped by recycled accounts of the Patriots' Deflategate scandal.

I turn off the set and join Ty in the kitchen, where he's chopping vegetables. He juliennes a yellow pepper and throws together a chicken stir-fry. The concoction sizzles in the wok, releasing the aroma of fresh ginger, combined with just the right amount of garlic. Not to be outdone, I show off my culinary talents by tossing a bag of brown rice in the microwave and opening a bottle of Malbec.

Ty plates the dishes while I clear my papers off the dining table.

"Anything going on with your investigation?" he says.

He rarely asks about my cases, which works out well since I can't reveal specifics, and even if I could, I don't like to burden him with the tragedy of it all. I'm at a standstill, however, and he's a good sounding board. Sometimes I test-drive arguments and theories on him before presenting them to my juries.

"Have you ever done online dating?" I say.

He takes a few bites of food and puts down his chopsticks.

"If you don't want to talk about work, just say so."

"I am talking about work. These women all posted ads and had their own websites."

I could have phrased the question differently, without making it sound personal, but this way it's a twofer. I can probe, without admitting I'm probing, and further my investigation, all at the same time.

"I've never done the online thing," Ty says.

I didn't think so. Handsome, sexy musicians don't tend to have problems meeting women; their challenge is fending them off. The few times I've shown up unannounced at Ty's performances, there has been at least one smitten fan, seeking his attention and affection.

"What about you? Have you ever met someone online?" he says.

I push aside the broccoli and take a bite of chicken.

"No," I say, which is technically true.

I've never actually gone out with anyone from the Internet. Once, however, after a month of too few dates, and a night of too much wine, a colleague and I posted our pictures on Tinder. We right-swiped and left-swiped and found some attractive candidates, but as soon as I sobered up, I deleted my account. I was petrified that a juror, defense attorney, or, worst of all, a defendant would see me on the site. For the next month, every time I came face-to-face with a felon, I'd wonder if his smirk or stare meant that he had seen my picture.

"Are you thinking about answering personal ads to try and find the guy?" he says.

"Why not? We do it to catch child predators," I say.

"Maybe you should go undercover, or whatever you call it, and post your own ad. You know—build it and they will come."

"I like the way you think."

There's a fine line between setting a trap and entrapment, but I think I can make a solid argument for the former. We finish dinner and clear the table. While Ty does the dishes, I open my office-issued laptop. If I use my personal computer, I'll never be able to disable the spam that will come from this kind of a search. The office account has a stronger filter.

I scroll through some of the sites that my victims posted on. Ty sits down next to me, hands me a plate of homemade apple crumble, and checks out the screen.

"I can't believe women are still hooking up with strangers," he says. "Everyone's got to know that there's a serial killer out there. What the hell are they thinking?"

"They're desperate, drug addicted, delusional, or all of the above."

In my tote, I find my file with the victims' ads and compare them with one another, searching for common threads, words or phrases that attracted the killer. If the FBI profiler had shown any insight or originality, I'd call for a consult. Instead, I stick with Ty.

"Here's what I'm thinking for a description," I say. "Five five, slender, blue eyes, blond hair."

"Babe, you're describing yourself. This is supposed to be a fake profile."

I devour the dessert, dropping clusters of brown sugar all over the keyboard.

"Hold on," I say. "I'm not done. Nineteen-year-old, Boston-area college sophomore, discreet and sophisticated, seeks arrangement."

"Sounds like a plan," Ty says.

I cast a wide net, covering all the sites that our victims used and throwing a couple of new ones to the mix. After I hit the send button, I take our dishes into the kitchen. A minute later, my phone sounds. It's the office IT specialist.

"Abby, did someone steal your laptop?" he says.

My Internet activity must have set off an alarm bell. He thinks I've been using my office computer to troll the Internet for dates. I decide to have a little fun with him.

"No, I have my computer with me. Why, what's up?"

"Um . . . I . . . don't mean to get personal."

"Is there a problem?"

"I get notified whenever someone uses an official government-issued computer for inappropriate personal use."

"Can you be more specific?"

"There's been some activity on your account," he says.

His breathing is shallow. I don't want to give him a coronary.

"Relax, I'm working on a case," I say.

"It's after hours, and what you do on your own time is none of my business, but you should know that your laptop is subject to public information requests."

Clearly he's heard this excuse a few times before, and he doesn't believe me.

"I really am working an investigation."

"Sure, okay."

He's still not convinced. I hang up, get back online, toss out the bait to a few more sites.

"Now what?" Ty says.

"We wait and see if I get any nibbles."

Chapter Thirty-Six

I'm out of bed at five, eager to discover if anyone responded to the ads. I brew coffee, open my laptop, and log on. My inbox is empty. Now I know what it feels like to be my old high school classmate Minnie Dorset when she had to take her second cousin to the winter ball.

When I get out of the shower, I notice a couple of missed calls from Kevin on my cell phone. As I'm about to hit redial, another call from Kevin comes in. I pick up on the first ring.

"This can't be good," I say.

"Are you sitting down?" he says.

I take a sip of coffee and prepare myself for the sting of bad news.

"Do we have a new victim?"

"It's not about our case. Why do you have to go to a dark place right off the bat?"

I stand and look out the window. The sun isn't up yet. There's a shadowy figure, a jogger, out on the footpath by the river. I can't tell if it's a male or a female, but I hope the person is safe, out at this hour.

"You're not calling me at five thirty in the morning to deliver good news."

"Remember the guy Cassandra prosecuted last year for extortion and identity theft?"

"The Houdini Hacker?"

"She must've pissed him off big-time, because he broke into the DA's computer system. He's threatening to release everything."

My mind races. Since Tim's murder and the threat of exposure about our relationship, I've been careful about electronic communications, but there are things from my past that I don't want to see on the Internet. There are deleted e-mails between me and Tim. And flirty exchanges between me and Ty from after we first met at a murder scene, before he testified in the grand jury, and while we waited for the jury to return their guilty verdict.

"Don't worry. So far it looks like the only account that's been compromised is Cassandra's." Kevin reads my silence. "Do I hear a smile?" he says.

"I'd never take joy in Cassandra's misfortune."

"Uh-huh. The guy sent a ransom note. He's asking for a hundred grand."

Cassandra must be in a panic. She's got to have something unsavory on her computer. At the very least, she's got snarky comments about difficult witnesses or parodies of incompetent judges—we all do. I can't imagine Max will ever kick in that kind of money to cover for her; she's a mediocre lawyer, easily replaceable.

I hang up with Kevin, grab my things, and Uber to the office. I was going to walk, but I want to get in to see Max first thing. Plus, a potential scandal involving my best frenemy is enough to get my heart pumping. I'm going to count that as my cardio for the day.

It's a little after seven when I arrive at Bulfinch, and Max isn't in his office yet. Upstairs, I pass Cassandra's door; it's closed, but the light is on. I remind myself not to gloat and devise a mantra for the day; I repeat it to myself, over and over. *I'm not the kind of person who takes pleasure in someone else's pain. I'm not the kind of person who takes pleasure in someone else's pain.*

I knock and listen for Cassandra's voice to tell me to come in, but the door swings open. Cassandra looks pale. Max, standing next to her, looks paler. She looks at him, he nods, and she steps aside so I can enter. As soon as I cross the threshold, she closes the door.

"You heard?" she says.

"Yes."

"I can't believe it's already out there," Max says.

Max loosens his tie. His face is splotchy and his forehead is damp with sweat. I haven't seen him this rattled since Tim was killed. Max cares about his employees, but there seems to be something bigger on his mind. Maybe the hacker got into his files as well.

"Who told you?" Cassandra says.

"Don't worry, it was a cop," I say. "He's discreet."

Max looks out the window and mumbles under his breath. "A discreet cop—that'd be a first."

He turns around and looks at Cassandra; they lock eyes for a few seconds. She touches his elbow. There's something going on between them, something intimate. Suddenly, it all adds up: the preferential treatment, the unexplained case assignments, the unearned support.

"You two are . . ." I can't even say it.

Cassandra finishes for me. "Screwing?"

"Jesus, Cassie," Max says.

"Get used to it. Soon the whole world is going to know," she says.

I'm as suspicious and cynical as they come, but I never imagined that Max and Cassandra were having an affair. He's got vices, including a long struggle with alcohol, but infidelity never seemed to be on the menu. Max and Cindy have been married for almost twenty years; they have a teenage son together. It feels like he's cheating on more than them; it feels like he's cheating on me.

"This couldn't have come at a worse time, in the middle of a mayor's race," he says. "Those e-mails are going to sink me."

I feel like telling him he's on his own, he got himself into this mess, but I'm not going to kick him when he's down.

"No one cares about sex scandals anymore," I say.

"My wife does." He chokes up. "She'll leave me. I can't do this without her."

"Thanks." Cassandra turns her back on him.

He walks to her, holds on to her shoulders, but she shrugs him off.

"Come on, Cassie, you knew I was never going to leave her. I told you from the start."

I don't need to be in the middle of this lovers' quarrel. I walk toward the door.

"Hold on, Abby," Max says.

I put my hand on the doorknob, ready to flee. Max puts his hand on the door to keep it closed.

"The guy is shaking me down, looking for a hundred grand."

"I know where this is going," I say. "Forget it."

Max looks at Cassandra and nods, signaling her to leave. She opens the door and turns to me.

"I wouldn't be too quick to say no," she says. "You owe us for keeping your mother's arrest under wraps."

Before I can respond, she's gone. Max tries to do damage control.

"She would never call the press. We're all friends. Please, I need your help."

"You're actually thinking about giving in to extortion? And you want me to help?" I say.

"It happens all the time. Big companies pay off hackers, so

do governments. Last year the Tewksbury and Swansea police departments paid ransoms. Abby, I'm desperate."

He takes my elbow, looks me in the eyes, and starts to cry. Like the skilled litigator that he is, Max has managed to put me on the defensive. He's the one who's done wrong, yet he's making me feel like the bad guy.

"I don't have the money," I say.

"You father could write the check without blinking an eye."

"Why should I help you?"

"We've got a long history."

This is exactly what I said to him when I wanted his support.

"We've been through a lot together," he says.

I remember the suffering Max and I endured after Tim and Owen were killed. We've both had a hard time trying to get to the other side of the trauma, and we leaned on each other for support. I have to believe that a year ago, Max never would have behaved like this. It doesn't excuse what he's done, but I do have empathy. I almost strayed myself.

"I'll talk to my father," I say, "but I want something in exchange."

I'm a friend, not a fool.

"Name it."

"Call the governor and tell him you support me. He's looking to you for a recommendation."

He drops his head.

"You've already endorsed Cassandra, haven't you?" I say.

"I'm sorry."

"Tell him you changed your mind, you discovered something in her past that could be an embarrassment to him. Tell him you're throwing your support to me."

He doesn't even pause to think about it.

"Done," he says.

There's no honor among thieves, and there's no loyalty among lawyers, even when they're sleeping together.

Chapter Thirty-Seven

When my father and I make plans to meet for lunch, there's no need to specify a time or place. It's always the same: one o'clock at the Downtown Harvard Club. There was a brief period when he stopped dining here, in protest to the new policy that granted Yale, MIT, and Fletcher School alumni membership privileges, but after a couple of months at the University Club, he relented.

It's a short walk from my office in Government Center to the Financial District. In less than a block, the landscape shifts from drab concrete bunkers to sleek steel skyscrapers. Not many of my law school classmates practice law in Boston, but those who do work in this part of town.

Inside One Federal Street, I find the bank of elevators designated for the upper portion of the building. When I get off on the thirty-eighth floor, I see my father at the bar, reading *The Wall Street Journal*. Our short walk across the main dining room takes about ten minutes; he stops at every other table to shake hands and exchange pleasantries. Finally, we take our seats at his usual window table.

The waiter is ready for our arrival, with two Arnold Palmers on his tray.

"Haddock for you, Mr. Endicott?" the waiter says.

My father, a creature of habit, smiles and nods.

"Ms. Endicott, what can I get for you?"

"Lobster salad, please."

Since I can't afford to pay for lobster these days, I order it whenever someone else is footing the bill.

After the waiter is gone, my father leans in and speaks quietly. "What's on your mind, muffin?"

"Max is in a bind."

"How much does he need?"

No surprise that my father, famous for his negotiating tactics, cuts to the chase.

"One hundred thousand."

He doesn't flinch.

"Should I ask what it's for?"

I explain the problem.

"It's best to pay the extortionist off," he says.

"I'm not sure if Max plans to pay you back," I say.

"I'd rather he doesn't. Let's consider it an investment in good government."

My father doesn't care about government; he cares about access. And $100,000 will get him a lot of access. The waiter serves our lunch, which, like all club food, is acceptable but bland. As we finish our meal, a couple of fledgling venture capitalists stop by the table and fawn over my father. I smile and nod until they leave. Then I turn the discussion to family matters. My father hasn't brought it up, but I know he'll be disappointed if I don't ask.

"How's Mom?" I say.

"She's coming home from the Vineyard tonight. You should come by the house."

"I'll visit her when she's an inpatient at McLean's."

He snaps, a rare occurrence, especially in public. "I am acutely aware of your mother's situation. I don't need instruction from you."

My father signals for the check. As we wait, each of us want to smooth things over but are unsure how. My father looks up and smiles at someone who is standing behind me. I turn to see Chip Aldridge. My heart beats a little faster. He looks handsome in a blazer; his tie matches the exact color of his sapphire-blue eyes.

"I don't mean to interrupt," Chip says. "I saw you over here and wanted to stop by and say hello."

"Don't be ridiculous. Pull up a chair," my father says.

My father is a terrible actor. This is a setup. My father's attempt to force me into a new job has failed; now he's trying to find me a new boyfriend. He claims he likes Ty, but really he's just tolerating him until someone else comes along. My mother probably has a role in this, too; she's always nagging him to fix me up with a suitable suitor. Finding me a husband and a good winter coat are her ways of showing she cares.

When my father stands and shakes Chip's hand, I remain seated, avoiding the awkward, should-we-hug-or-shake-hands dilemma. Once Chip is settled, I put my napkin on the table and reach for my tote. I'm tempted to stay and flirt a little, but I refuse to be manipulated.

"I've got to get back to the office," I say. "It's nice to see you, Chip."

"Muffin, stay for coffee," my father says.

"Can't the criminals wait a few minutes?" Chip says.

I don't want to seem ungrateful—my father has generously agreed to supply a sizable amount of cash to help my boss and, by association, my career. That doesn't, however, give him license to interfere with all aspects of my life.

"Please, don't get up," I say.

Ignoring me, they both stand.

"Great seeing you," Chip says.

He puts his hand on my arm and squeezes. I feel the electricity that seems to live in his magical, healing hands. He smiles and kisses my cheek. Everything about him exudes confidence, including his kiss. I see why patients trust him.

When I get outside, I start to compose a text to Max, to let him know that my father is on board, but decide to call him instead. It's better not to leave a trail of evidence; that will only land us deeper in the quicksand. Max picks up on the first ring.

"How'd it go?"

"Mission accomplished."

I hear Cassandra in the background. *"What? What did she say?"*

Max talks to her. "It's all set."

I want to get off this call.

"From here on out, it's between you and my father," I say.

Max excuses himself from Cassandra. I hear a door slam. He turns on a faucet, presumably so the water will drown out his voice.

"Jesus, Max, are you in a hotel? It's like you're begging to get caught."

"We're not in a hotel."

He must be in Cassandra's apartment. I've never been there, but I know she lives outside the city, in Watertown. I picture Max, standing in her bathroom, among the cheap perfume bottles, coral lipsticks, and sticky hair products.

"I'll see you back in the office," I say.

"Thanks, Abby. I'm going to call the governor and remind him about your competence and loyalty. He'd be lucky to have you serve as the interim district attorney."

Max and Cassandra deserve each other. I've been involved in politics enough to know it isn't for the faint of heart, but hiding in your girlfriend's bathroom and conspiring with her enemy are elevating things to a whole new level.

As I ascend the steep steps behind city hall, a man on his way down the stairs brushes up against me. He rushes away, without looking back. It's too late to get a look at his face, but I make a mental note of his height and weight, his oily reddish hair and dirty windbreaker.

I dig into my tote to see if he's taken anything. I find my wallet and badge, but I notice something else, an object that I haven't seen before. It's a black case made out of plastic, small enough to fit in the palm of my hand. It looks like a car remote. I struggle to pry off the cover; inside there are some wires and knobs. I try not to panic, put the contraption down in some bushes, carefully, away from the foot traffic. Then I rush toward the street, take out my phone, and call 911.

"What's your emergency?"

"This is Abigail Endicott, Suffolk County DA's Office. I need the bomb squad."

When I get off the phone, I see a security guard behind city hall, wave him over, and fill him in. We try to evacuate the area, warning people to move away. I text Kevin, who is nearby, at the courthouse. A uniform arrives quickly, followed by other detectives, technicians, firefighters, and Kevin.

Within minutes, Congress Street is shut down and traffic is diverted. City hall is emptied of government workers, politicians, and visitors. The tourists, vendors, and restaurant workers at Faneuil Hall are pushed back, in the direction of the harbor. News crews arrive and set up nearby.

When the bomb squad arrives, they use a robot to retrieve the device and drop it in a secure tank. It's x-rayed and inspected. I wait across the street until an officer, clad in a white spaceman suit, takes off his headpiece and waves to his sergeant. Some police brass join them, and they inspect the monitor and confer. Kevin is among the group. A couple of minutes later, a sergeant emerges, thumbs up.

"False alarm," he says.

Kevin moves toward me.

"What was it?" I say.

"A tracking device," he says.

I'm humiliated for overreacting, calling in the bomb squad over a misplaced GPS. Kevin leads me to his car.

"You did the right thing," he says. "It was a lose-lose situation. If you didn't call it in and something happened, it would have been worse."

"I'm an idiot," I say.

Kevin touches my arm. "It could have been an explosive. Last year, underreacting almost got you killed."

"I shut down Government Center."

He smiles. "Those hacks loved the distraction. If they knew how to write, they'd send you thank-you notes for getting them out of another boring city council meeting."

When the embarrassment subsides, a swell of panic hits.

"This means someone has been following me."

Kevin doesn't disagree. He drives to headquarters and, when we get out of the car, I remember that my old Prada tote is in his trunk. I pull it out, dig under the gloves and wrappers, and don't feel anything. I tip it upside down and empty the contents. Mixed among the loose change and dry cleaning tickets is another GPS.

"He must've been watching me for a while and lost track of me when I changed bags."

Kevin takes the device.

"Banging into you like that, out in the open, he turned it up a notch."

"Maybe he knows I posted the ads on the Internet."

I meet with detectives and give a detailed description of the back of the man's head; a positive identification is impossible. Kevin and I assemble a list of possible suspects: a Greenough; an Alpha Beta fraternity brother; a member of the senator's staff; or someone who attended the sex parties, like a federal agent. Whoever it is, he knows we're getting closer, he's angry, and he's coming after me.

Banter is not my forte. I can plea-bargain a murder case in my sleep, but negotiating a date is another matter.

Kevin has a better read on the clientele. "I don't think they need to get warmed up with verbal foreplay. We just need to give a time and place and seal the deal," he says.

"Then let's keep it short and sweet," I say.

We decide on a simple response, one that leaves no room for misinterpretation. *Would luv 2 meet. Where and when?* I hit the send buttons on all five, and we call it a night.

It's been a long day; the GPS discovery was scary, and the e-mail exchange was creepy. I don't want to go home to an empty apartment. I think about stopping by to visit my brother and Missy, when I remember Ty isn't scheduled to perform tonight.

"Drop me off at home?" I say.

Kevin drives to my front door and waits for me to get inside. Upstairs, I'm happy to find Ty in the living room watching a rerun of *Law & Order.* I kick off my shoes and snuggle in next to him on the couch. He doesn't seem to know about the bomb incident, and I don't bring it up. There's no point reliving it; it'd just make us both feel bad.

When I move to kiss him, he doesn't lean in to accept.

"Is something wrong?" I say. "You seem preoccupied."

"Babe, I have to tell you something." He lets out a yoga sigh. "I got a call today."

I immediately think something happened to my mother, and feel flashes of anger and concern.

"Is everyone okay?"

"Everyone is fine." He gathers his thoughts. "It was from the governor's office. They're doing your background check."

I stand up, excited, and start to pace.

"If I made it to this stage, that means they're serious about my candidacy."

Max must've made good on his promise to screw over his girlfriend. I hope my father's $100,000 check is as untrace-

Chapter Thirty-Eight

Kevin and I go upstairs, to his office, where I hide in his cubicle and check my e-mails. The box is flooded with responses to the Internet postings. This morning I was worried no one would answer the ad, but now I'm overwhelmed by too many responses. It's disheartening to learn that my fake Backpage profile attracted more men than my real one on Tinder.

I scroll through the messages.

"It'll take weeks to meet up with all these freaks," I say.

Kevin looks over my shoulder. "Let's do a compare and contrast."

We catalog the e-mails and create an Excel spreadsheet. All the men are looking for pretty much the same thing: sex with a sexy coed. There's a similar theme to most of the screen names, with monikers like BigDaddy101 and GenerousToAFault. Some of the men ask directly about services and prices; we classify these as amateurs and set them aside. Several e-mails have similar grammatical errors, misspellings, and emoticons; we bunch them together as one, since they're likely coming from the same person. When we're done, we select five men, those who most closely match our victims' profile responses, and use them as our starting point.

"What should we write?" I say.

able as my serial killer's e-mail account. Otherwise, I'll have to explain to the nominating committee what the money was for and why it's not illegal. If anyone finds out about it, I hope it's after I'm elected and sworn into office.

I look over at Ty. "This is good news. Why do you look worried?"

"The dude is digging deep." He gets up and puts his arms around me. "They know about my conviction."

"It came up in my interview. It's okay."

"It wasn't the only time I sold drugs," he says. "It was just the only time I got caught."

"I figured."

"They're gonna find out. They're turning over rocks. Someone has it out for you."

Outside, the sky is blanketed with puffy clouds. A sliver of moon is trying to shine through. I don't have a right to be angry. Ty has never made a secret of his past. I knew what I was getting into when we started dating. I didn't know, however, that I would have political aspirations, and that his past would impact my future.

He steps back, away from me.

"I know how much you want this," he says.

I try to imagine how someone with a healthy perspective on life might react, someone whose entire existence doesn't revolve around work. After a decade of investing all of my passion and energy into my career, I realize how stunted I am in other areas. I do my best imitation of a normal, healthy, thirty-five-year-old woman.

"It's only a job," I say.

"We both know that's not true. Your murderers are like my music."

"Whatever happens, I'll survive."

Looking at Ty, I almost believe what I'm saying.

"I think we should cool it for a while," he says.

My stomach drops. "What's that supposed to mean?"

"If you don't get this appointment, you'll start to resent me." He hesitates. "I can live someplace else until we sort things out."

For a second, I think about agreeing. It would solve a lot of problems. For one, our relationship is getting stronger, which makes me want to sabotage it. Sometimes the pressure and burden of intimacy are too much. If Ty moves out, the balance that he brings to my life will go with him, and I'll lose perspective. At some point, I'll probably cheat on him, or I'll do something else to destroy what we have. If we get it over with and break up now, I'll be able to focus on things at work and the election. There's only one problem: I love Ty.

Chapter Thirty-Nine

The next morning, I go directly to my computer, anxious to discover if any of the creeps took the bait and accepted our date proposals. My inbox has messages from four out of the five men. I open the responses, reading each one carefully, trying to temper my excitement. Our perp could be one of these men, or not.

Each prospective suitor suggests a different hotel: the Cambridge Marriott, the Sheraton on Route 128, the Lenox, and the Taj. The decision is easy. If I have to spend an evening sitting around a hotel room, waiting for a serial killer to strike, I prefer to do it at the Taj.

I call Kevin, fill him in.

"The Taj?" he says. "Leave it to you to set up a sting in one of the priciest joints in Boston."

"You'd rather drive out to Dedham?"

"Fine, but we're going to have to go dutch on this one," he says. "Your office pays half, the department pays half."

"If we nail the guy, Max will cover the whole thing."

The prospect of catching the killer has me so jazzed up that, after one cup of coffee, I can't sit still. I shower and dress; since I'll be spending the day at a five-star hotel, I allow myself to wear a more extravagant outfit than usual. I opt for a cranberry

Saint Laurent sheath and black suede Manolos. The frock is from last year's collection, and the shoes are a little scuffed, but I'll make do.

I walk over to the Taj, which sits on prime real estate, at the corner of Arlington and Newbury Streets, across from the Public Garden. I haven't been inside the hotel since it was the Ritz-Carlton, over a decade ago. It used to be a family favorite. My parents hosted countless Saturday-night dinners in the second-floor dining room and brunches in the street-level café. My mother still reminisces about the good old days, when the elevator operators wore white gloves and unaccompanied women weren't allowed in the bar.

I speak with the hotel manager about room availability, withholding the specifics until after I've secured the reservation. At best, a surveillance operation is a hassle, involving security concerns and unsavory characters. At worst, it poses a danger to everyone in the vicinity. There's no way to predict everything that could go down. The perp could be armed; he could open fire in a crowded area or take a hostage.

"I have two lovely rooms, adjacent to one another," the manager says.

I give her the office credit card, and as soon as she completes the transaction and hands me the key cards, I explain that we'll be using the rooms as part of a sting operation. She immediately tries to backtrack.

"I'm sorry, I've made a mistake. The computer is showing that we're fully committed."

I've been through this before.

"If I have to, I'll go to court and seek an emergency judicial order. You'll have to retain a lawyer to oppose the request, and I promise you'll lose."

After more back and forth, she concedes defeat and introduces me to the head of hotel security, a retired state police lieutenant. I don't give him details about the case, but he's been around the block and can probably figure out what we're up to. I'm not worried about him leaking information, since it's in his interest to protect the hotel from this kind of publicity. The last thing the Taj wants to be associated with is a serial killer.

Our undercover officer is barely recognizable. When I saw her at the station a few hours ago, she was in a police uniform. Now, she's wearing heels and a low-cut blouse. I hate that men get to go undercover as tough guys, Hells Angels, and Mafia wannabes, while women are stuck being prostitutes. Nonetheless, she looks like a pro in every sense of the word.

The detectives survey the layout of the first-floor lounge, which has a clubby atmosphere with upholstered armchairs, mahogany furniture, and a fireplace. The undercover takes a seat, alone, at the bar. She grabs a handful of nuts from a bowl and pops them in her mouth, one by one. Plainclothes detectives are scattered around the room, with glasses of ginger ale and club soda with lime, to look like they're drinking cocktails. Since Kevin and I are recognizable from news reports of the investigation, we go upstairs.

A forensic team plants audio- and video-monitoring devices in the takedown room. We settle in next door, in the observation room, with the technicians. Kevin paces; I sit in front of the one-way mirror. We wait for word of his arrival, hoping he's our guy.

An hour later, we get a text from one of the detectives downstairs in the lounge. *Target entering.* I want to get up and go downstairs, but stay in my seat.

A few minutes later, another text comes in. *They're on the move.* I imagine the undercover and the creep leaving the bar, getting on the elevator together, pressing the button, and walking toward the door. I can't wait to get a look at him. Our audio picks them up as soon as they reach the room. The heavy door opens and closes with a thud; the lock clicks.

"Would you like a drink?" LoveToLoveYou2100 says.

His voice is softer than I had expected, and he has a European accent, possibly German. He comes into view, and I can see that he's about six foot two, two hundred and fifty pounds; he's heavier and taller than the man who brushed up against me on the steps behind city hall. He takes a nip bottle from the minibar and pours them both rum and Cokes. The undercover never puts the glass to her lips; she isn't going to risk getting roofied.

He downs his drink in two gulps and loosens his tie. She gets down to business. "It's a thousand for the night," she says, "plus four hundred for the room."

"Yes, I understand," he says.

She sticks her hand out. "Cash up front."

He looks through his wallet and removes a few bills. She counts the money and stuffs it in her pocket. Then she pulls her handcuffs out from the small of her back. "Hands where I can see them, asshole."

"Hold on," the man says. "I'm not into that kind of thing."

The guy thinks that she's a dominatrix and this is part of her repertoire. He starts to put up a struggle, twisting his body and trying to free his hands from her grip, but he's no match for her. Even though he's got more than a hundred pounds on her, she's fresh out of the academy, well trained in defensive tactics. She grabs his wrist and elbow, applying pressure in opposite directions, and brings him to his knees. I feel a sense of pride, seeing her in control of the suspect.

Suddenly, the door to the room blasts open, followed by the satisfying sights and sounds of a well-executed takedown. The securing of the room: *All clear.* The arrest: *On the floor, keep your hands behind your back.* The denial: *You got it all wrong. I didn't do anything.*

The man is arrested for soliciting a prostitute and transported to police headquarters. Kevin and I follow behind the cruiser. The trip is a blur. We speed through stop signs and traffic lights, until we reach One Schroeder Plaza. The detectives take him inside and put him in an interview room, and Kevin goes in to talk to him. I take a seat behind the one-way glass to watch. The man clears his throat, runs his fingers across his acned forehead. He's not the cold-blooded killer I was expecting.

"Officer, I apologize." His accent is thick. "Prostitution isn't even a crime where I come from."

"Where's that?"

"Amsterdam."

"How long have you been in the country?"

He rubs his wrists. "I arrived two nights ago."

"From where?"

"Canada. I was at a dental convention."

In all the time I spent picturing the killer, imagining his voice, I never once thought of a Dutch dentist. The man shows Kevin his passport, who inspects it and leaves the room to verify its authenticity. We call Homeland Security and are not really surprised to learn that his travel documents check out, and so does his alibi. This man is not our killer.

Even though we could prosecute him for soliciting a prostitute, we don't press charges. He's had enough punishment. And, more importantly, it could blow our cover and compromise the investigation.

After he leaves, Kevin and I sit, unsure of what to do. The surge of adrenaline ends in a crash, sapping my energy and enthusiasm. Kevin offers me a bottle of water.

"We'll find our guy," he says. "It's a numbers game. Like real Internet dating, you have to kiss a bunch of frogs before you find Mr. Right."

Chapter Forty

Kevin and I meet in my office, and we get back online. A dozen more messages have come through since yesterday. We sort through them, add the data to our spreadsheet, and select our next candidate. One man stands out from the pack, PlatoAt-Play, who sounds anything but playful. He's aggressive, having responded three times; he sent two e-mails yesterday, and another today. His final e-mail ends with an admonition: *It's rude to ignore me. At least you could respond.* He sounds promising: hostile, sanctimonious, and desperate.

He suggests we meet at the Lenox Hotel, on Boylston Street in the Back Bay. We engage in a brief e-mail exchange. Me: *I'll text you the room number when I get there.* Him: *No, meet me in the piano bar. See you soon, sexy.*

My chest tightens, and I have a hard time breathing. I calm myself by remembering he can't see me and he doesn't know who I am.

A couple of hours before the scheduled meet, we head over to the hotel and scope out the lounge. It's only eight o'clock, but there are already about ten patrons, drinking and waiting for the show to begin. The manager is less than thrilled when I tell her why we need to secure the lounge and that we need two hotel rooms.

The patrons don't seem to notice when the detectives discreetly position themselves around the lounge and set up surveillance. A few plainclothes detectives are stationed on Boylston Street in case the perp tries to take off. The undercover settles in at a table, away from the lights and the piano, and nurses a Coke.

Soon the pianist starts to belt out show tunes, and people sing along; most are off-key, but it's a nice distraction. I stand off to the side and try to regulate my breathing as I listen to the familiar songs: "Somewhere Over the Rainbow," "Charlie on the MTA," "You Give Love a Bad Name." When I feel Kevin's elbow in my rib cage, I notice that my foot is tapping. I hope I was only singing in my head and not out loud.

"It's time to turn into a pumpkin," he says.

We both have a bad feeling about this guy and decide to stay close to the action. Reluctantly, the manager lets us wait in her office. A few minutes later, we get a text. *Target is on site.* I put my ear to the wall to listen, but all I can hear is music.

After about fifteen minutes, we hear loud voices and banging. Kevin opens the door, and we see the back of a man's head; he's being pulled outside by detectives. The man resists, but after a few futile attempts to break free, he surrenders.

Kevin steps into the hallway and signals me to follow.

"The coast is clear."

Outside, the suspect is standing on the sidewalk in front of the hotel. He's surrounded by police; I can only see the top of his head, his reddish hair and glasses, similar to the man who planted the GPS in my tote. The rest of my view is obstructed by the swarm. An officer guides him into the back of a cruiser and slams the door. The driver whisks him away.

On our way to headquarters, I call Max, and Kevin calls the commissioner. We're cautious not to brag. This could just be another creepy john. When we arrive, we sprint inside and take the stairs to the third floor; it's faster than the elevator, and it will help burn off some adrenaline. I peer in the glass opening of the interrogation room; the suspect is seated, his back to the door. His disguise, the reddish wig and glasses, are on the table. His hands are clasped behind his head, his fingers interlaced.

These could be the hands that strangled the life out of Caitlyn, Rose, Britney, and Valerie. They look strong, powerful, and eerily familiar. I feel a pull in the pit of my stomach. Before I can say a word, Kevin taps on the glass, and the man twists around. I take a hard look at his face, but it's not really necessary. I already know who he is. I freeze, try to speak, but my throat constricts. I can barely eke out a whisper.

"Oh my God," I say.

"What?" Kevin says.

"I know him."

The man sees me standing outside the door, looking in. He grins and waves.

"Who is he?" Kevin says.

"His name is Chip Aldridge," I say.

Chapter Forty-One

I tell Kevin everything. Chip's bogus story about our families summering near each other on the Vineyard. The accidentally on purpose encounters at the Mass General and Starbucks. And, most humiliating of all, our lunch at the Four Seasons. As soon as I'm done, I go to the bathroom and throw up. Then I wash my face and look at my reflection in the mirror. I have a new understanding of victims who fall prey to catfish scams and Ponzi schemes. I'll no longer ask myself: How could she be so stupid?

Kevin is predictably nonjudgmental.

"You're in good company. This guy fooled a lot of smart people over the years. So far we've tied him to eleven aliases."

I nod, but there's nothing he can say to make this right. I've been conned by a con man. While I was regaling Chip with stories about my grandmother, over a bowl of blood orange sorbet, he was sizing me up and planning his next move. The question is: Why? It's possible he's just a stalker. Or he could be a swindler with bad timing. More likely, he's our killer.

I drop my head in my hands. When Kevin starts to speak, I look up, hoping for words of wisdom and compassion, anything that will make me feel less awful.

"Don't take this the wrong way," he says, "but you got to get your head on straight. In a few hours, we can drink a bottle of booze or eat a bucket of ice cream, but right now, I have to interview him. We need to prepare."

I take a breath, shake my head. "What else do you want to know?"

"Where were you the first time he talked to you?"

"Near my apartment, walking to my car on Clarendon Street."

"When?"

"It was the day after I picked up Caitlyn Walker's case."

"So he probably planted the first GPS right around that time." He smiles. "How many times have I been on you to clean out that clown car of a pocketbook?"

Chip is in the interview room, drumming his fingers on the table. He looks directly into the one-way mirror and flashes a toothy smile at his own reflection. I take a step backward. He can't see me, but he knows I'm on the other side of the glass, watching.

"I'm going in," Kevin says.

When the interview room door opens, Chip looks over, expectantly. His expression sours when he sees it's only Kevin. I turn on the audio.

Chip keeps his eyes trained on the mirror and smooths his hair.

"Why isn't Abigail here?" he says.

Kevin turns on the recorder and Mirandizes him. *"You have the right to remain silent; anything you say can and will be used against you."* If ever I've wanted a suspect to waive his *Miranda* rights, it's now. *"You have the right to speak to an attorney, and to have one present during questioning."* Please don't ask for an attorney. *"If you cannot afford a lawyer, one will be provided at government expense."* This is taking forever. Hurry up and close the deal. *"Do you understand these rights?"* Chip thinks for a minute and nods. *"Knowing these rights, are you willing to answer my questions without an attorney present?"*

Kevin takes out the form and slides it across the table, along with a pen.

"I'll talk, but under one condition." Chip's Yankee accent has developed a midwestern tang.

"What?" Kevin says.

"I want Abigail in here."

Just when I thought this couldn't get any worse, it does.

"ADA Endicott can't represent you, she's a prosecutor," Kevin says.

"I'm fully aware of her position."

"Then why do you want her?"

"She's an old friend. If you want to talk, she has to be here."

Kevin cuts the recorder and comes out to consult with me. Participating in a prep meeting, a proffer, or an interview is acceptable practice. But prosecutors don't sit in on postarrest interrogations with suspects. We don't want to make ourselves a witness in our own case.

"It's your call," Kevin says.

"I don't have a choice. We want to get a statement, and he won't talk unless I'm there."

"It'll give him a soapbox so he can embarrass you."

"That ship has sailed."

Chip stands when I enter. He moves to pull out my chair, but Kevin blocks his path.

"Don't make me shackle you to the floor," Kevin says.

"I was taught to stand when a lady enters the room."

I move quickly and purposefully to a chair. When I sit, I clasp my hands in my lap so he can't see them shaking.

"How is your mother?" Chip says. "Has she recovered from her accident?" I start to talk, but Kevin cuts me off. "If you're trying to threaten ADA Endicott, you oughta know that case has been resolved."

"The Breathalyzer was thrown out," Chip says, "but no one

seems to have followed up on the blood tests. We both know what they'll show."

I don't believe a word he says anymore. There was no blood test. I hope.

"You've been stalking a county prosecutor," Kevin says. "Keep it up and I'll put a tag on your file. Corrections officers have a special place for prisoners like you."

I could press charges for stalking and intimidation, but that would be playing into his hands. It would force me to walk into an open courtroom and testify about what will be described as our blossoming romance. Worse, it could conflict me out of this case.

Kevin takes Chip's brief silence as a sign of retreat.

"We're going back on the record, and you're going to behave," Kevin says.

He turns on the recorder, and Chip signs the *Miranda* waiver.

"What's your true name?" Kevin says.

"I'll take a pass on that question."

"Your date of birth."

"Pass."

Chip could have declined to speak with us altogether, but he didn't want to miss an opportunity to show how clever he is, and to further embarrass me. This is fun for him, part of whatever sick game he's playing.

"Are you employed?" Kevin says.

"Some people think I'm a surgeon."

I search my memory. When I saw Chip at the hospital, he wasn't wearing scrubs, he didn't have an ID badge clipped to his jacket. I assumed he worked at the Mass General; there was no reason to doubt it. I wanted him to be a successful surgeon. It made me feel more desirable.

"Where do you live?"

This one he answers. He can't resist.

"In the C Street projects."

I was so swept up in the illusion that Chip was some kind of Ivy League knight in shining armor that when I stood outside the townhouse on Comm Avenue, I never bothered to check the name on the buzzer. Again, I had no reason to distrust him.

"Do you know Tommy Greenough?" Kevin says.

"Sure, he's the guy who's been all over the news." Chip stops talking, looks at me, clenches and unclenches his jaw.

I shouldn't speak, but I've broken a lot of rules already.

"Did Tommy Greenough introduce you to anyone?" I say.

Chip leans in. "Like who?"

"Females. Victims," Kevin says.

"Victims?"

Kevin plants his elbows on the table and extends his forearms. For a second, it looks like he might reach over and strangle Chip. If he does, I won't intervene.

Chip shifts in his chair, turns, and looks directly into the camera. "I'm invoking my right to remain silent. This conversation is over."

Kevin looks at me: *Now what?*

It's a tough call. Without a confession, we don't have much to arrest him on, but we can't release him back out on the street. Not until we have proof that he's not the killer. I nod, giving Kevin the go-ahead.

He turns off the camera and looks at Chip.

"Richard Aldridge, or whatever your name is, you're under arrest," Kevin says.

"For what?" Chip says.

"Soliciting a prostitute, resisting arrest, and whatever else we decide to charge you with," I say.

Chapter Forty-Two

Kevin gives me a ride home and watches me step into the lobby of my building. As soon as he drives off, I go back outside. I'm not ready to face Ty. I'm going to have to fess up, but not yet. I walk across the street, get in my car, and dial Max.

He answers on the first ring. "Did he confess?"

"No, he invoked."

Chip took the Fifth, but the right to remain silent doesn't apply to me. The words don't come easier the second time. Max listens, silently, and I have no idea what he's thinking. When I'm done talking, I expect him to yell or swear, but he doesn't.

"What did you charge him with?" His tone is quiet, detached.

"So far, just a bunch of misdemeanors."

"How are you going to play it?"

"I was looking for your thoughts, boss."

"It's your case, your call."

This is worse than a lecture; I'd rather be reprimanded than hung out to dry.

"The arraignment is tomorrow," I say. "We need to come up with a plan. Should I recuse myself?"

Max takes a beat. "Jesus, Abby. Men hit on you all the time—lawyers, cops, judges. You could date anyone."

"We didn't date."

"Delay the trial until after the election," he says. "That way, I'll be long gone when this keg of dynamite explodes." He hangs up.

That was tough, but the worst is yet to come. When I walk in my apartment, I find Ty in the living room, drinking a Rolling Rock, hunched over his laptop. He sits up, gives me a kiss, and helps me slip my arms out of the sleeves of my coat.

"You look stressed," he says.

"We did a takedown tonight."

"You caught the guy?"

"We're not sure yet."

I busy myself by hanging my coat in the closet and getting a glass of wine from the kitchen. When I return to the living room and sit on the sofa, I avoid eye contact.

"Do you remember Chip Aldridge?" I say. "That doctor we ran into in the hospital?"

"The dude who was checking on your mother?"

"Turns out he's not a doctor. And he was stalking me."

He studies my face. "For real?"

"We arrested him tonight."

"What do you mean, stalking?" Ty knows I'm holding back. He watches me closely as he speaks. "Did he try to hurt you?"

My mouth is dry. "He just kept turning up places—Starbucks, the Harvard Club."

"Why?" He closes his laptop and sits up.

I can't meet his eyes. "I don't know," I say.

"Hold on," he says. "You told me that you knew that dude from work."

"I didn't want you to get jealous."

My head throbs as I watch him stand and prepare himself for what he knows is coming.

"Jealous about what?" he says.

I speak quickly. "He's a con man. He was persistent. We had

lunch. It was nothing, just lunch with a guy who said he knew my family."

"But you didn't do anything to stop him."

"I told him all about you." I stand to face him.

He pauses. "Did you want to mess around with him?"

I hesitate. If I don't come clean, there's no hope for us.

"I guess I liked the attention. Nothing happened. I swear."

"Okay," Ty says.

"That's it?"

"You've probably got a big day tomorrow."

He leaves the room, and I hear him undress and get into bed. I brush my teeth and wash my face. When I get out of the bathroom, he's lying down, his eyes are closed. I pull down the covers on my side of the bed and move toward him.

"I'm going to recuse myself from the murder investigation," I say. "Chip Aldridge is probably going to turn out to be the killer."

Ty opens his eyes, sits up straight, and leans against the headboard.

"Don't do that," he says.

I'm surprised by his reaction. He's always interested in my cases, but the only time he voices a strong opinion is when he thinks I'm in danger.

"Cassandra can take the case," I say. "She's been salivating over it since it came in."

"You're not a quitter."

Ty knows this will break me, that I can't let the families down.

"I'm sorry," I say. "I should have told you about him."

I move to snuggle in next to him, hoping for a sign of forgiveness, but at the exact moment that I lean in for a kiss, he twists away and reaches over to turn off the lamp. I move back to my side of the bed, and we both pretend to fall asleep.

After lying awake for a few hours, trying to will myself to sleep, I give up and slip out of bed. Ty is facing the wall; I can't tell if he's sleeping or faking, but either way, he's not looking to chat.

In the kitchen, I pop a K-Cup in the Keurig and nibble on the stale Starbucks scone that I've been carrying around in my tote for the past three days. When I log on to my laptop, I'm not surprised to see that Chip's arrest has gone viral. There are news reports, tweets, and posts from dozens of women who recognize his picture but know him by other names: Ben Cabot, Spencer Coolidge, Sam Emerson.

There are stories about his background; he's been honing his con for years, moving around the country, expanding his repertoire, and growing increasingly bold. CNN is reporting that, as a teenager, he was thrown off campus at two schools, Groton and Andover, where he had convinced students to let him live in their dorm rooms. Fox News has a piece about his early adulthood, when he was caught sneaking into lecture halls at Princeton, Columbia, and Yale Law School, even though he was never enrolled. *The Huffington Post* reports he's been engaged three times, married twice, and stolen from countless women. Most were too embarrassed to press charges, opting to cut their losses instead.

I see an e-mail from Kevin, detailing two active arrest warrants out for Chip. He's wanted for identity theft in Denver and investment fraud in Grosse Pointe. Neither charge merits more than a few months of jail, but if we're desperate, it'll be something we can pursue.

Just as the sun is starting to rise, a call from dispatch comes through to my cell phone.

"Abigail Endicott, homicide."

"Are you the ADA looking for Valerie Jackson?" the dispatcher says.

I take a breath, sit back on the sofa.

"Did they find her?" I say.

"The Coast Guard picked her up."

"Where?"

"The Graves," the dispatcher says.

"She was in a cemetery?" I say. "Which one?"

"No. Not a grave—the Graves."

"The island?" I say.

The Graves is a small, privately owned island in Boston Harbor. It's less than ten miles from downtown, known for its one-hundred-year-old granite lighthouse, the Graves Light.

"Yes," he says.

"Has the medical examiner been called in yet?"

"Medical examiner?" He pauses. "No, she's headed to the Mass General."

I stand so quickly that I feel a little dizzy.

"Valerie Jackson is alive?"

"Her pulse is weak, her blood pressure low, and she's suffering from hypothermia and dehydration, but, yes, Valerie Jackson is alive."

Chapter Forty-Three

The Coast Guard spotted Valerie on the rocky edge of the Graves; she was naked and dazed. As soon as the officer was able to get her name, he knew she was our fourth victim. Everyone had been on alert, searching for her, but no one expected to find her alive.

Dispatch connects me with the detective, who is riding in the ambulance with Valerie.

"Do you want me to take a statement?" he says.

"No, the less said, the better. I'll meet you at the hospital."

I want to minimize the number of times Valerie has to repeat her story. Defense attorneys will pick apart whatever she says, using it as fodder for cross-examination. *In the ambulance, you said that your assailant was wearing blue pants. In the hospital, you said he was wearing blue jeans. Which was it, pants or jeans?* In court, the lawyer will argue that Valerie's inconsistent statements prove that she was too frightened or injured to remember clearly, and therefore she's not reliable.

That's the strategic reason to restrict the number of interviews. There's also a psychological one: every time Valerie describes what happened, she'll have to relive her trauma, over and over again. She's already been wounded. I don't want to inflict more pain than is absolutely necessary.

I jump in my car, head to the hospital. On the way, I call Valerie's father to deliver the first piece of good news I've had since we met.

"She's alive." I get the words out quickly, knowing that's all he cares about right now.

"Where is she?" He fumbles with what sounds like keys.

When I reach Mass General, I think about the last time I ran into Chip Aldridge, when he was masquerading as a compassionate physician. His strong hands and his confident smile, once so appealing, now make my stomach turn. My anxiety level surges; maybe I should stop by the pharmacy and fill the Ativan prescription I've been carrying around in my tote.

I arrive at the always-busy emergency room, where I find a familiar nurse and give her the heads-up. She reserves an exam room, sets up IV fluids, and finds a rape kit.

When Kevin arrives, we look around and see a few empty seats in the waiting area. No one is coughing or scratching, but you can't always tell who's carrying a communicable disease.

"Let's wait outside," I say.

"It's freezing out there."

"I'd rather catch a cold than contract a case of C. *diff.*"

I pump a dollop of hand sanitizer from a wall dispenser, and as soon as we step through the automatic doors, an ambulance pulls up to the bay and the driver jumps out. We move closer and watch the EMTs open the back door and slide the gurney out, expecting to see Valerie. False alarm; it's an elderly woman with a gash in her head. We back away.

"You look tired," Kevin says. "You're running yourself ragged."

"I can't believe I thought Chip Aldridge was a doctor. I should have made him as the crook that he is."

"Let's get something at the coffee shop, my treat. If you ask nice, I'll even get you a chocolate chip cookie."

He puts his hand on my back and tries to lead me inside. I shake him off.

"I came back to work too soon. Maybe I shouldn't have come back at all."

He faces me, puts his hands on my shoulders. "If you're going to kick yourself, you're on your own," he says.

"I lost my edge."

"Baloney."

"All the signs were there, and I missed them."

"You didn't do anything wrong. In fact, you did everything right. You solved this case."

My phone sounds; it's Carl Ostroff. He probably got a tip about Valerie's rescue and wants to confirm it. I ignore the call.

Another ambulance pulls up. A trooper jumps out and waves to us. It's Valerie, on the gurney, hooked up to a monitor with an IV drip in the fold of her arm. Her hair is matted, her lips are blue, and there are ligature marks around her neck.

We follow the EMTs as they wheel Valerie into the exam room. They grab the sides of the sheets and lift her off the gurney, onto the hospital bed. She looks like she's in shock.

We wait in the hallway, while the nurses and doctors examine her and do a rape kit, an internal and external examination. They're looking for anything that could contain DNA; they swab for semen, comb for stray hairs, and clip her nails for skin cells. But we all know that whatever might have been there has since been washed away.

Soon the doctor comes out. "You can see her, but only for a few minutes."

I inch into the room and look at her, trying to mask any hint of fear, horror, or pity. She looks small and fragile in her blue hospital gown. They've cleaned and stitched her wounds, including the ligature marks, and applied a few bandages.

I speak softly, introducing myself and Kevin. She seems to understand what I'm saying, but doesn't respond. Kevin asks if it's okay to take pictures, and she nods. He snaps photos of everything, the cuts and swelling on her face and hands. There's a bruise the size and color of an eggplant on her arm. She's in no condition, physically or emotionally, to give a full statement.

"Can you tell me your name?" I say.

"Valerie Jackson." Her voice is barely audible.

There's a cup of ice chips on a tray near her bed; I pick it up, and she nods. Using the tiny plastic spoon, I carefully deposit a sliver of ice in her mouth.

"Do you know where you are?" I say.

She looks at the IV tube, as though noticing it for the first time.

"The hospital," she says.

"Who introduced you to your attacker?" Kevin says.

She takes another ice chip. "Green . . . Greenough," she says.

"Can you identify the guy who did this to you?"

She repositions her body and grabs the bedrails until her knuckles turn white. "He's not here, is he?" she says.

I put my hand on hers.

"No."

"He thinks I'm dead." Her scratchy voice grows louder. "Please, don't let him know where I am. He'll kill me."

"A police officer will be stationed outside your hospital room," Kevin says. "You'll be safe."

I want to allay her fear, tell her I think we have the guy, that he's locked up, but I can't. First she has to make an identification. She's my only surviving witness; her testimony could make or break the case. If I tell her anything about Chip ahead of time, his lawyer will argue that her identification is tainted, and it could be suppressed at trial.

"I'm going to have another detective show you pictures. I'll be right outside the door."

Per police protocol, an officer who doesn't know the details of the case and has never seen Chip will conduct the photo array. It has to be a blind ID, and since the officer doesn't know who we hope she picks out, he can't be accused of trying to suggest a particular picture.

We step outside and listen to the officer instruct Valerie.

"I'm going to show you a series of pictures. Please look at all of them, one at a time, and tell me if you recognize anyone. The man who assaulted you may or may not be included in the group."

A few seconds pass. Then we hear a scream. The sound is shrill and loud. Even though there are no words, it's very certain. We got him.

Chapter Forty-Four

Chip's murder arraignment is delayed a couple of days so the victims' families can be here. I arrive at the courthouse early; there's a long wait at the security check, people hoping to catch a look at the handsome con man, the heartless killer.

Inside, the courtroom is at capacity. The front row of the gallery is occupied by the families of my victims. I say hello to Rose's parents, Ed and Delia Driscoll, who are seated on the aisle. When they speak, their eyes remain fixed on the empty judge's bench, as though they don't want to miss a second of the proceedings. Caitlyn's mother, Karen Walker, has her arm around Caitlyn's former roommate, Nadine Franklin. Valerie's father, Walter Jackson, is surrounded by support. He introduces me to his priest, his employer, and his poker buddies. Britney's sister is alone, arms crossed, leaning against the wall.

I move past the bar and set my files on the prosecutor's table. There's no sign of a defense attorney.

"Who represents him?" I say to the court officer.

He checks his roster and shrugs. "No one filed an appearance."

"Has probation done an assessment?"

"You'd never know by looking at him, but he qualifies for public counsel."

I call the Committee for Public Counsel Services and ask to speak with the assignment coordinator.

"We sent someone to talk to him last night," he says. "He said he's not a member of the *unwashed public*, and won't be treated as such. Good luck to whoever gets stuck with him."

Murder cases are expensive; we ran Chip's financials, and it doesn't look like he has the funds to retain his own lawyer. Either he conned someone into footing the bill, or a he found a defense attorney willing to represent him at a reduced fee, because of the free advertising the case will generate. I hope it's one of the less offensive defense attorneys, someone I can reason with.

Chip shuffles into the courtroom, handcuffed and shackled, flanked by court officers. He sits and grins at me. The fluorescent glare bounces off the back of his head, exposing a bald spot I never noticed. He looks older than I remember, but his charisma is still palpable, even in an orange jumpsuit. My stomach churns, but I hold his eyes. I want him to know he's misjudged me. His girlfriends and ex-wives may have been too humiliated to stand up to him, but I'm not. Or at least I don't want him to think I am.

The Greenoughs, father and son, are ushered in next. They keep their heads down and make a point of looking away from the audience. Josh takes a seat and positions his chair to block the Greenoughs from the camera.

The deputy goes into the judge's chambers, to tell her we're ready. When I found out Judge Hynes had been assigned the case, I was ecstatic. It's been a while since Kevin and I went to her house, seeking authorization to search the Greenoughs' homes, but she'll remember the case. When we were asking for permission to bust down doors without probable cause, her legal acumen and evidentiary expertise were obstacles, but that phase of the investigation is over. She's the perfect trial judge, one who will ensure an unassailable verdict, one of the few jurists who will keep a tight rein on these defendants.

The deputy comes back and bangs his knuckles on the wall. "All rise."

The door opens, and I do a double take when Judge Charmaine Swanson enters the courtroom. A Tiffany-blue scarf is knotted around the collar of her black robe, but it doesn't detract from the film of sweat above her lip. The camera light flashes; she gazes longingly at the door to her chambers, then inches toward the bench. She's in over her head, and she knows it.

"Initially, Judge Hynes was assigned this matter, but she's become unavailable." She clears her throat. "I will be presiding."

The fix is in. Judge Swanson is one of the greenest and most biased jurists in the Commonwealth. She was appointed to the bench two months ago, at age thirty-five, with the support of her father's former law partner, who is married to the attorney general. She is the worst possible choice—political, manipulable, and single.

The room quiets, and the clerk announces the case. Josh files his appearance, which makes him the lawyer of record for the Greenoughs.

"My clients plead not guilty and waive argument on bail."

Josh wants to prevent the facts from coming out for as long as possible.

Judge Swanson turns to Chip. "Where . . ." Her voice catches, making her sound like she's choking. "Where is your lawyer, sir?"

Chip jumps out of his chair. "Most respectfully, Your Honor, I wish to assert my rights, under the Sixth Amendment to the United States Constitution, and represent myself."

I'm impressed. Chip's attendance at Yale Law School was unauthorized, but it was time well spent. I'm also nauseated. The only thing worse than a sleazy defense attorney is no defense attorney. Chip's decision to go pro se will force me to interact with him and treat him like any other lawyer. It'll be intimidating to my witnesses, who will be subjected to his cross-examination. I should have anticipated this move. He's played pretend doctor;

of course he thinks he can play pretend lawyer. For a guy like Chip, scamming a jury is the ultimate con.

Chip hands his appearance slip to the court officer, who passes it to the judge. She picks up the water pitcher; her hands are unsteady, the liquid sloshing around as she fills her glass. She's buying time, unsure of how to respond. This gives me an opportunity to take control.

"Your Honor, since the defendant has waived counsel," I say, "perhaps we could proceed with the arraignment and resolve the issue of representation at another date."

I refer to him as the defendant more times than necessary, knowing it must sting.

She nods, grateful for my assist. "How do you plead, Mr. Aldridge?"

He stands and pivots to face the back of the courtroom, staring directly into the TV camera. "I am 100 percent not guilty." His voice is forceful and seductive, like a radio personality.

He faces the judge and smiles. Her eyes follow his hand as he brushes a stray hair into place. She tucks her own hair behind her ears. He's reeling her in, and she doesn't even know it. Like so many others, myself included, she's captivated by his casual charm. I want to scream. *Don't fall for it.*

I try to break the spell. "Your Honor, may I be heard on bail?"

She looks at me, then the audience, as though she forgot we were here, and shakes her head. "Yes, proceed."

"If convicted, the defendant faces three concurrent sentences of life in prison with no possibility of parole. He has no roots in this, or any other, community. We don't even know his true name. He has no family ties and no work history. If released, he has no incentive to return to court and answer to these charges. He is the ultimate flight risk. The Commonwealth submits that no amount of bail is sufficient to guarantee his appearance, and we ask that he be held without bail."

I take my seat. If I were wearing a mic, it would pick up the sound of my heart pounding.

"This is a witch hunt." Chip pauses to look at me. "The prosecutor's allegations are unfounded. She has no direct evidence, no DNA, no fingerprints, no eyewitness identification, no confession. Her entire case is based on a personal ad posted on the Internet. I give you my word that I will return to court. I have every incentive to come back and prove my innocence."

His argument is effective, designed to both get himself out of jail and fire a warning shot at me. He hasn't mentioned Valerie. If he doesn't know she survived his attack, he'll know soon. I'll have to provide her name as part of discovery.

"May we approach sidebar?" I say.

She nods. Chip follows me to the bench. As we stand in front of the judge, Chip brushes his elbow against mine. I try to ignore him, not wanting to give him the satisfaction of knowing how much he's getting under my skin.

"Your Honor, I want to inform the court that the defendant and I have had several interactions."

Judge Swanson looks at Chip, then at me. "Are you saying there was a personal relationship?"

"I believe it was part of a calculated plan to extract information, threaten me, and possibly inflict harm. He surveilled my neighborhood, and he planted a tracking device in my bag, twice."

"You forgot about lunch." Chip looks at the judge. "I took her to lunch at the Four Seasons."

Judge Swanson opens her mouth, but no words come out.

I power on. "I considered seeking indictments for stalking and intimidation of a witness, but decided not to file charges."

Chip interrupts. "Charges? I paid for that lunch. It cost me a hundred and fifty bucks."

Finally, Judge Swanson finds her voice and cuts to the chase. "Mr. Aldridge, if you believe that the prosecutor has a conflict of interest, I'm prepared to recuse her from the case."

There is clearly a conflict, but if Chip agrees to waive it, the judge can allow me to remain on the case. If Chip refuses, he'd take me out of my misery. I'd be free of this nightmare. I could focus on my political plans, my family, and Ty. In the alternative, I could simply concede and put an end to it myself.

I glance over at the victims' families, who are leaning forward, straining to read our lips. Even from across the courtroom, I can see the toll that this has taken on each of them, how much they've aged over the past six months. Delia Driscoll's brown bob has grown shaggy and gray. Walter Jackson has gained about thirty pounds. Cheryl Walker's complexion has become wrinkled and sallow.

I don't wait for Chip's response. "I would submit there is no conflict."

Chip nods. "Agreed."

As he speaks, I can smell peanut butter on his breath. They must have given him a sandwich for breakfast.

"Sir, I can give you time to think about it and consult with experienced counsel." Judge Swanson sounds like she wants to recuse herself.

"That's not necessary," Chip says. "I look forward to going toe-to-toe with Ms. Endicott. She is, by all accounts, a worthy opponent."

Judge Swanson stares at him for a minute.

"The bail, Your Honor?" I say.

"Mr. Aldridge, I'm holding you without bail until trial. You are remanded to the Nashua Street Jail."

The court officers swoop in and move him back into the dock, with the other criminals. I exhale and keep my head down, relieved that he's out of reach—not his reach, *my* reach. Otherwise, I might throttle him.

Chapter Forty-Five

After Judge Swanson gets off the bench, I steer the families to a conference room, away from the crowds. The room is quiet, unsure how to interpret what just happened. Delia is holding a notebook; she flips a page and starts a new section: *Meeting with ADA*. Everyone settles around the table.

Rose's father, Ed Driscoll, speaks for the group.

"We couldn't hear what went on up there with the judge," Ed says.

"She ruled in our favor and denied bail," I say.

Ed's shoulders relax a little. "So he'll be locked up?"

"Yes, and the same goes for the Greenoughs."

Caitlyn's former roommate, Nadine Franklin, raises her hand, as though she's in one of her seminars at Wellesley. Her coat sleeve is matted with dog hair. I resist the urge to offer her the lint brush I keep in my tote.

"If he doesn't have a lawyer, then who will ask us the questions when we testify?" she says.

"He will." I don't try to sugarcoat it. "He'll cross-examine you."

"That doesn't sound fair." Nadine tears up.

Fairness rarely applies to victims. The game is rigged in favor of the accused: He has the right to confront his accusers. He has the presumption of innocence. He has the right to a trial by jury. And as much as I'd like to let Nadine know I share her sentiment, ethics rules strictly prohibit prosecutors from speaking negatively about the defendant or his lawyer, so I keep my disgust to myself.

"What about my girl's case?" Valerie's father, Walter Jackson, says.

Walter is a solid six foot three, and it looks like, up until his daughter went missing, he hadn't missed a day in the gym. Sitting here, he looks small and powerless. I want to give him a hug, but now is not the time. This is the time to present the facts, let everyone know what to expect.

After the meeting, the room empties slowly, except for Caitlyn's roommate, Nadine. She sits, shell-shocked.

"How are you holding up?" I say.

"I can't testify," Nadine says.

"I need you to give background about Caitlyn, identify her photograph, and provide a timeline for her movements that night. You were the last person to see her alive. I wouldn't ask if it wasn't important."

She puts her hands to her face and starts to sob. Her moans escalate into wails, and she sounds like she might hyperventilate. I dig in my bag for tissues and water.

"I'm going to get you through this," I say.

"I can't face him."

"You'll be safe."

I put my hand on her forearm. She's shivering—with grief, or fear, or something else. It could be a delayed response to the trauma, but it seems more urgent. After she leaves, I slump in my chair, feeling like I just climbed Mount Washington, in stilettos, carrying a backpack full of pain.

When I get outside, Max's communications director is organizing a presser. The last time we held a formal briefing on the case was the night Caitlyn's body was discovered in East Boston.

At that time she was the second of two victims. Now she's the second of four.

A black SUV pulls up, and Max steps out of the passenger side, greets a few police officers, and moves behind a jumble of microphones. He delivers a canned speech about the diligence and determination that went into solving the case, as if he had anything to do with it.

When he's done, he waves me up to the podium; I step in front of the firing squad and field a few questions. The rules only permit me to repeat what I've already said in the courtroom, so I don't reveal anything new. After a few minutes of *I'm sorry, I can't comment on that at this time*, the conference ends and reporters set up their live shots.

Max jumps back in his SUV and takes off. He's too self-absorbed to offer me a ride, which is fine. I don't want to sit in a car with him either. I barely make it a few feet when Carl Ostroff steps in front of me, blocking my path.

I don't wait for his question. "I can't talk about the case."

"This isn't about the arraignment." He holds my eyes, stone-faced. "I'm looking into a story, and I suspect you're going to want to know about it."

I hesitate, then step around him.

"It's about your family," he says.

I stop, look around, and consider my response. Press vans are parked up and down the street. A reporter from the *Herald* is keeping a careful watch on us. I can't be seen huddled with Carl. People already suspect we feed each other information.

"Call me," I say. "We can talk on the phone."

I leave him, head back toward my office. As soon as I round the corner onto Cambridge Street, my phone vibrates.

"Did your father write a check to Max?" Carl says.

Suddenly, I long for the time when Carl was obsessed with my alcoholic mother. I'm glad he can't see my face. I maintain a steady tone of voice and try to blow it off.

"It's no secret my father is a generous donor when it comes to political campaigns."

"I'm not talking about campaign donations."

Even though we didn't do anything illegal, I want to talk to Max and my father before responding. Otherwise, I risk getting caught up in a lie. Lying is never the best route, especially to a major news outlet.

"I'm not sure why you think this has anything to do with me," I say.

"You're the common denominator," he says. "I can hold off running with it for a day or two, but this story isn't going away."

Chapter Forty-Six

My father's offices occupy a nineteenth-century McKim, Mead & White building on the sunny side of Commonwealth Ave. Out front, the landscaping is meticulous but simple, with flowering shrubs and evergreens. Inside, the lobby has a white marble fireplace and a Simon Willard grandfather clock. There are no shiny sculptures or massive art installations. My father doesn't shout money. He whispers wealth.

The firm is a lean operation, employing about two dozen full-time investment managers and analysts, including my brother Charlie. According to *Forbes* magazine, it turns quite a profit. My father inherited a sizable fortune, but he's successful in his own right. Over the years, he's managed to parlay tens of millions into half a billion, give or take.

After my street encounter with Carl, I call to see if my father and brother have time to talk. I want to fill them in and come up with a plan. When I call my father's private office line, it goes to voice mail.

I dial the main number, and his assistant, Kiki, picks up on the first ring.

"Hi, Abigail. They're both in meetings. Can we return?"

"Can you squeeze me in this afternoon?"

"Come by, we'll figure something out."

When I arrive, I press the buzzer, and Kiki, who is two years out of Bryn Mawr and earns more than most of the senior lawyers in the DA's office, comes down to greet me. In a couple of years, she'll apply to Harvard Business School, my father will support her application, and the firm will pay the tuition. For now she's learning the ropes; by the time she's my age, she'll be a fund manager, raking in millions.

Kiki takes my coat, and we ascend the grand oak staircase to the second-floor landing. She tells me my father is finishing up a phone call and offers me an espresso, which I accept, even though I'd prefer a shot of whiskey.

As she grinds the beans and tamps the coffee into the filter, I can't help but wonder what it would be like to work in a place like this, where it feels like a private home, and employees don't have to worry about leaving their coats unattended. Here the executive suite has a Palladian window rather than bulletproof glass, and a successful day is measured by the number of dollars earned, not the length of prison terms imposed. It would be nice to host visitors who have come to discuss acquisitions, rather than losses.

My father walks into the room, looking almost casual in shirt-sleeves, the cuffs of his blue Turnbull & Asser rolled up. When he gives me a hug, I'm comforted by the familiar lime scent of his shaving cream. He leads me into his office, and we take seats at the conference table.

"What's on your mind, muffin?"

I start to answer but am interrupted when Charlie strides in, wearing the Hermès tie I gave him as a stocking stuffer last Christmas. My eye follows the glint of platinum on his ring finger; I'm still not used to seeing him wearing a wedding band.

"Abs, it's always great to see you, but I'm pressed for time." Charlie remains standing. "I can guess why you're here, and there's nothing we can do. Mom isn't going to rehab."

If I had been meeting with a victim, this is the point where I'd reach into my tote and pull out one of the pamphlets I keep on hand. I travel with a stash of information on everything from battered women's shelters to methadone clinics. I'm tempted to offer my brother the brochure on codependency, but I didn't come here to recommend an alcohol counselor. We need an accountant.

"This isn't about Mom," I say. "Can we see if Prescott is available for a conference call?"

My father leans back and shakes his head. "We've talked about this. I'm not going to green-light the release of funds unless and until you're out of the murder business. If you become the district attorney, with a full-time security detail, we can revisit the issue."

"I came to talk about your finances, Dad, not mine."

Charlie, now interested, takes a seat. "What about his finances?"

"Dad transferred a lot of cash to Max."

He turns to my father. "How much are we talking?"

I'm surprised my father didn't mention the payment to Charlie.

"A hundred grand." My father shrugs: *no biggie*. "His computer system was hacked, he was afraid people would find out that he was playing footsie with his secretary, so we paid the ransom."

Charlie doesn't see the problem. "If Max is going to be the next mayor, then it sounds like a solid investment."

"Not if everyone gets indicted," I say. "Carl Ostroff from Channel 7 found out about it. You have to be sure everything is aboveboard and declare it on your taxes as a loan, rather than a gift."

My father laughs and waves his hand, as though swatting away a small nuisance. "This isn't my first rodeo."

"Aren't you worried about bad publicity?" I say.

"In my line of work, an overly generous contribution is viewed as a savvy business decision."

"People won't be as impressed with Max. He's a public official."

"That's his problem."

"He probably would have been better off if he hadn't paid the extortionist," Charlie says. "If word of his affair had leaked, the only person who'd care would be his wife."

I'm not entirely comfortable with Charlie's cavalier attitude toward the affair, but he's right. These days, financial deceit, not consensual extracurricular sex, is what brings politicians down.

Kiki taps on the door. "Hong Kong is on the line."

My father moves to take the call at his desk.

"If I were you, Abs, I'd worry more about myself," Charlie says. "You're smack in the middle of this mess."

While Charlie isn't exactly offering words of comfort, I'm glad someone has thought about how this could impact me. As I stand to leave, my father puts his caller on hold.

"I spoke with the governor," my father says.

"Thanks, but I think it's a lost cause. I'm too controversial."

"Thomas Greenough is trying to sabotage your prospects," my father says, "but since he's been arrested and arraigned, his influence is waning. You're still in contention."

My father returns to his call. Charlie walks me out into the foyer.

"You're forgetting something," Charlie says. "The governor's term is almost over. He's going to be looking for a job, and I'm sure he'd love to land here."

This is veering into felonious territory. The mention of quid pro quo, even among family, makes me nervous. It's one thing to imply it; it's another to articulate it. I hug Charlie good-bye, grab an espresso for the road, and head back to work.

Chapter Forty-Seven

When Valerie is discharged from the hospital, she takes the semester off from Tufts and moves into Walter's apartment in Somerville, not far from campus. I give her a few days to rest and then call her. I tell her I'm going to stop by, see how she's doing, and prep for grand jury. She tries to put it off, but I press. The next court date is looming, and as much as I hate to contribute to her anxiety, there's a limited amount of time to secure a superseding indictment. Chip was indicted on three counts of murder; I have to add the rape and kidnapping charges.

When I pull up to the Jacksons' triple-decker, there's a black-and-white Somerville police cruiser stationed out front. The media ignored Valerie's request for privacy, and reporters have camped out across the street. The local PD agreed to provide a security detail, and a uniform stands watch on the front porch.

I flash my badge, and the uni nods me through, avoiding eye contact. I don't know why he's giving me the cold shoulder; maybe it's because I prosecuted a Somerville detective for a domestic assault a few years ago.

I push on the doorbell. Walter's voice crackles through the intercom.

"She's asleep." He's more dismissive than informative, a far cry from the man who was seeking my comfort and reassurance a few weeks ago.

I'm not dissuaded. "I'll wait until she gets up. I brought work with me."

There's a long pause before he speaks again. "Please, come back another time."

After some back and forth, he buzzes me in and directs me to the parlor, a room filled with balloon bouquets, floral arrangements, and a couple of teddy bears clad in *Get Well Soon* T-shirts. I use the time to work on my grand jury presentation.

After almost an hour passes, my stomach grumbles, and I start to feel light-headed. I haven't had anything to eat today; I'm tempted to break into the Whitman's Sampler on the coffee table and steal a few vanilla butter creams, but settle for a couple of Tic Tacs from my tote.

Finally, Valerie emerges from her bedroom. Her bruises have matured into the color of ripe bananas, and most of the swelling has subsided. As she sits, she moves her hand to her throat and rubs her fingers gently over a thin line of scabs. She seems disappointed, as though she expected the wounds to have healed during her nap.

I ask her how she's doing and give her information about survivor groups, for when she feels ready to leave the house. For now, all she can handle is phone therapy with a rape crisis counselor.

"I don't want to testify. He almost killed me." Her words express fear, but her affect is flat, probably from Valium or Ambien.

I think about motioning the court for an extension, but that will only delay the inevitable.

"I know you're scared, but you can do it."

"You have no idea what it feels like."

"Trust me, I know what you're going through."

She rolls her eyes, crosses her arms. "Yeah, right."

I haven't shared my feelings about my own brush with death,

not even with Ty or Kevin. I'm not sure I've fully sorted my emotions out in my own mind, but I know that fear is at the top of the list. It's unprofessional to talk to a victim about my own personal experiences, but it seems selfish to withhold it from her.

"Last year someone tried to kill me. For months I wanted to jump out of my skin when a neighbor's door slammed. My heart raced every time the phone rang. I broke into a sweat when a strong breeze rustled the trees. Last winter a snowstorm knocked out our power, and when the sun went down, I had a panic attack. I got in the car and drove all the way to Rhode Island, in the middle of the blizzard, until I saw lights on in a hotel."

She studies my face. I've struck a chord. "What do you need from me?"

"Chip Aldridge is in jail. I want to keep him there."

"What do I have to do?"

As I start to explain the process, she yawns and her eyelids grow heavy. She hit the wall and won't remember another word of what I'm saying. Walter is in the kitchen, clanging pots and pans, cooking something garlicky.

"Valerie, we're eating in ten minutes," he says.

She promises to appear for grand jury, but I can't risk taking her at her word. Without her, my case will get directed out at trial; the defendants will argue there isn't enough evidence to convict, the judge will agree, and the charges will be dismissed before the jury has a chance to deliberate. I serve her a subpoena and tell her Kevin will be by in the morning to pick her up.

I head back to Boston. Driving through Porter Square, I notice a Somerville police car behind me. The lights blink, and the siren blips. I move to the right side of the road to let the car pass, until I realize the signal is directed at me. I pull over, and the cruiser follows.

The officer approaches. "License and registration."

We've crossed the city limits, into Cambridge, which is beyond her authority, but the best course of action is to comply with her order, rather than debate jurisdiction. I reach into my tote and feel around for my wallet; it takes me a minute to find it, buried under a few loose Junior Mints and an empty pretzel bag. I pop one of the melty chocolates in my mouth and hand her my registration.

She examines the document with disdain, as though she suspects it's counterfeit.

"Have you been drinking?" she says.

"No, Officer."

She shines a flashlight in my face, then indicates the stripes on her sleeve. "It's Sergeant. You failed to signal when you turned onto Mass Ave. Where's your license?"

I've always scoffed at ADAs who stash their IDs in their badge cases, so they can not-so-subtly flash their tin at times like this. Now I wish I hadn't been so sanctimonious. I pull the license from my wallet and hand it to her.

"I don't think we've met before. I'm Abby Endicott, chief of homicide at the Suffolk County DA's Office," I say.

That should settle things. She should extend some professional courtesy, maybe even apologize, and let me go.

"Wait here." She's not impressed.

She returns to her cruiser to run a check, taking more time than she needs, probably calling her spouse to ask what's for dinner. Just as I'm about to call Kevin to ask who he knows at Somerville PD, she's back.

"ADA Endicott, you of all people oughta know better. You were going forty in a thirty-five zone. You could've killed someone."

This is the first she's mentioned speeding or vehicular homicide. This has to be about more than my prosecution of a colleague. I can't imagine that punishing a man for pummeling his wife would elicit this much animosity, even if the defendant was a detective. This could only be about one thing: Senator Greenough.

I'm done playing nice. "Issue me a citation and let me go."

"Not so fast. Your insurance has been canceled."

I'd completely forgotten. I haven't paid the car insurance in months; the policy must have lapsed. My financial insolvency is impacting more than my shoe collection.

"I'll straighten it out when I get back to the office."

She opens my door. "Step out of the car."

"What the hell are you talking about?"

"Operating uninsured is an arrestable offense."

"You don't have authority to make an arrest. We're in Cambridge."

"Get out of the car, or I'll write you up for resisting."

Short of stepping on the accelerator and triggering a high-speed chase, there's nothing I can do. I get out of my car. She pats me down, running her hands up and down my body, which is humiliating, and then she cuffs me, which is more painful than it looks. The back of the cruiser is hot and claustrophobic.

When we arrive at the station, I'm booked. My property, including my phone, is confiscated. As I roll each finger onto the glass to have my fingerprints taken, I look around for a familiar face but don't see anyone I know. After my mug shot is snapped, I demand to speak with the chief but am told he's unavailable.

An officer walks me to a holding cell, where six women are seated on concrete slabs that line the wall. The door slams closed; I find an open spot and sit down. It's my luck that I don't know any of the police officers, but I do recognize one of my cellmates, a bank robber I prosecuted a few years back. Her head flops over to the left; she's dozing, unaware of my presence, until—splat! She vomits all over my Jimmy Choos.

She opens her eyes, wipes her mouth with her sleeve, and looks up at me. "Hey, I know you."

"Shhh." The last thing I need is for the rest of my fellow prisoners to know I'm a prosecutor. "I'm working undercover."

Her head drops; she goes back to her drug-induced reverie. When I'm finally given access to a phone, I think about calling Ty to come get me and make me feel safe and human again. Instead, I call Kevin, the more practical choice, the most likely to get me out of this place in one piece. He picks up on the third ring.

"Can you pick me up at the Somerville PD?" I say.

"What the heck are you doing there?" His voice is gravelly, like I woke him.

"Don't ask."

"I'm staying at my in-laws, down the Cape. Sit tight. I'll be there as soon as I can."

I spend the next hour in a panic, alternating between sitting and pacing, experiencing a panoply of my phobias: claustrophobia, entomophobia, and germophobia. Finally, an officer unlocks the cell. I follow him to the booking area.

Kevin is at the desk, mouthing off to a lieutenant. "I hope that none of you are planning to come to Boston anytime soon. If you are, here's a piece of friendly advice: don't drive, take the T."

Out of the corner of my eye, I see the sergeant at her desk; a photo hangs on the wall behind her. It's an autographed picture of Senator Greenough with his arm around a teenager.

"Senator Greenough is good people," she says. "He got my boy an internship at Homeland Security."

Kevin turns to the sergeant. "If you're trying to strong-arm ADA Endicott, thinking she'll cave and go easy on that sleazeball, forget it. She's not that kind of prosecutor."

I collect my tote, check to be sure my wallet and phone are inside. On our way out of the station, Kevin hands me the most thoughtful gift I've ever received: a pocket-size bottle of hand sanitizer.

"I know how you are," he says. "I always keep a spare bottle in the glove box."

"I could kiss you," I say and then immediately wish I could take it back.

There's a moment of awkward silence as he unlocks his car with the remote and opens my door. As soon as I settle in and buckle up, I unscrew the top of the bottle and bang it against my palm, until a glob comes out. It smells better than any expensive perfume. I put the top back on and stuff the bottle in my tote. We drive back to Boston, more resolved than ever to catch the bad guys.

Chapter Forty-Eight

There isn't enough time to go home and shower, so I head directly to the office. When I arrive at Bulfinch, wrinkled, smelly, and exhausted, I try to make myself presentable with a spritz of dry shampoo, a fresh coat of lipstick, and a smear of deodorant. I slip into one of the clean white shirts that I keep on hand for inappropriately dressed witnesses and head to court.

On the way, I stop by Starbucks, order a double latte and heart-healthy bowl of oatmeal. As the cashier rings me up, I change my mind and ask for a cranberry scone. After a night in a jail cell, I deserve a fat-filled, nonnutritious breakfast.

Inside the courthouse, I pass through security and jump on an empty elevator. I push the close button, but someone jams in a briefcase, and the doors bounce open. Cassandra hops in and sniffs the air.

"Ewww, it smells like someone barfed in here," she says.

I cleaned off my shoes as best I could, but apparently I missed a spot. I look at Cassandra and raise my eyebrows, like I don't know what she's talking about, like she's nuts.

"I don't smell anything," I say.

On the sixth floor, I'm surprised to find all twenty-three grand jurors seated and waiting. They're nearing the end of the term, a time when attendance usually becomes spotty, but when I scheduled the case, the foreman told me they were itching to hear from Valerie.

The room is somber, with none of the usual sounds. No idle chitchat, clacking knitting needles, or crunching popcorn. The retired postal worker and the graphic designer have relocated from their seats in the back up to the front row. The landscaper from Revere is sporting a jacket and tie. Even the nurse's aide from Chelsea is here; she's been a no-show for weeks.

I set a cup of water and a box of tissues on the ledge of the witness-box and get Valerie, who is seated in the waiting room between her father and Kevin. She follows me, and as she takes her seat, she stumbles and knocks over the water, spilling liquid onto the carpet. Her eyes well up, and she drops her head, looking more defeated than before she walked in.

The postal worker picks up the cup and refills it. "Don't sweat it. People do that all the time. Yesterday, a guy knocked over the whole pitcher."

I'm grateful for his fib, and so is Valerie; she hugs her purse and settles in. I pull my chair out from behind the table and drag it next to the witness-box. This way, maybe she won't feel so alone.

When I raise my right hand, she mirrors me.

"Do you solemnly swear that the testimony you are about to present to this grand jury will be the truth and nothing but the truth?"

She leans into the microphone, so close that she bangs it with her tooth, then lurches back.

"Yes. I swear."

She coughs, clears her throat, then coughs again. The nurse's aide offers her a lozenge, which she accepts. The grand jury is an awkward forum for all but the most experienced police officers. It's formal, with rules and procedures, but the absence of judges and defense attorneys allows interaction between jurors and witnesses, including expressions of empathy.

Valerie starts to relax her shoulders as I direct her through background questions: name, age, address, education.

"Were you receiving financial aid at Tufts?"

"Yes." She chomps on the cough drop.

"Did you work?"

She lifts her gaze from the floor. "Yes."

Valerie looks and sounds robotic, which isn't lost on the jurors, who are getting fidgety. I cut to the core of her testimony.

"Were you a paid escort?"

"Yes."

A couple of jurors sit up straighter.

"The weeks before your abduction, did you post an ad on backpage.com?"

"Yes."

"Did Thomas Greenough Jr. respond to the posting?"

"Yes."

"Did he pay you to attend parties?"

"Yes."

At this point, I have to stop leading the witness with yes-or-no questions. If she doesn't tell her story in her own words, I'll be accused of misconduct and the indictment could be dismissed.

"Where were the parties?" I say.

"Mostly at hotels around Boston. A couple of them were in Washington, D.C."

"Who attended?"

"Lobbyists and people who worked for the government. Some were kind of famous. One of them looked like that guy who used to be governor of New Jersey. Some of the girls said FBI and Secret Service agents were there."

"Tommy Greenough organized the logistics and the invitation list?"

"I think so. He screened the women and introduced us to men."

The postal worker blurts out, "So you're saying that Greenough was a pimp?"

Valerie looks at me, startled. The jurors know to wait for my cue before asking questions, but sometimes they can't help themselves. Admonishing the juror for interrupting will slow things down, so I keep going.

"Did you ever see Senator Greenough at a party?"

"A couple of times. He steered me to some of the men, told me to be nice."

"How did you meet Chip Aldridge?"

"Tommy set me up with him, on a date."

"Can you tell us what happened?"

Her hand trembles as she rubs it across the ridges in her throat. We sit in silence for a few seconds. She exhales.

"I agreed to meet him at the Sheraton on Route 128. When I got to the room, he was walking around in circles, looking out the window. He seemed weird, maybe like he was on something, and it kind of freaked me out."

"Did you tell him you wanted to leave?"

"Yes. He blocked the door and wouldn't let me go."

Valerie stops, gnaws on a cuticle.

"Did Chip Aldridge attack you in that hotel room?" I say.

"He raped me."

The landscaper interrupts, "What do you mean, he raped you? How could he rape you, when he paid for it?"

A couple of jurors in the back exchange looks. The nurse's aide whispers to her neighbor, who nods; I can't tell if they're being supportive or judgmental. I decide to let Valerie answer the question; it's a question a lot of people will be asking.

"I know I was there for sex, but it was rape. I didn't consent." Her voice is confident and resolved, and I'm proud of her.

"Did you tell him to stop?"

"Yes, definitely."

"What did he do?"

"He put a pillow over my head. I thought he was going to suffocate me."

"Tell us what happened afterward."

"I put on my clothes and left the hotel. I went into the parking lot and was about to call for a ride. He grabbed me from behind and covered my mouth."

She looks at the landscaper, who nods: *Okay, I get it. He raped you.* The other jurors, the skeptics, seem to have softened, too.

"Did he force you in the car?" I say.

She takes a breath, then speaks slowly. "Yes, we drove for a while. When we stopped, he put a cloth over my mouth. It smelled like chemicals, and I passed out. When I woke up, we were on a boat, and I was naked. I tried to fight with him. He wrapped a string around my neck, it was like a shoelace or something, and he pulled and pulled and pulled until I blacked out. I guess he thought I was dead."

"When did you regain consciousness?"

"I was in the water." She looks directly at the jurors. "I almost drowned. I saw the lighthouse, and I swam to the rocks. I don't know how I did it."

We're in the home stretch. Now I have to give them a chance to make inquiry.

"Does anyone have any questions for this witness?"

I say this for the record, but glare at them and issue a silent plea. *Please, no questions.* No one says a word. I excuse Valerie, turn off the recorder, and give the foreman the letters of indictment.

"I'll be outside," I say.

In the waiting area, I take off my suit jacket and sit down. I could be here awhile. To issue indictments, grand juries only have to find probable cause to charge, not guilt beyond a reasonable doubt, and they only need a majority vote, not a unanimous one. But they have a few charges to consider, and the evidence is scant.

After a minute passes, I'm surprised when the foreman comes out and hands me papers.

"We voted," he says. "It's a true bill."

I sign the indictment forms, then walk to Valerie. I give her a hug, and she almost hugs me back.

Chapter Forty-Nine

When I get back to the office, there's a logjam at the elevators, and the fourth-floor library is packed with reporters. Max is delivering a speech about the opiate addiction crisis, but no one is listening; the cameras and microphones don't even seem to be turned on. Everyone is biding their time, waiting for him to wind down, so they can ask about the mushrooming allegations of corruption. Cassandra probably planted the rumor as payback to Max for dumping her. Sabotaging my candidacy is an added bonus.

My father, who is at the center of the controversy, conveniently jetted off to Hong Kong, or at least that's what his assistant is telling people. He's probably where he always is at this time of day—in the steam room at the Harvard Club. I'd like to avoid the reporters, too, but that would make me look complicit, and I have a political career to worry about.

Max is at the podium, with a well-crafted response. He must have ice blocks in his shoes, because he's the only person not dripping with sweat. To discourage lingering, his campaign manager cranked up the heat and removed the water cooler. Some of the reporters take off their jackets and roll up their sleeves. An audio technician fans herself. A cameraman looks like he's about to faint from heat exhaustion.

As soon as Max finishes talking, Cassandra's favorite *Herald* reporter pipes up. "Can you explain the financial transaction with ADA Abby Endicott's father?"

Max is defiant. "Nothing illegal or unethical transpired. Our computers were hacked, and it was in the best interest of the people that we serve to protect the confidential information."

"What kind of information?"

"Names and addresses of rape victims, testimony of gang members who turned government witness, strategies about capturing drug traffickers." He omits the part about an extramarital affair between himself and a member of his staff.

Carl raises his hand but doesn't wait to be called on. "Then why not be open about it and pay out of office funds?"

Max grins. "That's a first, the press complaining that I'm saving the taxpayers money."

A few people in the audience laugh. Carl isn't one of them.

"ADA Endicott, since this involved your family, do you think it will impact your chances of getting the appointment?" Carl says.

"What I think isn't relevant," I say. "It's what the governor thinks and, ultimately, what the voters think that matters."

"You already sound like a candidate," Carl says.

I flash a smile, cameras click. A couple of reporters try to follow up with questions about my candidacy.

Max steps back up to the podium. "ADA Endicott has a big trial coming up, and she needs to prepare. Today is about the opiate crisis, not unsubstantiated rumors. Thank you all for coming."

An aide whisks Max away, into a locked stairwell. The hot, hungry reporters move in and surround me.

"Sorry, I've got a meeting," I say.

I jump into an elevator; Carl manages to slip in with me. I swipe my badge over the security sensor and push the button for the eighth floor.

"I spoke with your boyfriend this morning," Carl says.

He looks at me, wants me to think he has information about something outrageous—something about my father or mother or Ty. I'm not biting. Ty isn't politically shrewd, but he's smart, not one to be lured into giving away secrets, and he's a performer. He can hold his own against Carl.

"Stay out of my personal life." I watch the floor numbers flash: 5, 6, 7.

"It's a valid story. *Candidate for DA was living with a convicted drug dealer.*"

He was bound to ask about Ty's drug conviction, but I'm not worried. I've already discussed it with the governor's committee. We reach my floor, and the elevator doors slide open.

"Wait . . . *was* living with a drug dealer?" I extend my arm to prevent the doors from closing.

"Your boyfriend told me he moved out."

This can't be true. I hope. Either Carl misunderstood or Ty just said that to get Carl off his back. The elevator door timer runs out, and the alarm bell sounds. I step into the hallway and rush past the receptionist.

"Jack Rater is waiting for you in your office," she says. "He brought the evidence from the crime lab."

"I'll be with him in a minute."

I'm late for my trial-prep meeting with Jack, but I won't be able to concentrate until I talk to Ty. I duck into an empty conference room and phone him. When the call goes to voice mail, I hang up. After two more tries, he answers.

I forgo the pleasantries. "Did you tell Carl Ostroff you're moving out?"

He hesitates. "Babe, I tried to talk to you about it, but you wouldn't listen."

The room feels like it's spinning. "So it's true?"

"I was going to tell you when you got home. I sublet a place in Brighton."

The receptionist is standing outside the conference room. She taps on the glass, startling me. I look at her and hold up two fingers.

"Give me two minutes," I say to her.

Ty thinks I'm talking to him. "We can talk later," he says.

I start to tear up. "You don't have to move. I can handle Carl."

"It's more than just him. Two radio stations and a newspaper called. Some guy from *The Harvard Crimson* was out front of our apartment building this morning."

The receptionist waves her arms over her head, like a football referee signaling to stop the game clock. I swivel my chair around so she can't see my face.

"It'll blow over," I say.

"We should both lie low for a while."

"It's okay. I don't mind the scrutiny."

"Well, I'm not okay with it," he says. "First I get grilled by the governor's people, then reporters start calling. This is taking on a life of its own."

"You're breaking up with me? Over that?"

"It's not just your job. I love you, but let's face it—you came pretty close to cheating on me."

"But I didn't."

This isn't how it's supposed to go. He's not supposed to leave me. I'm supposed to leave him. In all of my past relationships, except for Tim, I've always been the one to cut and run.

There's another tap on the window; it's Jack. He points at his watch. *I have to go.* I hold up a finger. *I'll be right with you.*

"I'll call you later," Ty says.

The line goes quiet. I can't lose Ty. I take him for granted sometimes, but I can't imagine life without him. I look up and see Jack, still outside the window. I find a tissue and blow my nose. There's no time for self-pity; three women are dead, and their families are counting on me. I open the door and let Jack in the room.

We sit around the conference table and review the evidence. A milk carton, streaked with Caitlyn's blood, from the alley in East Boston. Links of Rose's necklace, from Christopher Columbus Park. Pieces of Britney's scalp from King's Chapel Burying Ground.

Jack is imparting important information, but my head is throbbing. As he talks about body fluids and hair samples, I imagine Ty, packing up his reeds and sheet music. By the time Jack starts to talk about Valerie's rape kit, I have a migraine. Somehow I make it through the meeting.

When I get home, my apartment is dark and empty. There's no light on in the hallway, no food sizzling on the stove, no music wafting through the air. I check the closets; Ty's clothes are gone. He's taken all of his things, everything but the leather coat I gave him for his birthday, which is still folded neatly inside its glossy red box.

Chapter Fifty

The trial is still months away, but pretrial motions are scheduled for this morning. The courtroom is at capacity. My victims' friends and family members take up about a third of the gallery. Reporters, lawyers, and court watchers fill another third. The Greenoughs occupy the rest. As far as I can tell, no one is here to support Chip, at least not openly.

I take my place in the front of the room. Behind me, there are two tables; one has three chairs, for Josh and the Greenoughs, and the other has one chair, for Chip. Some defense attorneys would opt to push the tables together, allowing the parties to consult and present a united front, but Josh doesn't want the visual of his clients sitting next to Chip.

The courtroom quiets as the three defendants are escorted in through a side door. The contrast between lawyer and defendant is usually obvious, but not in this case. All four men show signs of privilege. The Greenoughs look pasty and thin, but they still have expensive dental work, good posture, and quality wing tips. And I have to admit Chip cuts a fine figure in his navy-blue pinstripes. The telltale sign of incarceration, however, is the haircut, and Chip's has turned the corner from thick and wavy to bushy and unkempt. Prisoners don't have the benefit of Newbury Street stylists.

The court officer gives each prisoner their files, along with pads of paper and pens. While Chip thumbs through his papers, I sneak a look at his hands. They're no longer smooth and manicured but still could pass for the strong and steady hands of a surgeon.

"All rise," a court officer says.

Judge Swanson emerges from her chambers, takes the bench, and eyes Chip. She was practically swooning over him at the arraignment, when he was outfitted in an orange jumpsuit. Now that he's dressed for success, she looks at him wide-eyed, like she thinks he's dreamy. I want to scream at her: *I thought he was handsome, too. Remember: He's not really a lawyer. He's a cold-blooded killer.*

Josh and I wait for her to acknowledge us, but Chip either doesn't know or doesn't care about courtroom decorum. He jumps out of his seat, careful to position himself so he's facing forward, toward the bench, while also allowing the cameras in the back of the courtroom to capture his perfect profile.

"Your Honor, may it please the court, I have filed a motion for a speedy trial. Most respectfully, I ask to be heard." In an instant, Dr. Aldridge has transformed himself into Attorney Aldridge.

Judge Swanson doesn't scold him for speaking out of turn; in fact, she encourages him.

"Certainly, Mr. Aldridge, I'll hear you." There's a lilt in her voice.

"Rule 36 of the Massachusetts Rules of Criminal Procedure, as well as a significant body of case law, mandate that the defendant receive a trial free of unnecessary delays," Chip says.

He puffs out his chest, proud of himself. His oratory skills are eloquent. If you scratch the surface, however, his legal reasoning doesn't hold water. When he was sneaking into classes at Yale Law School, he should have paid more attention to criminal procedure. The rule he cited doesn't apply, but I'm not going to quibble with him. My victims' families want to move on with their lives, and so do I. The investigation is complete, and my witnesses are ready; this is as good as it's going to get. Unlike First Growth Bordeaux, murder cases don't improve with age.

"The Commonwealth answers ready for trial," I say.

Not one to give up the spotlight to anyone, least of all an ex-girlfriend and a fake lawyer, Josh is on his feet. "I filed a motion to sever. My clients should have their own separate trial. Otherwise, there's a substantial risk of guilt by association."

Chip backs him up. "I concur with my cocounsel."

Josh flinches when he hears Chip refer to him as his *cocounsel*.

Judge Swanson looks to me. "What's your position on severance?" she says.

He's on solid legal footing, but this would be a disaster. Two trials will double my workload, the witnesses will have to testify twice, and the families will have to sweat it out while they wait for two verdicts.

"It will be a waste of time and resources," I say.

Chip takes a deep breath and exhales loudly, as though I've offended his sense of justice. "Protection of the defendant's rights, not economy and expediency, should be the primary consideration for this court."

Not bad for an amateur.

Josh picks up the baton and sprints to the finish line. "The evidence in the Greenoughs' cases is irrelevant and unduly prejudicial to Mr. Aldridge's case, and vice versa."

Judge Swanson nods. "We're going to have two trials—one for the Greenoughs and one for Mr. Aldridge."

I've been ambushed. The Greenoughs smile in victory. Josh gives the appearance he wants nothing to do with Chip, but clearly they strategized and plotted this out ahead of time. I never would have agreed to Chip's request to fast-track the cases if I'd known that they were going to push for separate trials.

Josh and his clients start to pack up their papers. Judge Swanson eyes the door to her chambers, ready to bolt. Chip isn't done.

"One more thing," he says. "I filed a motion to exclude the alleged use of aliases."

I stand. "Mr. Aldridge's false identities are relevant and an exception to the hearsay rule," I say.

The judge fiddles with her pen as she scans Chip's rap sheet. Hopefully, his sex appeal drops a notch with each false name and date of birth. She looks up and checks her watch, as though she has someplace more important to be than here, at the biggest trial that will ever come across her desk.

"I agree with Mr. Aldridge. The proffered evidence is excluded from the trial," she says.

"Your Honor, may I—"

"No. I don't want to hear about aliases or dates of birth. We impanel in the morning."

The ruling is a huge loss. It means the jury won't learn about Chip's past and his experience in the art of the con. Some may take him at his word. Chip doesn't need a lawyer—it looks like Judge Swanson is going to assume that role. She might as well get off the bench and take a seat next to him at the defense table.

When I get home, I go straight to bed. It's only nine o'clock, but I need to rest up while I can. The past few days have been brutal, but the next few weeks are going to be worse. The only upside to being on trial is it gives me a valid excuse to let everything else in my life fall by the wayside. I don't have time to think about my family, my relationship with Ty, or the election. For now, my sole focus will be on convicting Chip Aldridge and sending him away for life.

Chapter Fifty-One

The next morning, a tent and staging area are set up in the middle of Pemberton Square. The case is a boon for local merchants who, unlike me, would like the trial to go on in perpetuity. An enterprising vendor is selling two styles of T-shirts. One has a photo of Chip's face behind bars, with *GUILTY* stamped across his face. The other has a picture of Chip, surrounded by a picture frame, with the word *FRAMED* on his forehead.

Choosing a jury is always a crapshoot, but this one will be even more so. It seems that anyone with a pulse has already formed an opinion, which means selecting a so-called fair and impartial jury will be nearly impossible. The only people likely to declare they can keep an open mind are either lunatics or liars.

The jury commissioner issued summonses to seven hundred Suffolk County residents. From that group, we select sixteen jurors for the panel, twelve of whom will ultimately deliberate. Under the rules, we each have eighteen preemptory challenges, jurors we can eliminate without giving a reason.

Voir dire is tedious. Potential jurors file into the courtroom in groups of fifty and fill out twenty-page questionnaires. They're supposed to report any prejudices or biases, for or against the defendant, and we're supposed to take them at their word. As if.

When they're done checking boxes and scribbling answers, they look up and wait for Judge Swanson to emerge from her chambers. She takes the bench, fidgets with her lavender infinity scarf, and asks a litany of questions: *Do you understand the defendant is presumed innocent? Are you related to a police officer? Have you ever been the victim of a crime?*

Anyone who raises a hand is called up to sidebar for further inquiry. Judge Swanson seems more interested in what the men have to say, particularly the single advertising executive who lives in the South End and the divorced dermatologist from the Seaport District. Someone should remind her: it's a jury pool, not a dating pool.

When she's done, she allows us to inquire. No surprise, Chip's questions are clever, charming, and superficial. He addresses the first juror with confidence, as though he's done this dozens of times before.

"I noticed that you've brought reading material with you. May I ask, who is the author?"

The woman holds up her book and smiles. "It's a novel by Danielle Steel."

"My sister's favorite. Excellent choice."

Well played. It sounds like a throwaway question, but during this little exchange, Chip accomplished two things: he humanized himself and bonded with the juror. He made himself out to be a loving brother, and he also flirted a little. He's probably never heard of Danielle Steel, and I doubt he has a sister.

He moves on to the next juror. "I see you're not married. Have you ever stretched the truth to impress a date?"

The man shrugs. "Hasn't everyone?"

"Yes, I suppose so."

Chip uses most of his preemptories to eliminate men from the panel, but he holds on to this one. They've formed a connection over deceptive dating practices.

My voir dire questions are designed to do three things: elicit information, establish my theory of the case, and begin the process of persuasion. It's like a push poll.

I start with the question that the grand jurors had grappled with. "Some people think a prostitute can't be the victim of a sexual assault. Do you?"

Many of them respond by saying they're not sure, which gives me latitude.

"Do you believe if a woman says no, the man has an obligation to stop, regardless of her occupation or station in life?"

"Yes, sure."

"Because no means no, right? No matter if you're a prostitute or a physician."

"Right."

I move on to another juror. "Could you convict someone based purely on circumstantial evidence?"

"I think so."

"Even if the defendant has destroyed the DNA?"

"Sure."

When we're done with impanelment, the final sixteen jurors don't appear pleased to have made the cut, particularly number five, a high school teacher from Mattapan, who rolls her eyes and mutters under her breath. Judge Swanson appoints the dermatologist foreperson. She seems to fancy him, which is fine by me. Better that she favor the real dermatologist than the fake lawyer.

First order of business is to take the jury on a view. I give a brief view opening, to let the jurors know what we're about to do, and then we set out to visit the four crime scenes. First stop is the Graves, the island where Valerie was picked up by the Coast Guard. We travel to the harbor by bus. Chip and I sit up front with the judge, clerk, and stenographer. The jurors are in the back.

When we reach the harbor, a Boston police boat transports us to the island. It's a twenty-minute ride; the air is cold, and the sea is choppy. As a child, I was a competitive sailor, accustomed to rough waters, so I planned ahead and popped a Dramamine before we left the courthouse. As we near the rocky shore, some jurors take in the skyline and others watch the harbor seals frolic, but as we start to loop around the island, jurors number four and seven complain that they feel seasick, Chip looks a little green, and Judge Swanson leans over the side of the boat and throws up. Not a good way to start a trial.

The next day, we visit King's Chapel Burying Ground, where Rose was dumped, and Christopher Columbus Park, where we found Britney. Then we set out to our last stop, the alley in East Boston, where Caitlyn was discovered.

When we arrive, the jurors look out the windows and hesitate. They're not eager to get off the bus. A couple of them give me the stink eye. They should blame Chip, not me. I didn't pick the location; he's the one who killed Caitlyn and left her here. As soon as everyone is off the bus, a rat scurries by, and the schoolteacher stumbles and slips on a splotch of slime. Chip comes to her rescue and catches her, preventing her from falling.

"Thank you," she says as though he's her hero.

On the way back to Boston, we get stuck in rush-hour traffic, and people grumble. Jurors number three and four have child care responsibilities; the judge lets them make phone calls, and I can hear them frantically asking people to pick up their kids from school. When we finally get back to the courthouse, Judge Swanson is worried they'll leave and never come back.

She admonishes them in advance. "If you're not here at nine o'clock tomorrow morning, I'll send the police to find you."

The next morning, they straggle in, and we start opening statements. I have the burden of proof, so I go first. I stand and look around the courtroom, at my victims' families, the reporters, the court watchers. Kevin is seated in the back. Cassandra is front and center, whispering to her favorite reporter from the *Herald*.

I plant myself in front of the jury box, then turn and point at Chip. "This man is a triple murderer. He may not look violent or menacing, but he is. He is a cold-blooded killer, a man who murdered three women and tried to murder a fourth."

When I look at Chip in disgust, he holds my eyes. I turn back to the jury and recite the facts of each murder, highlighting the most horrific parts. I apologize in advance for what they are about to experience and warn them that the details will be gruesome. When I'm done, I sit down, shaking from anger, nerves, and adrenaline. Chip rises. Everyone is eager to hear his response, but no one more than I.

"Respectfully, ladies and gentlemen, this prosecutor is mistaken. I didn't do what she's accused me of. And because she has arrested the wrong person, the real killer is still out there."

His tone is moderate, his demeanor even tempered. The contrast is obvious. He's trying to make me look like an overly emotional woman.

He continues. "But don't take my word for it. Look at the facts. You will see that there is nothing tying me to the murders. No witnesses, no scientific evidence, no videotape, no DNA, and no confession. Their entire case rests on one person, Valerie Jackson, a woman who was herself the victim of a brutal attack. She was vulnerable and confused, and now that she has regained her strength, her story will change. When she comes in this courtroom, she will not identify me as her assailant. You'll see, I am an innocent man."

As he returns to his seat, I glance over at the jury box. Two of the women won't meet my eyes; a third glares at me. When we take the morning recess, I find Kevin in the hallway.

"Why is he so confident Valerie isn't going to make the ID?" I say.

"He's bluffing," Kevin says.

"I hope he hasn't threatened her."

"You worry about the trial, I'll talk to Valerie."

"Our whole case rests on her. If she doesn't identify him, it's game over."

Chapter Fifty-Two

I always kick off my trials with an emotional witness, preferably a member of the victim's family. Before the jurors learn anything about the crime—how, what, when, where, why—it's important for them to feel the full impact, the loss. This ups the chances that they'll pay closer attention to the evidence, and it will make them more likely to despise the defendant.

I turn to the court officer. "The Commonwealth calls Delia Driscoll to the stand."

Witnesses are usually sequestered during the trial, but the judge allowed my motion to exempt my victims' parents from the order. Delia is seated in the gallery, in the middle of the front row. Ed gives her a hug, others in the row stand to give her room to navigate, and she moves toward the front of the courtroom. Her right hand trembles as she holds it in the air and listens to the clerk administer the oath. Her eyes are red and unfocused; she probably hasn't slept in months.

"Yes, I promise to tell the truth."

She takes a seat, looks at the jurors, and starts to tear up. Judge Swanson looks down on her and wags her finger.

"Ms. Driscoll, I don't allow displays of emotion in my courtroom. I am ordering you not to cry."

Everyone is taken aback. Delia looks at the judge, her eyes

and mouth open wide, unsure of how to respond. If by ordering a grieving mother not to cry, the judge's intention was to remove emotion from the proceedings, it's having the opposite effect. Two of the jurors remove tissues from their purses and wipe their eyes. Delia blows her nose.

"I'm sorry, Your Honor. I'll do my best."

She takes a breath and bows her head. When Delia looks back up at me, I guide her through questions about Rose's background: what year she started at BU; what she was studying; and when she went missing. I display a photograph on a TV monitor, and Delia identifies Rose as her *beautiful, sweet girl.* In an attempt to stifle a sob, Delia puts her hands over her mouth, looks down, and snorts. Three of the jurors in the front row glare at Judge Swanson. I don't mind that they hate her, as long as it doesn't take any animus away from Chip. There's no way to control the loathing; juries are fickle.

I leave the photograph of Rose on the screen and sit down.

"Any questions from the defense?" Judge Swanson says.

"No questions. My sympathies for your loss."

Chip isn't an experienced lawyer, but he is a master manipulator who knows how to read his audience. Next up is the first responder to Caitlyn's murder scene. I question him for about an hour and show crime-scene photographs. Once I've sufficiently horrified the jury with the grim pictures of trash, vermin, and dead body, I round off the morning with a technician who talks about evidence collection.

When we recess for lunch, Kevin texts me. *Valerie is not a happy camper.* I go to the waiting room, where Valerie is seated next to her father, Walter; they both have their arms crossed, backs to Kevin.

Walter gives me a tentative hello. Valerie gives me nothing.

"You're up next, after the lunch break," I say.

"Uh-huh." She avoids eye contact.

"Can I get you something for lunch?"

"No, thanks." She looks up. "I don't mean to be rude, but I'd rather be alone."

I look at Walter.

"We'll be fine," he says.

I move toward the door. "Text me if you need anything."

Kevin and I settle into an empty office. He takes out a sandwich, wrapped in a Subway bag. As he's about to take a bite, he notices I'm not eating.

"Is your boyfriend on strike?" he says.

"He's out of town."

I'm not ready to tell him that Ty moved out and he'll probably never make me lunch, or anything else, again.

"I got a tuna sub. Take it." He slides the sandwich across the table. "I can get another one when you're in court."

I take half of the sandwich and pass the other half back to Kevin.

"How are the families holding up?" I say.

"Britney's sister is a Monday-morning quarterback, with lots to say about everything. She hates juror number seven, thinks you should call the ME next, and she loves your shoes. The rest of them are pretty quiet."

"Valerie seems jittery."

"She's having second thoughts about testifying. We have to get her in and out, pronto."

I finish the sandwich, find a tin of Altoids in my tote, and pop one in my mouth. I walk toward the visitors' room, to offer Valerie some words of encouragement, but as I round the corner, I'm summoned into the courtroom.

I turn to Kevin. "Swanson is ten minutes early."

"It's that dermatologist? The judge can't get enough of him. Do you see the way she's always making goo-goo eyes at him?" he says.

"Better him than the defendant."

When we get in the courtroom, Judge Swanson is already on

the bench, drumming her fingers. It looks like she gave herself a manicure during the recess; her nails are bright red, and the room smells of acetone.

As soon as the jury is seated, the judge says, "Ms. Endicott, call your next witness."

"The Commonwealth calls Valerie Jackson."

The court officer goes into the hallway. We hear him shout. *Valerie Jackson.* He waits a few seconds. *Ms. Jackson.* The door swings open. We all turn, expecting to see Valerie. It's Kevin. He looks at me and shakes his head.

"Your Honor, may I have a moment?"

"Quickly."

Everyone watches as I walk over to Kevin; my heart is pounding. I cup my hand over my mouth.

"Where is she?" I say.

"She's gone, and so is her old man," Kevin says.

"Like to the bathroom or the coffee shop?"

Kevin takes a silent breath. There's no need for him to respond because I can tell by the look on his face. Valerie Jackson is gone.

Chapter Fifty-Three

When we adjourn for the weekend, I go back to the office and waste a few hours, trying to figure out where Valerie could be. There's a pile of papers on my desk, a backlog of other cases that need attention, but I can't concentrate, and I don't want to go home to an empty apartment. I lean back in my chair, close my eyes, and doze off.

At 3:00 A.M., the blare of sirens from the police station next door wakes me. I call Town Taxi and wait in the lobby of Bulfinch. Uber would be faster, but climbing into the backseat of a strange man's Toyota, in the middle of the night, doesn't seem like the best mode of travel right now.

I arrive home, exhausted and defeated, but adhere to my new routine; I check the rooms and closets for any sign that Ty has been here. Unfortunately, everything is exactly as it was when I left, about twenty-two hours ago. I fall into bed and get a couple of hours of restless sleep.

In the morning, after I shower, I dial Valerie's phone. The call goes to voice mail, and I leave a message. In the kitchen, I make coffee, and remove a bagel from a plastic bag in the freezer. The hole in the center is filled with ice; I poke out some of the crystals and pop it in the toaster.

When I'm into my second cup of coffee, my cell phone buzzes.

"We've been out all night," Kevin says.

"Any luck?"

"Nope. We sat on the house until Valerie's father came out."

"Did he give you anything?" I say.

The acid from my coffee starts to churn in my gut.

"He wouldn't tell me if my coat was on fire," Kevin says.

Victims take off during trial all the time, but they usually don't go far. I should have kept a closer watch. I was too focused on Nadine and didn't pay enough attention to Valerie.

"I know what you're thinking," Kevin says, "but this isn't your fault. You're juggling a zillion things. If this is on anyone, it's me."

Homicide detectives are responsible for finding witnesses and keeping them safe, but they're not babysitters. My victims' advocate has had her hands full with my families, arranging for transportation and hotel rooms, fielding questions, explaining the proceedings, and sitting with them in court. Valerie fell through the cracks.

"We're screwed," I say.

If don't we find Valerie and get her on the stand, my case will fall apart. She's my only living victim. Without her, I won't be able to make her case or tie Chip to the other women. I can prove that one man committed all of the crimes, that there was a modus operandi, but I need Valerie to identify Chip as the perpetrator.

"There are two other people who can get us over the rail," Kevin says.

"I see where this is going," I say. "No way."

"They're our best shot at getting to guilty."

"You seriously want me to cut a deal with the Greenoughs?"

Calling Josh and offering his clients a plea is repulsive. They don't deserve a break, especially after all the hoops I had to jump through to get them locked up in the first place.

"Take your personal feelings and your ego out of the equation. Think of them as a regular, run-of-the-mill mopes. We make deals with bad guys all the time."

I hang up and pace around my apartment. Anything is better than an acquittal; I don't have a lot of alternatives. I can let the trial play out and hope we find Valerie, or that something else breaks, but that's too risky. Kevin is right; working with the Greenoughs, getting Tommy to flip and testify against Chip, is my best option. And, if I'm successful, it'll be Chip's own fault for demanding two separate trials.

I phone Josh. He picks up on the fifth ring.

"Abigail?" He sounds groggy.

"It's after ten. Did I wake you?" I say.

"Yes."

Good—I caught him off guard. I hope he's hungover.

"Meet me for lunch?" I say.

I can hear the rustle of sheets. Someone next to him stirs, a woman's voice. "Josh, who are you talking to?"

"It's work," he says to his bunkmate.

"Bartley's at noon?" I say.

When we were dating, Mr. Bartley's Burger Cottage was our go-to place. It's exactly as billed, a burger joint, with an open grill and a lunch counter. Except this greasy spoon is in the middle of Harvard Square; in addition to locals and tourists, it also draws Nobel laureates and heads of state.

"Bartley's? That means you're looking to butter me up for something. What do you want?" Josh is pompous and annoying, but he's no fool.

"Let's conference the case, see if we can resolve it."

"You must be getting hammered at trial." I can hear the smile in his voice.

"See you at noon."

I call Kevin, and he offers to come, but I tell him I'll have more luck with Josh solo. I grab my car key, then change my mind and taxi to Harvard Square. Bartley's doesn't offer valet parking, and I don't need the added stress of fighting traffic and circling around, looking for an open meter.

We zip across the river, and the driver drops me off on Mass Ave. The line to get into Bartley's runs all the way past the Harvard Book Store and around the corner. I text Josh. *I'm in line.* He texts me back. *I've got a table.*

I make my way in the front door and take in the familiar smell of grease. The décor hasn't changed since we were in law school; it looks like a college dorm room, decorated with street signs and sports posters. The daily specials are written on a chalkboard. One thing that has changed, however, is the addition of gluten-free and vegetarian dishes to the menu.

I find Josh at a table in the back of the room. He stands when he sees me and pulls out my chair, like he did when we were dating. The gesture is both sweet and chauvinistic, the parts of Josh I remember fondly.

The waiter taps the top of his pencil against his green pad, anxious to take our order. Bartley's isn't a place to dawdle, which is one of the reasons I chose it. I get the Fiscal Cliff, well done, which comes with blue cheese and bacon, and a plate of onion rings. Josh asks for the Taxachuett, rare, which comes with baked beans and a side of fries.

"You're the only woman I know who is still a proud carnivore," he says.

"I'm thinking about taking up yoga," I say.

"I'll believe it when I see it. One of these days, your vices are going to catch up with you."

Our lunch arrives quickly, eliminating the need for more small talk.

"Thanks for meeting me." I dip an onion ring into a glob of mayonnaise.

"Watching you squirm is a bit of a turn-on," he says.

I bite into the juicy burger and chew slowly, preparing to negotiate. I wait for Josh to shovel a spoonful of beans into his mouth before talking.

"We have a strong case against your clients," I say.

He swallows and wipes his napkin across the lower half of his face.

"So you've said."

"We have computer records and financial statements. A bunch of fraternity brothers are lined up to testify. And the Greenoughs' client list will be exposed, causing a lot of problems for everyone involved."

"Fine by me." Josh smiles. "If people didn't have problems, I'd be out of business."

I push my almost untouched plate away. The smell of grease is suddenly making me nauseous.

"Are your clients interested in a plea?" I say.

Josh swallows carefully and takes a long haul on his vanilla frappe.

"I thought you'd never ask," he says.

The waiter comes by. "Anything else?"

"No, everything is perfect," Josh says.

The waiter clears the plates and drops off the check. Josh doesn't move to pick up the tab, so I take out my wallet.

"What are you offering?" Josh says.

"Is Tommy willing to testify?" I say.

"Sure, if you give him the right incentive."

"What will they take?" I say.

"Two years' probation."

The waiter returns and hovers, waiting for us to pay and leave. He clears his throat.

"All set here?" he says.

"Ten years in state prison," I say.

"I'll come back," the waiter says.

"Forget it," Josh says.

"I'm prepared to take out drug trafficking charges against Tommy."

"Based on what? No drug dealer will ever testify against a Greenough."

"Freddie Craven will."

"Who?"

"He's your client's drug supplier."

The last thing Josh wants to do is go back to the office and tell the Greenoughs that instead of getting a sweet deal, they're facing new charges of drug trafficking.

"Two years in the house of corrections," he says.

"Five years in state prison, and Tommy testifies against Chip."

"Deal."

His wipes his greasy paw with a paper napkin, but it still feels slippery when he reaches across the table, offers it up, and we shake.

"Deal," I say.

Chapter Fifty-Four

First thing Monday morning, Josh and I contact the court and arrange to come in early and meet with Judge Swanson. When we arrive, the clerk knocks on the door to her chambers and gestures us inside. She's standing in front of a full-length mirror, zipping a black robe over her loud floral dress. We tell her that the Greenoughs want to plead guilty, and she's so giddy with relief that, for a minute, it looks like she might kiss Josh on the lips.

"I knew you'd see it my way," she says as if she had something to do with it.

The Greenoughs are brought in from the lockup, and Judge Swanson keeps things moving at record pace, to assure that no one backs out of the deal. It's barely eight o'clock, too early for anyone but the most ambitious reporters and avid court watchers. As the clerk calls the case, Carl slips in the back of the room and throws me a look; he's annoyed I didn't give him a heads-up.

The clerk swears in the Greenoughs, and the judge makes the requisite inquiry. *Are you doing this freely and voluntarily? Have you had any medication today that could cloud your judgment? Do you understand the implications of a guilty plea?* And my personal favorite: *Are you pleading guilty because you are guilty, and for no other reason?*

They both say yes. Tommy is slightly hunched over; Josh nudges him to stand up straight. The senator speaks clearly and tries to project confidence, but neither man looks like he's been faring well in jail. Most of the inmates know about Greenough's tough-on-crime bill, seeking to eliminate good-time for prisoners and reestablish chain gangs. As a result, the Greenoughs are being held in solitary confinement.

"Ms. Endicott, I'll hear your statement of the case," the judge says.

I didn't have time to memorize my recitation of the facts, so I read from notes. "The defendants were engaged in a conspiracy, aimed at procuring prostitutes. They ran a lucrative business, profiting from the exploitation of young women, some of whom fell prey to a serial killer."

Josh can't help himself; he butts in. "May the record reflect that my clients had absolutely nothing to do with the murders of these unfortunate victims." His remarks are geared more to the audience than the judge.

I want to correct the record—Tommy Greenough did have something to do with the murders. Chip was Tommy's client; Tommy introduced Chip to my victims and charged a hefty fee. But I remain silent—I don't want to kill the deal.

Judge Swanson accepts the pleas and imposes our agreed-upon sentence of five years in state prison. By now, the gallery is full, and the chatter level rises, inducing the judge to gavel the audience.

"Silence," she says.

The voices quiet as the Greenoughs are cuffed. I let the chief court officer know we need Tommy to remain nearby, because I'm going to call him to testify this morning.

"What do you want me to do with the senator?" the court officer says.

"Send him to the prison." As I say this, an unexpected tinge of satisfaction catches me off guard.

Before he is shackled and taken away, the senator gives his son a bear hug. He owes him; without Tommy's cooperation, he'd be doing an extra five years. After a short recess, the jury is brought back to the courtroom, and the trial resumes. Chip tries not to appear flustered by the turn of events, but his eyes dart back and forth as he calculates his next move.

I stand. "The Commonwealth calls Thomas Greenough Jr. to the stand."

A couple of jurors take out their pencils and notebooks. The teacher puts on her glasses. The dermatologist leans forward. We all look at the door as it bangs open and Tommy Greenough is escorted in, flanked by two court officers.

He looks pathetic without his swagger. He stares at the clerk, hanging on to every word in the oath. Anything to avoid eye contact with the jurors. He swears to tell the truth, and I hope he means it.

As much as I want the jury to hate him, I need them to believe him, which is no easy task. As soon as he opens his mouth, he transforms from pathetic loser to pompous ass. His Boston accent has the stretched *a*'s of a Kerry or a Kennedy, not the chopped *ah*'s of an Average Joe. *I attended Haavaad*, not *I went to Hahvid*. For outsiders, it's a subtle difference, not so to a Suffolk County jury.

"Do you know the defendant, Chip Aldridge?" I say.

"Yes."

Josh, who is standing by his side, has clearly advised him to only answer the specific question, not to offer any extraneous information, making it as tough on me as possible.

"In what context did you know him?"

He sips water and takes his time putting down the cup. "We had a business relationship."

"Please explain what you mean by that."

"He was a client. I organized parties and invited women, and he paid to attend."

The jurors are listening, scribbling in their notebooks.

"Did you introduce him to Rose Driscoll?" I say.

"Yes, the night before she was found."

"You mean the night before she was found murdered?"

Tommy looks at Chip, then back at me. "Yes."

"What about Caitlyn Walker?"

"I introduced them two nights before she was found." He doesn't wait for my follow-up. "I mean murdered."

"And Valerie Jackson?"

He nods. "They met through me."

He is growing more unlikable by the minute. I drag as much as I can out of him and then sit down. I don't want him too closely associated with my victims.

Chip moves to the podium and launches into his cross-examination.

"Is it fair to say that you invited other men to these parties?"

"Yes."

"And you introduced the deceased women to other men as well."

"Yes." Tommy crosses his arms tightly across his chest.

"And you don't know much about those other men, do you?"

"Not personally, but I had an exclusive clientele."

"You don't know any more about them than you did about me, correct?"

"I suppose."

Chip lets that hang. He knows how to heighten drama and emphasize his point.

"You have no idea if any of those men are abusive," Chip says.

"I guess." Tommy shifts in his seat.

"Or sadistic?"

"No, not from personal experience."

"Any one of these men could have been the murderers, isn't that true?" Chip looks at the jury and raises his eyebrows.

"Objection. Calls for speculation," I say.

Judge Swanson is so mesmerized by Chip's finesse that she seems to have forgotten that it's her, not him, who is in charge of the proceedings.

"Your Honor?" I say.

"Overruled," she says.

Chip scored big, manages to keep the momentum. "In fact, you don't know who killed these women, do you?"

"No, I don't." Tommy looks like he'd rather go to prison and start serving his sentence than spend any more time in this courtroom.

"By the way, where is Valerie?" Chip says.

Tommy looks at me. "You'll have to ask the prosecutor."

I'd been hoping to string this out a little longer, but I can't lie.

"Valerie Jackson is a missing witness," I say.

The jurors exchange looks with one another. I have to get to sidebar.

"May we approach?" I start to move toward the bench.

Judge Swanson stops me. "No, you may not. Where is the witness?"

"We hope to produce her before the end of trial."

Chip throws up his hands. "This proves what I've been saying all along. She's been abducted by the real killer. Someone else committed these heinous crimes."

The jurors look at me. *Where is she?*

I feel my face heat up. "There is still time to locate Ms. Jackson. Our evidence is that she fled out of fear for the defendant."

No matter what I say, Chip has undone any progress I made on direct. I'd be better off if I'd never used Tommy as a witness. It was a waste of a plea.

"No further questions," Chip says. "Thank you for your testimony."

Chip has managed to make it look like Tommy was his witness, instead of mine. The judge excuses him and calls a recess.

On my way out of the courtroom, I nod at the families, trying to exude confidence, even though I don't feel any.

Kevin and I huddle in the stairwell.

"It wasn't that bad," he says. "You've still got a fighting chance."

"I'm losing to a fake lawyer," I say.

"He's a con man. There's a fine line between a liar and a lawyer." Kevin nudges me, tries to get me to smile.

I can't muster up any cheer, not even for Kevin. "I need Valerie."

Valerie has been through a lot, and I can't really blame her for not wanting to tell her story to a roomful of strangers and a national television audience. Unfortunately, while her absence is understandable, it's devastating to my case, and it could be the reason a serial killer is set free.

Chapter Fifty-Five

I'm up most of the night, spinning worst-case scenarios in my mind. I land on *Valerie is dead, and Chip is acquitted and kills again.* Sometime before dawn, my anxiety shifts to politics. It's election day, and if Max wins the mayor's race, the governor will appoint his successor within the next week or so. My life could change drastically. I've been so consumed with my trial that I haven't read or heard anything about how I'm doing in the polls. Maybe the Greenoughs' guilty plea gave me an uptick.

I get ready for court, but first make a stop at my polling place, the Boston Public Library. A dozen sign holders are standing out front; half are holding LOMBARDO FOR MAYOR signs, and the rest are split between the remaining candidates. If I weren't on trial, I'd be expected to spend today outside, in the cold, passing out literature and waving a sign, as I've done every election day since I joined the DA's office.

When I step in the booth and pull back the curtain, I examine the ballot: *Lombardo, Maxwell (D).* A shiver of excitement blasts through me as I imagine my name listed here.

After casting my vote for Max, I head to the courthouse. Crossing through the Public Garden, near the equestrian statue of George Washington, I see my brother. He's talking on his cell phone and doesn't notice me; I think about pretending I don't notice him. We've always gotten along well, but lately, there's been a lot of tension between us. Mostly, it's because we don't see eye to eye when it comes to my mother. We agree there's a problem, but disagree about the solution. I want to get her help. Charlie, a true laissez-faire conservative, has taken a more hands-off approach.

I shout out to him. "Charlie!"

He ends his call, comes over, and gives me a hug.

"Abs," he says. "I've been watching your trial on TV."

"Sorry I've been MIA."

"I hope you can still make it to dinner."

"Of course."

I'd completely forgotten Charlie and Missy are celebrating their first wedding anniversary this week.

"It's tonight, at our house, just family," he says. "Bring Ty."

I avoid eye contact. "Ty is out of town," I say.

Charlie and Missy love hosting dinner parties. There's only one reason they would limit the guest list to immediate family and hold it at a private venue: to avoid the embarrassment of being in public with my mother. Things must have gotten worse.

I promise to be there and continue on to the courthouse. When I arrive, Kevin tells me they haven't made any progress finding Valerie. Her father stopped coming to court and has made himself impossible to reach.

The first half of the day flies by. I start the morning with the creepy-crawler guy, who testifies about Caitlyn's and Britney's approximate times of death. Chip senses my squeamishness and drags out his cross-examination, taking particular sadistic pleasure during the show-and-tell portion of the testimony. He plops a jar containing live maggots on my table and doesn't retrieve it until the end of his questioning, which seems interminable. I almost gag watching a cluster of the slimy larva inch up and down the length of the glass.

I have no appetite for lunch, which works out, since Kevin is busy, looking for Valerie, and I don't have time to go out and buy a sandwich. During the break, I call Valerie a couple of times, just in case, and check my phone every five minutes, hoping for word, but nothing comes.

When we start up again, I summon FBI agent Stan Alvarez to the stand. He testifies about Chip's childhood, emphasizing that he didn't find any indications that Chip's parents were abusive.

"Chip grew up in Wisconsin. His father drove long hauls, and his mother worked on an assembly line. He ran away when he was sixteen. He came east, hid out in boarding schools, and leached off wealthy students, particularly girls," Stan says.

The jury seems interested to learn about Chip's college education, how he moved from one Ivy League school to the next, never gaining admittance or paying tuition at any. They exchange looks when they hear that he snuck into law school classes.

Stan isn't allowed to testify about Chip's criminal past; the previous allegations of rape and fraud are considered irrelevant and inadmissible. Stan also isn't allowed to testify about his conclusion that Chip fits the profile of a serial killer.

"That's for the jury to decide," Judge Swanson says.

Stan is, however, allowed to posit an opinion about Chip's mental state. "He is an extreme narcissist, with an IQ of 158, which puts him in the category of Very Superior. His sociopathic tendencies and high intelligence are a very dangerous combination."

"Is he also a pathological liar?" I say.

"Yes."

I've hit the high notes. I won't be allowed to get into detail about anything else, so I take a seat.

Chip rises. "Dr. Alvarez, are you familiar with a condition known as delusional disorder?"

"Yes."

"It's a form of psychosis?"

"True."

"A person suffering from this type of disorder has certain fixed beliefs, despite evidence to the contrary."

"Generally speaking."

"They actually believe that something is true, even though everyone else knows it's false." Chip is brilliantly morphing into his next career: forensic psychiatrist. "Delusional disorder is a very serious mental illness," he says.

Chip has cleverly turned my FBI psychologist into his own witness and, in doing so, has laid the foundation for an insanity defense. He snuck it in through the back door, without subjecting himself to a mental evaluation or examination. He's trying to plant the seed that he lacks the ability to form the mens rea, or specific intent, required for a premeditated murder conviction. He may have managed to fire the fatal blow to my case.

Chapter Fifty-Six

When Charlie and Missy announced their engagement two years ago, they bought a townhouse on the top of Mount Vernon Street, around the corner from my parents. It's five stories, with five bedrooms and seven baths, a little smaller than the house we grew up in.

When I arrive for the family dinner, Charlie comes down to greet me. I step inside, he looks behind me.

"Where's Ty?" he says.

"He's not coming." I consider lying, but there's no point. "I think he broke up with me."

"Sorry to hear it."

"You are?"

"I was starting to like him." Charlie sounds like he's actually disappointed.

I follow him up the sweeping spiral staircase, to the second floor. Missy is in the bar, unwrapping a block of Manchego. She gives me a hug, hands me a glass of wine. She forgoes alcohol and instead puts ice cubes in a tumbler and pours herself a Pellegrino.

"Are you pregnant?" I say.

"We're trying," she says.

Unlike me, Missy is a cautious and patient planner. She's

probably already interviewed nannies and sought advice from prenatal nutritionists and preschool educators. I have no doubt that if she wants a child, one way or another, she'll have a baby by this time next year.

We join the others in the library, where they're watching the election returns. My mother looks stunning in a quiet cashmere cardigan and gray dress. You'd never know she'd been in a major car accident.

My father gives me a kiss. "They declared Max the winner," he says.

"All that talk about corruption didn't amount to a hill of beans." My mother takes a sip of her martini.

Charlie puts a cheese platter on the glass coffee table. "The scandal probably helped raise his profile."

I shave a slice of Carmody and put it on a cracker. "Did they announce his successor?" I say.

"I thought you were going to get his job, dear." My mother sounds like she's had a few. She doesn't wait for an answer. "Oh, well, it's probably for the best."

"They couldn't pay me enough to do that job," Charlie says.

My father mutes the TV. "Speaking of paychecks. Muffin, you're overdrawn at the bank."

That's not really breaking news. Last year, this is something my father would have handled with a phone call. Not anymore.

"Prescott called," he says. "Your condo fees and car insurance are past due. Your credit cards are maxed out. You owe back taxes. Did you know that there's a lien on your apartment?"

My mother pipes in. "Sounds like it's reached the point of no return."

She has the smile of victory. She's not taking pleasure in my misfortune; my mother isn't evil. She wants me out of the DA's office, and she assumes that financial collapse is the only way to force my hand.

My father won't let it drop. "Your options are finite. Sell the condo or find a new source of income."

I sip my wine and pretend to concentrate on the election results until Missy's housekeeper calls to the dining room. We take seats around the antique rosewood table, set with my grandmother's leafy green Flora Danica china.

My father raises his glass. "Here's to Charlie and Missy, happy anniversary. May you have a future of wedded bliss."

"Just like us, right, dear?" My mother sounds more sarcastic than celebratory.

We ignore the comment and toast the couple. My mother empties her glass and asks for another.

"Mom, haven't you had enough?" I say.

Everyone looks at me as though I have three heads.

"Abigail, that's not your concern," my mother says.

"It's my concern when you almost kill someone and derail my chances of becoming DA."

"Darling, if you don't get that job, it'll be because of your ex-convict boyfriend, not because of me."

"Mom, Abs is right," Charlie says. "You've had enough."

"Fuck that," she says.

I'm stunned. I've never heard my mother swear.

My father stands. "I'm leaving."

"Don't be so dramatic," my mother says.

"Dad, sit down," Charlie says.

"I love you all," he says, "but I've had it."

"Good night, dear," my mother says.

My father leaves the room, and we listen to his footsteps echo on the marble floor in the foyer. The front door slams, and my mother takes a bite of her food.

"This veal is delicious," she says. "The Mableys are coming to dinner next week. I'll ask Claude to get the recipe."

Chapter Fifty-Seven

The next morning, everyone in the office is talking about Max's mayoral victory and speculating about who will be the next DA. What they're really thinking about, however, is how the change will impact their jobs. Depending on who takes over, some lawyers will be promoted, others will be fired, and the rest will remain unaffected. I avoid the chatter. It's a foregone conclusion: I'm not going to get the appointment. The best I can hope for is that Cassandra doesn't get it and I keep my position.

I walk across the Plaza to the courthouse and take the elevator up to the courtroom, where Kevin is waiting. He hands me a white paper bag; inside is freshly baked Irish soda bread.

"I stopped by Bread & Chocolate, on the way to Nadine's apartment," he says.

I take a bite. It's crusty on the outside, sweet and tender on the inside, kind of like Kevin.

"How is Nadine doing?" I say.

"I can't get a read on her. Something about her feels hinky."

I finish the soda bread, reach into the bag, and feel around for another, but it's just crumbs. I could have eaten three more.

"You think she's holding back?" I say.

"Something like that," Kevin says. "She'll come through."

"She'd better. She's all we got."

Kevin goes to the waiting room to get Nadine, and I grab a bottle of water for her and a Zyrtec for myself. The last time I met with her, I sneezed and coughed until I could barely breathe. When she comes in the room, she's accompanied by Cinder, a beloved member of the DA's staff. Cinder is a facility dog, part Lab, part golden retriever, trained to provide comfort to victims and to relieve their anxiety.

The dog plants himself at Nadine's feet. She rubs the scruff of his neck and pats his silky hair as we talk.

"You seem really stressed out," I say.

"I'm okay." Nadine keeps her eyes trained on Cinder.

The prisoner's elevator dings, and Chip gets off, shackled and surrounded by guards. Nadine jumps out of her seat, and Cinder stays close to her. Chip glares at Nadine.

"Eyes straight ahead," Kevin says.

Chip ignores the command and keeps staring. Nadine opens her mouth as though she might scream, then covers her face with her hands. Chip takes a step toward her, gets tangled in the shackles, stumbles, and loses his balance. The guards grab his arms to prevent him from falling.

After he steadies himself, he looks at Nadine. "I'm counsel of record, and I've been trying to get in touch with you. I want to conduct a witness interview."

"You don't have to talk to him," I say.

Chip smiles. "No, but *I'm* allowed to talk to *her*."

He's right. As a defense attorney, he can interview witnesses in preparation for trial. The guards pull him around the corner, and Nadine starts to tremble. We're so close to the end of the trial, I can't afford to lose another witness.

"I need you to tell the jury that you saw Chip and Caitlyn together, on the night she went missing," I say.

"What if I refuse?" Nadine says.

No one can force the words out of her mouth, but she could be held in contempt.

"It's up to the judge. She could send you to jail."

"For how long?"

"Until you change your mind and testify, or until the trial is over."

I don't tell her if she refuses to cooperate, the trial will be over tomorrow and she'll be out of lockup in time for lunch.

The court officer calls out. "All persons having anything to do with the matter of Commonwealth *v.* Aldridge, draw near, give your attendance, and you shall be heard."

Nadine isn't in the right mind frame to take the stand; she needs time to calm down. She stays with Kevin and Cinder while I go into the courtroom and call the medical examiner as my next witness. He testifies to the autopsy results, which are gruesome and compelling, but they don't help me prove that Chip was the killer.

When we break for the morning and the courtroom empties, I remain at the table and check my phone for any sign of Valerie. There's an e-mail, marked urgent, and an attachment from an unfamiliar name. It could be spam or a virus, but could also be about Valerie. I open it.

To: Abigail Endicott
From: Dr. Jeffrey Messner
Re: Nadine Franklin

My patient, Nadine Franklin, contacted me this morning regarding her condition. Please be advised that Ms. Franklin is suffering from depression and acute anxiety, including panic attacks. Her condition will be exacerbated if she is called to testify at trial. She has been prescribed Wellbutrin and Xanax and is undergoing intensive psychotherapy. It is my opinion that participating at trial will cause significant medical and emotional

damage. I request that she be excused from the proceedings
and allowed to continue with her treatment regimen.

I feel myself tearing up. I have to call Nadine to the stand. Eight months ago, she was a college student at Wellesley, looking forward to graduation and veterinary school. Chip Aldridge changed all that. He's done irreparable damage to her life. And now, here I am, about to make it all worse.

Chapter Fifty-Eight

Nadine makes her way to the witness stand; her steps are slow and tentative. She pulls out the chair and inspects it carefully, as though it might be rigged with dynamite. I take my place at the podium. Before I have a chance to start my questions, she looks up at the judge and speaks.

"Judge, I want to be excused," she says. "I have a note from my doctor."

As she hands the letter to the clerk, the jurors strain forward to try to get a glimpse of what's on the page. The clerk passes the paper to the judge.

"Have you shown this letter to Ms. Endicott?" Judge Swanson says.

"Yes, but she said I have to testify anyhow."

"Is that true, Ms. Endicott?"

I clear my throat. "Yes."

The clerk shows the note to Chip, who examines it and acts as though he has Nadine's best interest at heart.

"The doctor says it's detrimental to her health," Chip says.

The jurors look over at me with disgust. *Why are you torturing this poor woman?*

"The Commonwealth has an obligation to prove all of the elements of the crime," I say.

"What about me?" Nadine says. "Don't you have an obligation to me?"

Chip's self-representation continues to pay off for him. She's afraid to testify, because she knows he's going to question her, but I look like the bad guy. When I ask Nadine to introduce herself, she tears up. She gives her name, blows her nose, gives her address, blows her nose. This goes on for my next six questions.

"Do you recognize the defendant?" I say.

She looks at him, then looks away quickly. "Yes."

"Did you see him with Caitlyn the night before she disappeared?"

"Yes."

"What was the nature of their relationship?"

Nadine looks into the front row of the gallery, at Caitlyn's mother.

"Answer the question," Judge Swanson says.

"He paid her to go out with him," Nadine says. "Caitlyn was an escort."

I'm closer to guilty, but still have a ways to go. I sit, and Chip stands. Instead of planting himself at the podium, he moves closer to the witness-box.

I jump up. "Your Honor, could the defendant be ordered to move away from the witness."

"Step back." Finally, Judge Swanson acts like a judge, but it's too little, too late.

Nadine breathes heavily. I'm worried she might hyperventilate.

"You didn't see who killed Caitlyn, did you?" Chip says.

She hesitates and forces out the words. "I wasn't there when it happened."

"She provided her services to other men as well."

"Yes."

"One of them could have killed her."

I try to distract him. "Objection."

Judge Swanson doesn't know what to say. "Ask a question, Mr. Aldridge."

"You saw me at your house with Caitlyn?" Chip says.

"Once with her, and once . . ." Nadine stops midsentence.

I don't know what she was about to say, but something is happening between them. Chip's mouth twists slightly. He's angry and in a hurry to get her off the stand.

"Nothing further," he says.

"Ms. Endicott, any redirect?"

I can't tell if Judge Swanson picked up on the exchange. The jury doesn't seem fazed by it. Maybe I'm so desperate for a conviction I'm seeing things that aren't there. I turn to Kevin, who tips his head slightly. He saw it, too. I move to the podium.

"The defendant has been to your house on more than one occasion?" I say.

"Excuse me?" Nadine says.

"Did you and the defendant have some kind of relationship?"

Chip stands, anxious to cut this off. "Objection. Beyond the scope of cross-examination."

"It's a follow-up question."

"Overruled," Judge Swanson says.

"I met him before," Nadine says.

Most of the jurors are leaning in, staring at Nadine. A couple of them are looking at Chip, trying to gauge his reaction.

"When was the first time you met the defendant?" I say.

Nadine looks down and shakes her head back and forth. She's afraid, but I think it's more than that. Nadine is ashamed. A camera clicks, her head sinks a little lower, and her face reddens.

I fill the silence. "Were you an escort as well?"

She looks at me and starts to speak but can't get the words out.

"Did you have an encounter with the defendant?" I say.

She nods. "Yes."

Chip is on his feet. "Your Honor, this testimony would be tantamount to a prior bad act, and inadmissible under the law."

Judge Swanson, aware of the cameras and the scrutiny that will follow her ruling, puts it on me.

"What's your response?" she says.

I have no idea what Nadine is going to say, so I wing it.

"This witness is also a victim, a part of Mr. Aldridge's crime spree."

Before the judge rules, Nadine steels herself and turns to the jury.

"I had a date with him, a year before all this happened," Nadine says.

"Did he hurt you?" I say.

She pauses, takes a breath. "He tried to choke me. He said he was just playing, that's how he gets turned on, but it felt like more than that."

"Did you tell anyone?"

"No."

"Why not?"

"I'm so sorry." She looks at the families in the audience. "I had no idea he would kill anyone."

I sit, and Chip stands. "If I was such a bad man, why didn't you warn Caitlyn?"

Nadine tears up. "I didn't know you were coming. When I saw you out the window, I tried to tell her you were weird and she should be careful, but I didn't know you would—"

Chip interrupts, turns to the judge. "I'd ask that the witness's testimony be stricken from the record."

"Denied."

When Nadine is done, she gets off the stand and brushes past me. I look at her and smile in sympathy, but she doesn't meet my eyes. I hope it was worth it.

Chapter Fifty-Nine

On the way home from work, I stop by Macy's. I've walked past the store a million times, but have never been inside. I'm desperate; since I had to let go of my housekeeper, I haven't had time to do laundry, and I'm out of clean underwear. The last time I bought lingerie, I called my shopper at Saks, and she sent over an assortment of everything I needed, and more.

I stand in the middle of the intimates department among racks, tables, and walls of unfamiliar brands, searching for a name I recognize. I settle on CK by Calvin Klein; I select a couple of pairs and hand a twenty to the salesclerk.

"Would you like to open a Macy's credit card?" she says.

There's no way I'd qualify. "No, thanks, I'm all set."

I leave the Downtown Crossing area and walk around the edge of the Common. It's dark, and I want to stay on well-lit streets. Last week, a group of teenagers thought it would be fun to play knockout, a game where someone punches random passersby in the face and tries to knock them unconscious. A Japanese tourist wound up in Tufts Medical Center, where's he's still on life support.

As I pass the Commonwealth Ave. apartment building where Chip Aldridge pretended to live, I take out my phone and call the real estate agent who sold me my condo a few years ago.

The chirp in her voice makes me wish I'd called someone less enthusiastic. I'll miss living there but try to convince myself it's only a condo; there are more important things in life, like food and heat.

"Would you like to start shopping for a new place?" she says.

"Do you show rentals?" I say.

She pauses. "A penthouse in the Mandarin is on the market for a three-year lease. It's two thousand square feet and a steal at $35,000 a month. I can arrange a showing."

"I was thinking more like a one bedroom in Brookline."

Unsure if I'm kidding, she lets out a nervous laugh.

"I'm on trial, but I'll leave the key at the front desk," I say.

My building is a rare commodity, with a doorman, a gym, and spectacular views. Unfortunately, the unit will sell quickly.

When I arrive home, Manny greets me in the lobby. "I saw you on the news tonight. Are you gonna nail that creep?" he says.

"I hope so."

I'm going to miss my daily chats with Manny, his running commentary on my trials.

"My Realtor may come by this week," I say. "I'm putting my apartment on the market."

"You're selling your place?" He sounds hurt, like my decision to relocate is a form of personal rejection. "How come?"

"Money." I sound breezier than I feel.

I don't have the energy to console him. I don't have the energy to console myself. I pass the mailboxes, not bothering to check on the contents, knowing it will be a stack of bills, mostly second and third notices. When I get into my apartment, I call Valerie. The phone rings, and just as I'm about to hang up, someone picks up. No one speaks, but I can hear sobbing.

"Valerie?" I say.

"Why do you keep calling me?" Valerie says.

"Are you okay?"

"I saw the girl, Nadine, on TV." She sniffles. "I'm sorry. I let everyone down."

"The trial isn't over. There's still time."

"I can't do it."

"Yes, you can."

She sobs, then takes a deep breath. "I'm sorry."

I fish through my purse and find a pen and paper.

"Where are you? I can send someone to get you."

"I know you can trace the call, or whatever, but I won't be here for long."

"Please, I can help. You'll be safe."

"It's more than that."

"I know it's humiliating."

"You have no idea."

I could argue with her, tell her I do have a sense of what it's like to be taken in by Chip Aldridge, but I keep it to myself. I've already revealed enough about my personal life.

"You're a good lawyer," she says. "The news reporters say you're the best. You'll get him."

The line goes dead. I put in a call to the cell phone company, to find the location, but we won't find her in time. I open the lid to my washing machine, toss in my new underwear, and pour in detergent. In the bathroom, I pull my hair into a ponytail, wash my face, and brush my teeth. Then I get into bed, curl up, and start to cry.

Chapter Sixty

The next morning, Kevin is waiting for me in front of the courthouse. A couple of reporters, looking for comments, try to intercept us as we make our way past the security gate. *What are you going to do if there's an acquittal? Is Valerie Jackson really dead? Are you worried that he'll kill again?*

We duck into the stairwell.

"Let's hoof it," Kevin says. "We could use the exercise."

By the time we reach the third-floor landing, I'm winded.

"I'm falling apart," I say. "I found a clump of hair in the shower this morning."

"I'm no barber, but losing your locks at age thirty-six can't be good."

"I'm thirty-five." I elbow him gently. "It's nerves. I'll be okay."

"That's not nerves, that's nutrition. You've probably got scurvy." He pulls a Granny Smith from the accordion folder he's carrying and offers it to me. I take a couple of bites. When we reach the door to the courtroom, I stop.

"Remind me," I say, "why don't I work at one of those law firms where nobody dies, and the most stressful part of the day is tallying up your billable hours?"

"Because you don't want to sit around on your duff all day, counting money."

"Right now, that doesn't sound so bad." I nibble around the core of the apple.

"You'd go nuts."

"Give me one reason to back go in that room."

"There's a million reasons. To stand up for the little guy. To give a voice to the voiceless. To make the world a safer place." He smiles. "To lock up the evildoers and give them their due. You tell me."

Kevin gets a call, talks briefly. He hangs up and turns to me.

"There's a couple of people downstairs. I gotta go talk to them," he says.

"You're not going to miss closings, are you?"

"I'll be there. Shake a leg."

"It's break a leg."

"Yeah, you fractured your leg during your last trial. This time, just shake it."

I take a cleansing breath and prepare myself to be infuriated by Chip's words. I took a meditation course a couple of years ago, but I never quite found my inner peace, and I stopped trying after a bullet almost ripped through my chest.

When I walk into the courtroom, the families are clustered together in the gallery. I want them to remain hopeful, but have also done my best to prepare them for the worst. A camera clicks as Chip is brought in and uncuffed. He's worn the same suit three days in a row, and there's a sweat stain around the collar of his shirt. He's lost his last shred of sex appeal.

The court officer calls out, "All rise."

The jury enters, and then Judge Swanson walks in, takes a seat.

"Good morning, members of the jury. Have you followed my instructions and avoided news reports and social media about this case?" She looks at each juror, waits for them to nod in response. When she reaches the dermatologist, she lingers for a few extra seconds. "It's time for closing arguments. Mr. Aldridge, you may proceed," she says.

Chip stands, moves to the jury box, and plants himself front and center. His life is on the line, and he knows it. He's amped up, ready to do battle. He seems less concerned with camera angles, opting instead for eye contact and connection with the people who will decide his fate.

"The prosecutor had no evidence, so she did what lawyers do: she made things up. She needs this conviction to bolster her candidacy for DA, and she'll do anything to get it, including offering perjured testimony. She didn't have the real killer, so she did the next best thing: blame the man who turned down her advances. She wanted to date me, and I wasn't interested, so I was as good a target as any."

"Objection! That's a complete fabrication, with no basis in the evidence," I say.

Objecting during closing arguments is risky; it could make me look like I'm afraid of what he's saying, but I can't let this go. He's pushed it too far. The only thing that keeps some lawyers honest is the threat of disbarment. Since Chip isn't a real lawyer, he has nothing to lose. Judge Swanson isn't sure what to do, so true to form, she doesn't speak.

Chip continues. "The real killer is still out there." He lowers his voice, as though he's sharing a revelation. "That's why Valerie Jackson isn't here. He got to her. And soon he'll get to someone else. The prosecutor should be out looking for the real murderer, not in here, trying to convict an innocent man."

Chip sits. When I reach the podium, I put my prepared remarks aside. I look into the audience and notice that Kevin isn't here. It's not like him to miss closings. I try not to let it distract me.

"It's true, no one saw Chip Aldridge commit these heinous crimes, but you don't need an eyewitness. You've heard from dozens of people, civilians, scientists, and police officers, and the most important witness of all: Nadine Franklin. She was his first victim. She was his test run, to see how far he could take it and how it felt. Judging by the horror that she displayed from the witness stand, he was terrifying, and he enjoyed every minute of it. Then he took it a step further."

I describe the four attacks, then display photos of my four victims on the screen, starting with Rose and ending with Valerie.

"Make no mistake, we got the right man. These crimes have Chip Aldridge's signature all over them. Please, convict him."

Some of the jurors seem to be with me, others not so much. I didn't have a lot to work with, and I don't know if I have been able to pull it off. As I take a step back to my table, the door swings open, and Kevin walks in. He signals to a woman, who is behind him. I do a double take. It's Valerie Jackson.

I stand in the middle of the courtroom; the jurors follow my eyes from Valerie, to the photographs on the screen, and back to Valerie. Since she didn't testify, the jurors have never seen her in person, but it's clear they recognize her as the woman in the picture, victim number four.

Valerie's presence makes the most compelling argument of the day. She sits in the front row, next to Delia Driscoll. There are tears in her eyes, underscoring what I just said: *Please, convict him*. Kevin looks at me, unveils the hint of a smile.

After Judge Swanson gives her instructions and the jury is sent out to deliberate, I find Valerie in the waiting room.

"I'm glad you came," I say.

"Thanks for not giving up on me," she says.

Chapter Sixty-One

Hours turn into days, and there's no verdict. I think about using the time to sort through bills and call the Realtor, but mostly I pace around the corridors of the courthouse with Kevin, debating whether or not it's a good sign that the jury is taking so long. He says yes; it's harder to convict than to acquit. I say no; they want to convict, but there isn't enough evidence.

"I'm going stir-crazy," Kevin says. "Let's get out of this joint."

We can't go far—the phone could ring at any time—so we walk in circles around the courthouse.

"Everyone who's paid any attention to this case knows you gave it your all. And I'll be standing right next to you, whatever happens," he says.

He puts his arm around my shoulder and pulls me in. Even through his suit jacket, I can feel the flawless definition of his biceps and pecs. I stop, sink into his strength, and he wraps his other arm around me. When I look up, we lock eyes for a beat too long, and I start to vibrate. It's my phone.

"Your cell is blowing up," Kevin says.

I don't move to check it. I want the moment to last a little longer. Kevin leans in and kisses me softly, on the cheek.

"You did good," he says.

"You're my best friend," I say. "Sometimes it feels like you're my only friend."

"Back at you," he says.

"Do you ever think about what it would be like if, you know . . ."

"Yup." He releases me and takes a step backward. "But I'm married, and you're with . . . what's his name." He smiles playfully.

"You're a wise man." I don't tell him that Ty and I are through.

"As much as I mess with you, I think Ty is a keeper. You need someone who isn't in this crazy business. Someone who doesn't deal with death all day long. Someone who can lighten your load."

My phone vibrates again, and I take it out of my pocket. My heart is already in overdrive, but it pounds a little faster as I check the screen.

"Do they have a verdict?" Kevin says.

I'm surprised to see the governor's counsel number come up on the screen. I shake my head, take a breath, and raise my voice an octave, to make it sound like I'm smiling.

"Lennie Potter here." It's the man with the polka-dot tie. "We all watched the closing on NECN. You did a helluva job."

"I didn't expect to hear from you, at least not until after the jury comes back." I immediately realize this sounds snarkier than I had intended.

"You haven't made it easy for us. You've got a lot of personal liabilities."

I shift into autopilot. "My personal life shouldn't be an issue." I can't help it; I argue when I'm nervous. "I'm the most qualified candidate you have."

"Yes, I know." Suddenly, he doesn't sound like someone about to deliver bad news.

"You do?"

"We're prepared to offer you the position."

"You are?"

This is going too well; there's got to be a catch.

"There are a couple of conditions," he says.

Here it comes.

"Okay, what are they?" I say.

"Your father has to recall the loan to Max."

"I can arrange that."

"We understand you've broken it off with your fiancé, so that issue has resolved."

Ty and I may be through, but it's not going to be because Mr. Polka Dot demanded we break it off. I take a deep breath.

"You're mistaken. Ty and I are very much together. In fact, we've been talking about setting a wedding date."

The line goes silent for a few seconds.

"Then I'm sorry, that's a deal breaker," he says. "I wish you all the best."

I think for a minute, decide not to argue, and say good-bye. When I hang up, Kevin is a few feet away, reading his texts.

"They're about to name Max's replacement," Kevin says.

"That was fast," I say. "Please, tell me it's not Cassandra."

"It's not Cassandra. She's going to be Max's chief of staff at city hall."

I'm thrilled, give him a high five. It's probably misplaced joy, since I don't have a verdict to celebrate.

"If it's not me, and it's not Cassandra, then who got the job?"

"They're bringing in someone from the outside: Stan Alvarez."

"An FBI profiler is going to be the new district attorney?"

"Turns out, he's a shrink and a lawyer."

The fact that it's not Cassandra almost makes up for the fact that it's a fed.

"Yippee. And ugh," I say.

"Be straight with me. You never really wanted that job. You

toyed with the idea, and you're not one to turn down a challenge, but you love what you do too much to do anything else."

My phone vibrates. It's the clerk.

"We need you in the courtroom," he says. "The jury's back."

Chapter Sixty-Two

As soon as we get word there's a verdict, Kevin and I text the families, most of whom are in the victims' waiting room, to tell them to meet us outside the courtroom. Kevin senses I'm too distracted to make small talk; he takes over and fields their questions.

"It took a long time. What does that mean?" Delia Driscoll says.

"It's impossible to know."

"Will he be sentenced today?" Valerie says.

"If he's found guilty, yes."

"Do you think he's going to be found guilty?" Karen Walker says.

"We'll know in a couple of minutes."

Kevin is patient with them, even though they've already asked these questions a thousand times before. It's hard to retain information when you're waiting, unsure if your child's murderer is going to be held to answer to his crimes.

When we get in the courtroom, the room is jam-packed, but eerily quiet. No one is moving or talking. Except Nadine, who lets out a series of explosive sneezes.

"All rise, jury entering," the court officer says.

The jurors look tense and serious, and don't make eye contact with either me or Chip. I can't get a read on anyone. The foreman hands the verdict slip to the court officer and scans the audience. When his eyes search the gallery and stop at Valerie, I let out a sigh of relief.

"How do you find? Is he guilty or not guilty?" Judge Swanson says.

"Guilty."

A few people applaud, some cry. Valerie and Nadine hug each other. Walter Jackson shouts: *We got the bastard!*

I stand. "The Commonwealth moves for sentencing."

The judge turns to Chip. "Do you have anything to say for yourself, Mr. Aldridge?"

For the first time since I met him, Chip isn't interested in talking. He sits silently, looking down at his papers, probably plotting his next con. The judge imposes four consecutive life sentences, and Chip is hauled off to prison.

We're all in a bit of shock as we say our good-byes. I'll likely hear from some of them in the future. A few will check in regularly; others will want nothing to do with me.

On my way home, I think about my own family and decide to stop by my parents' house. My mother is in her bedroom, on a chaise longue, reading *Vogue*. She's alone and, shockingly, she looks sober. Her eyes are clear; her hands are steady. I give her a kiss and don't pick up the familiar smell of alcohol on her breath. Neither one of us mention my trial.

"Where's Dad?" I say.

She flips the page, to an article about destination spas, then looks up.

"He's been staying at the club."

She nods at his closet; the door is ajar. Half of his clothes are gone. The last time I saw him, he was angry, but I didn't think was going to move out.

She puts down her magazine. "He filed papers."

"Divorce papers?"

She nods and sighs. "I won't do well without him."

I give her a hug and am surprised when she hugs me back.

"He'll come home," I say.

"I hope so," she says, "but I've contacted an attorney, just in case."

After I leave my mother, I stop by Gary Drug for a bottle of Poland Springs and a tin of Altoids, and as I cross Charles Street, I see Judge Swanson and the dermatologist juror duck into Bin 26 Enoteca. He holds the door for her, she pauses to look at him and smile, and he gestures her inside. They look tentative and awkward, like something fantastic is about to unfold between them.

When I reach Beacon Street, I take out my phone and call my father.

"You can't just abandon Mom," I say.

"Muffin, I know you're a problem solver, both by nature and by trade, but our marriage isn't yours to fix."

I think about trying to argue with him, but he's right. Stepping into the lobby of my building, I run into my Realtor, who is at the reception desk with Manny.

She's all smiles. "We got an offer."

I look at Manny, who busies himself returning the spare key to a lockbox.

"Did they meet our asking price?" I say.

"They came in over asking."

"When can they close?"

"It's a cash deal," she says. "They're ready whenever you want to move out."

"I'll start packing in the morning."

I go upstairs and look around my living room—at the mid-century modern furniture: a $15,000 cowhide Egg Chair; an $8,000 plum Pelican Chair; a $9,000 walnut-and-lacquer credenza. It all seems so ridiculous—stylish and smart, but ridiculous. In my bedroom, I open the door to my closet and survey the contents. Tens of thousands of dollars' worth of Armani suits, Fendi bags, Prada shoes. Wherever I end up living, it's unlikely that I'll have space for all of this stuff.

I grab my tote, get in the car, and call Kevin.

"Do you have a guy at the Registry?" I say.

"What do you need?" he says.

"Change of address info for Tyson Clarke."

Kevin doesn't comment or probe.

"Give me three minutes," he says.

Two minutes and fifty seconds later, he calls me with the information. I program Ty's new address into my GPS and head up Beacon Street. It's late, but Kenmore Square is teeming with college students, entering and exiting the bars. They look carefree and happy. I can never quite imagine how that must feel.

I locate Ty's new apartment building, a triple-decker, and circle the block until I find a parking space. Standing on his front porch, I worry about what to say and how he'll react when he sees me. I hope he's here and that he's alone.

I press on his buzzer, wait a minute, and buzz again. There's no sign of anyone. As I consider whether or not to leave, I hear footsteps, and the doorknob turns.

Ty opens the door. My heart sinks as he gives me a blank stare.

"I miss you," I say.

"I miss you, too."

Ty takes my hand and leads me upstairs. I survey the living room: the wallpaper is faded, the furniture is shabby, the rooms are cramped, and there's no place I'd rather be.

Acknowledgments

Victoria Skurnick, my fabulous agent at Levine Greenberg and Rostan, thank you for your insight and expertise. And thanks to everyone at Minotaur, especially the supremely talented Kelley Ragland and Hector DeJean.

Thanks to my generous community of writers in Boston, especially Bonnie Waltch, Lisa Borders, and my Grub Street classmates.

Joan Rater, Tony Phelan, Jenny Kane, Beth White, Chris White, Erin McDonough, and Alex René—thanks for your friendship, enthusiasm, and all-around awesomeness.

A shout-out to my former colleagues and friends in the Suffolk County District Attorney's Office, the Boston Police Department, the Massachusetts Trial Court, the Attorney General's Office, the Massachusetts State Police, the U.S. Department of Justice, and the FBI. Especially Ursula Knight, who has been so supportive and a constant sounding board.

Billy Bob Thornton, thanks for sharing your wisdom and for inspiring me to keep telling my stories.

And to my father, Henry Wechsler, and my brother, Peter Wechsler. I'm so grateful for your infinite supply of encouragement, confidence, and counsel.